CATCH THE MUNCHIES!

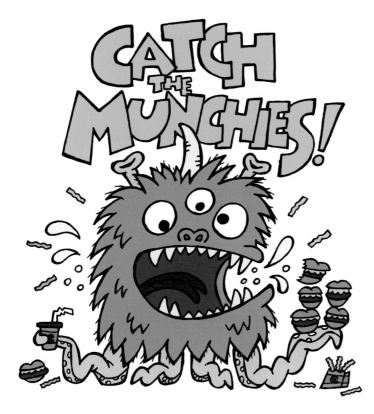

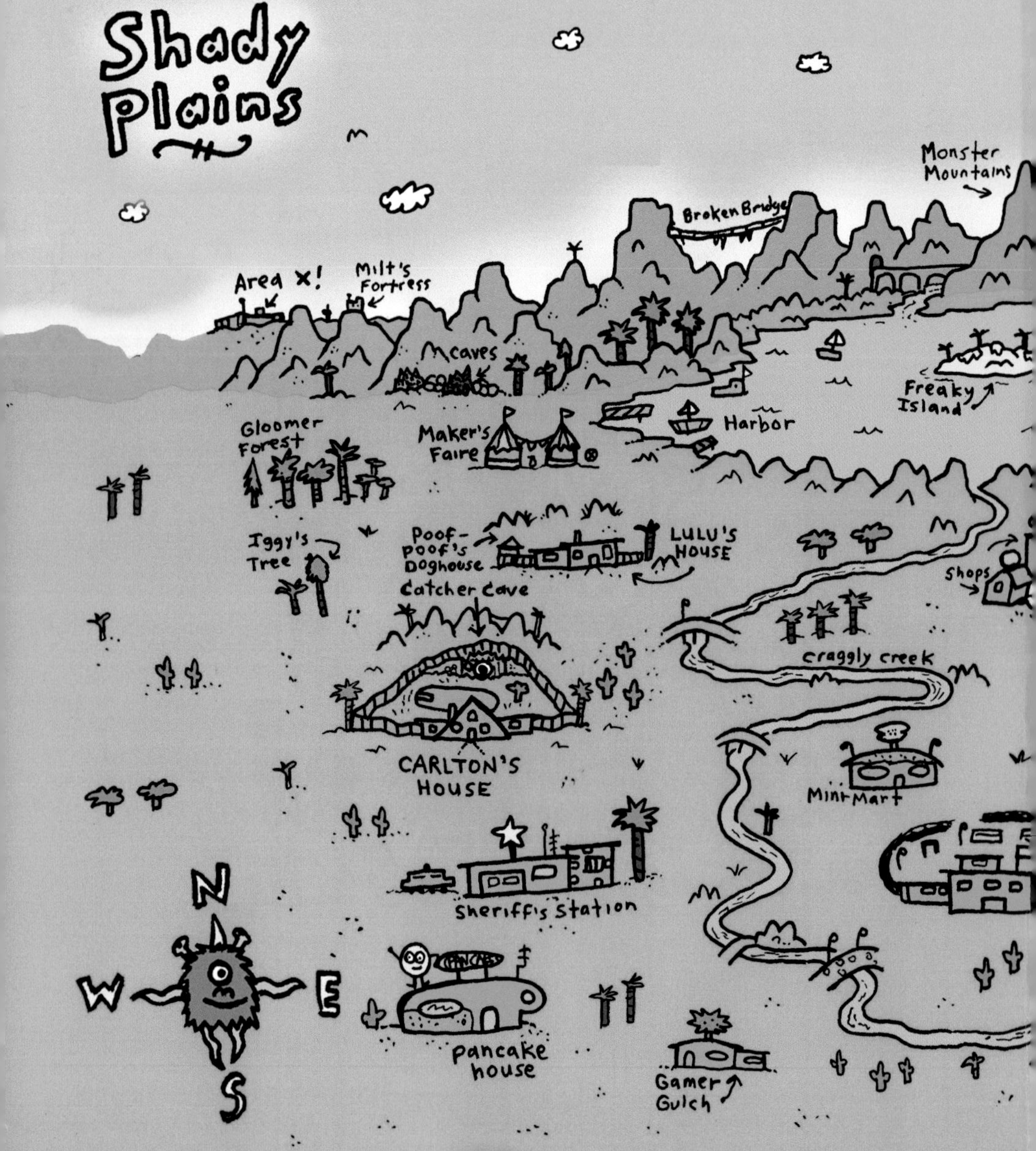
Shady Plains
Monster Mountains
Broken Bridge
Area X!
Milt's Fortress
caves
Freaky Island
Gloomer Forest
Maker's Faire
Harbor
Iggy's Tree
Poof-poof's Doghouse
LULU'S HOUSE
Shops
Catcher Cave
craggly creek
CARLTON'S HOUSE
Mini-Mart
Sheriff's Station
N
W
E
S
pancake house
Gamer Gulch

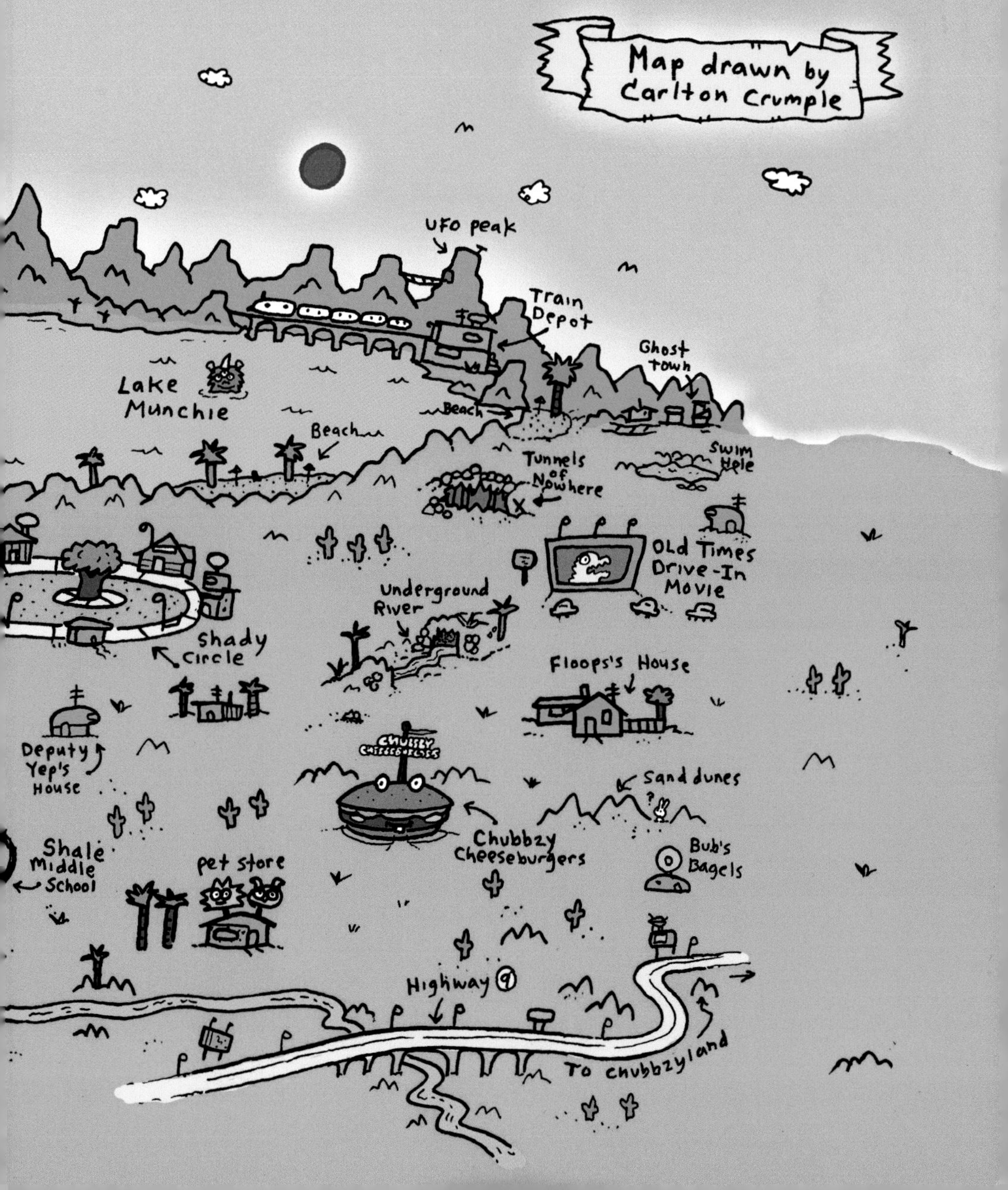

Map drawn by Carlton Crumple
UFO peak
Train Depot
Ghost town
Lake Munchie
Beach
Beach
Swim Hole
Tunnels of Nowhere
Old Times Drive-In Movie
Underground River
Shady Circle
Floops's House
Chubbzy Cheeseburgers
Deputy Yep's House
Sand dunes
Chubbzy Cheeseburgers
Bub's Bagels
Shale Middle School
pet store
Highway 9
To chubbzyland

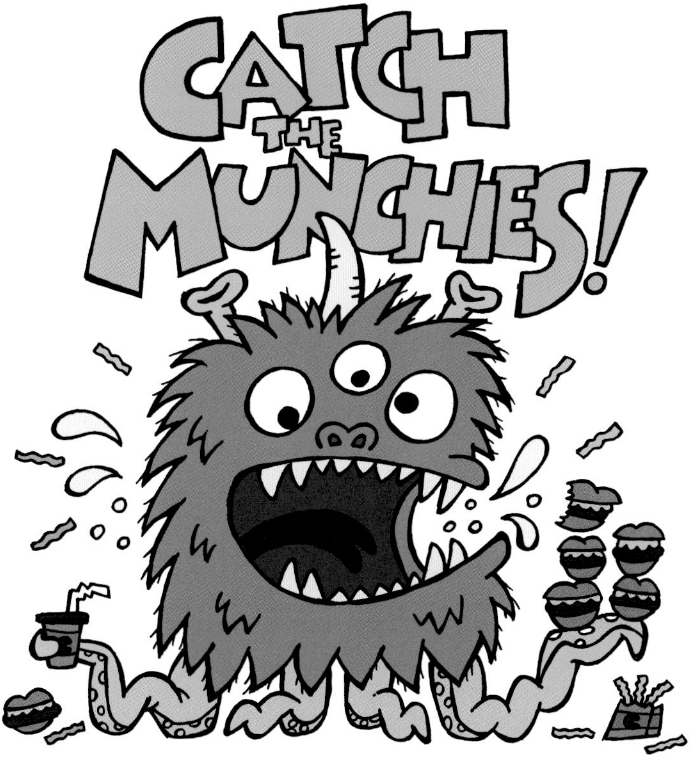
CATCH THE MUNCHIES!

Read all the books in the
Carlton Crumple Creature Catcher series:

#2 Tater Invaders!
#3 Reptoids from Space!

CATCH THE MUNCHIES!

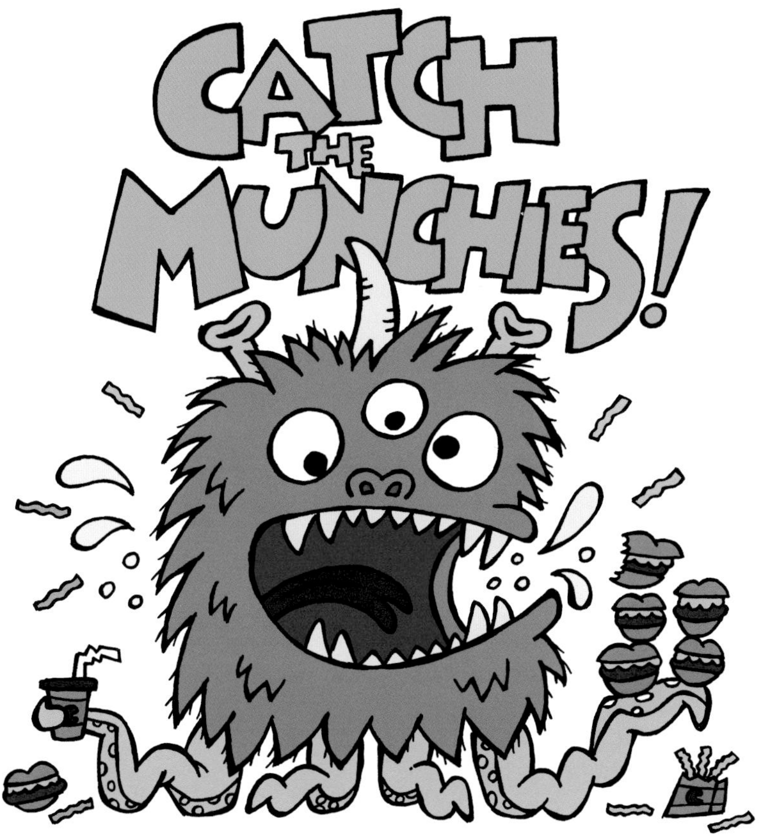

Written and Illustrated by David Fremont

Color by Jimbo Matison

PIXEL+INK

PIXEL+INK

Text and illustrations copyright © 2020 by David Fremont

All rights reserved

Originally published by Pixel+Ink August 2020

First paperback edition May 2022

Pixel+Ink is a division of TGM Development Corp.

Printed and bound in February 2022 at Toppan Leefung, DongGuan, China.

Color by Jimbo Matison

Book design by Sammy Yuen

www.pixelandinkbooks.com

The Library of Congress has catalogued the hardcover edition of this work as follows:

Library of Congress Control Number: 2020938106

Paperback ISBN: 978-1-64595-005-9

eBook ISBN: 978-1-64595-056-1

1 3 5 7 9 10 8 6 4 2

For my beautiful creatures, with love:
Carol Tree Monkey, Milo Wolf,
and Greta Fox

CHAPTER 1

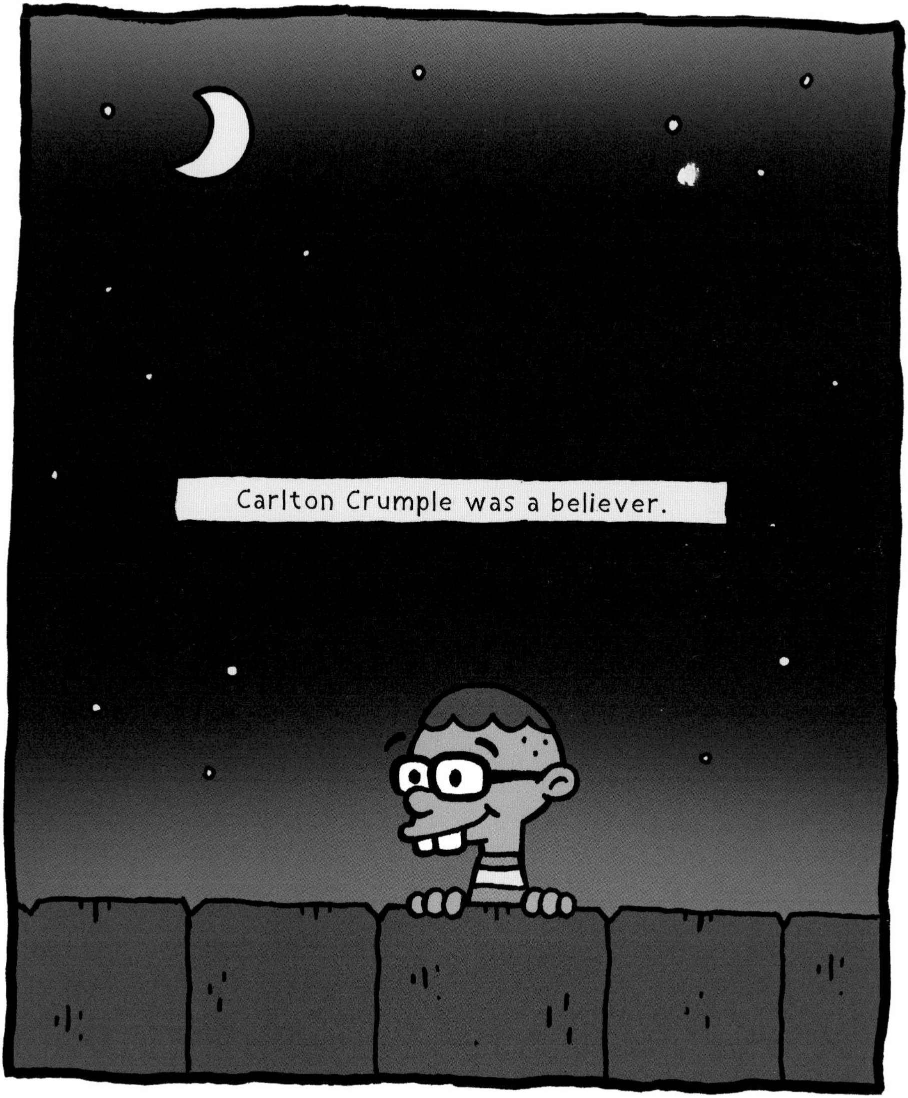
Carlton Crumple was a believer.

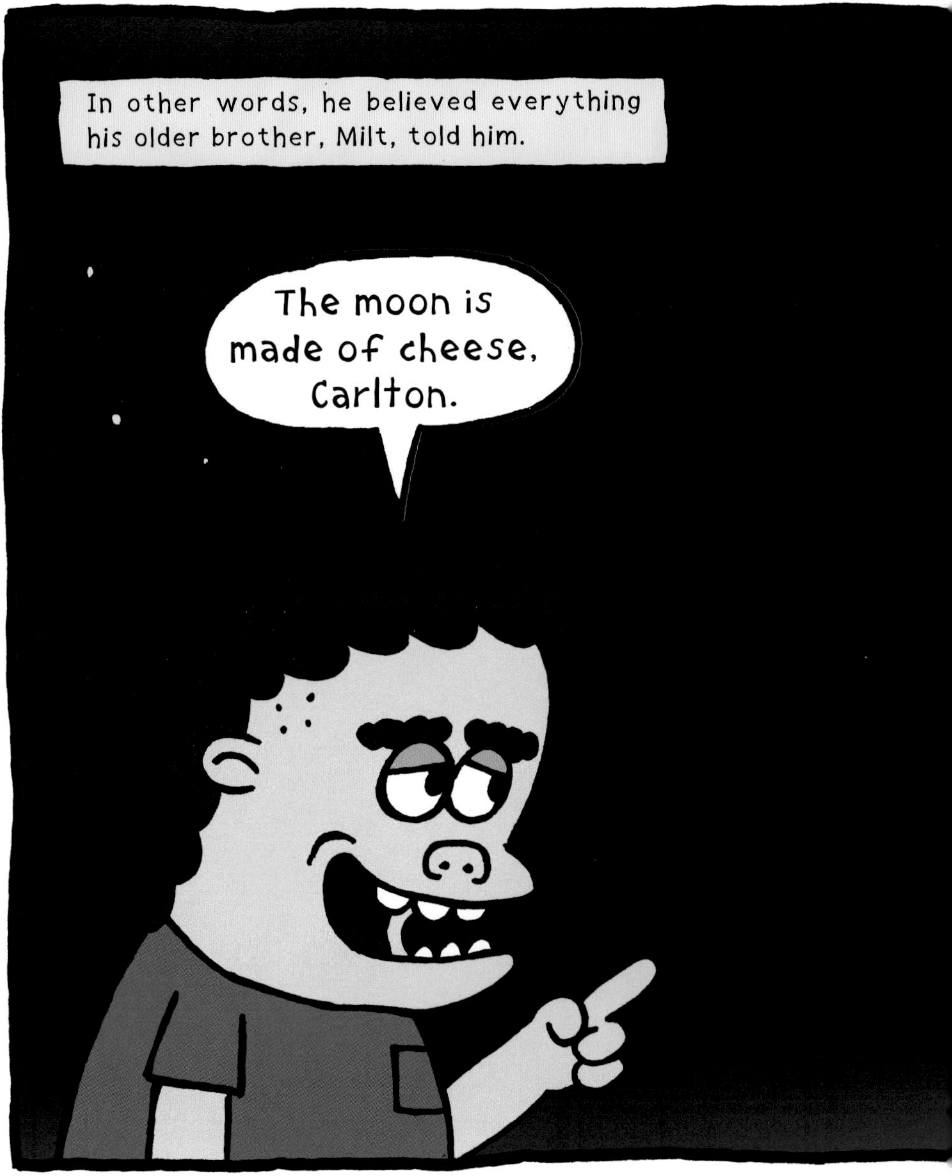
In other words, he believed everything his older brother, Milt, told him.
The moon is made of cheese, Carlton.

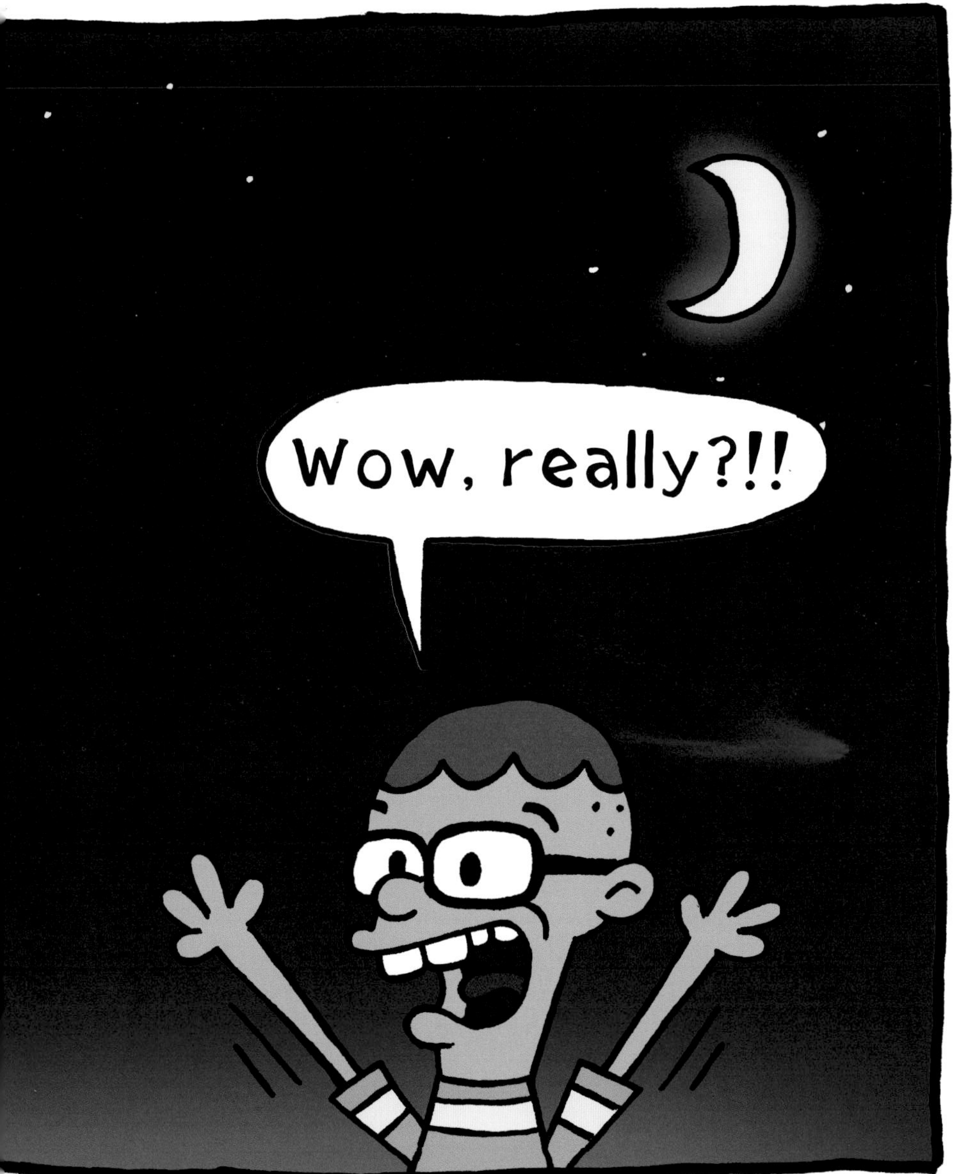
Wow, really?!!

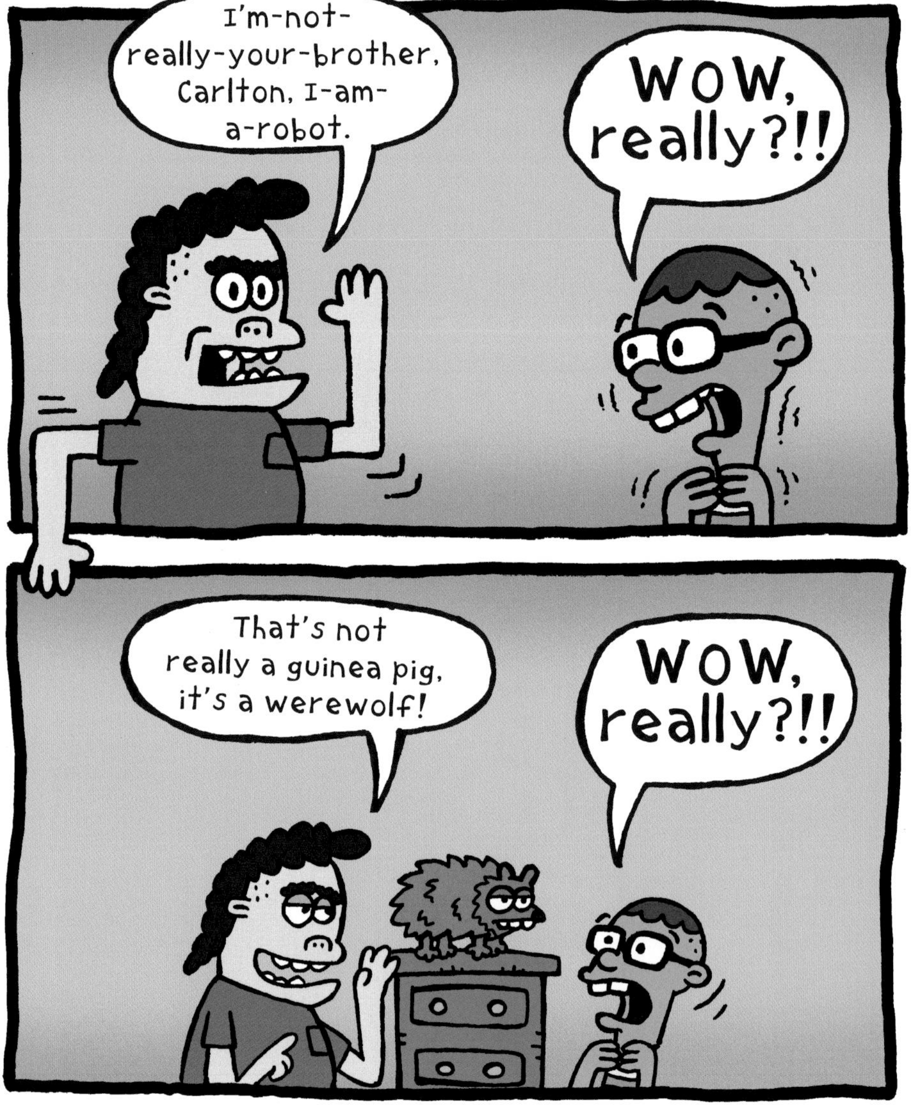
I'm-not-really-your-brother, Carlton, I-am-a-robot.
WOW, really?!!
That's not really a guinea pig, it's a werewolf!
WOW, really?!!

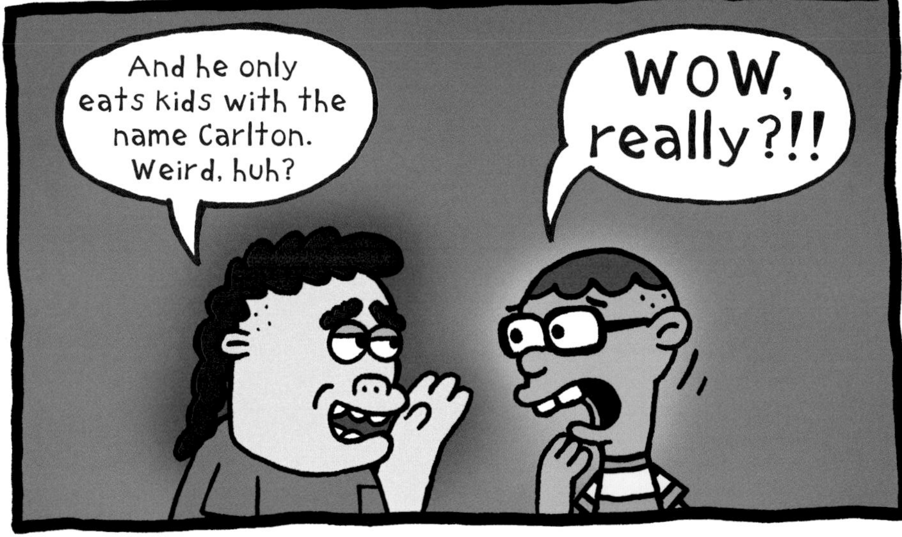
And he only eats kids with the name Carlton. Weird, huh?
WOW, really?!!

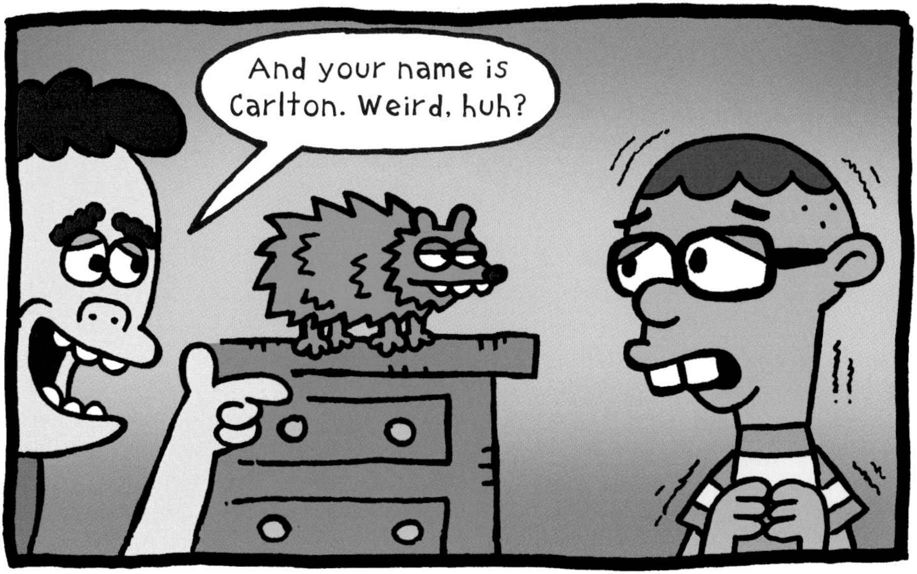
And your name is Carlton. Weird, huh?

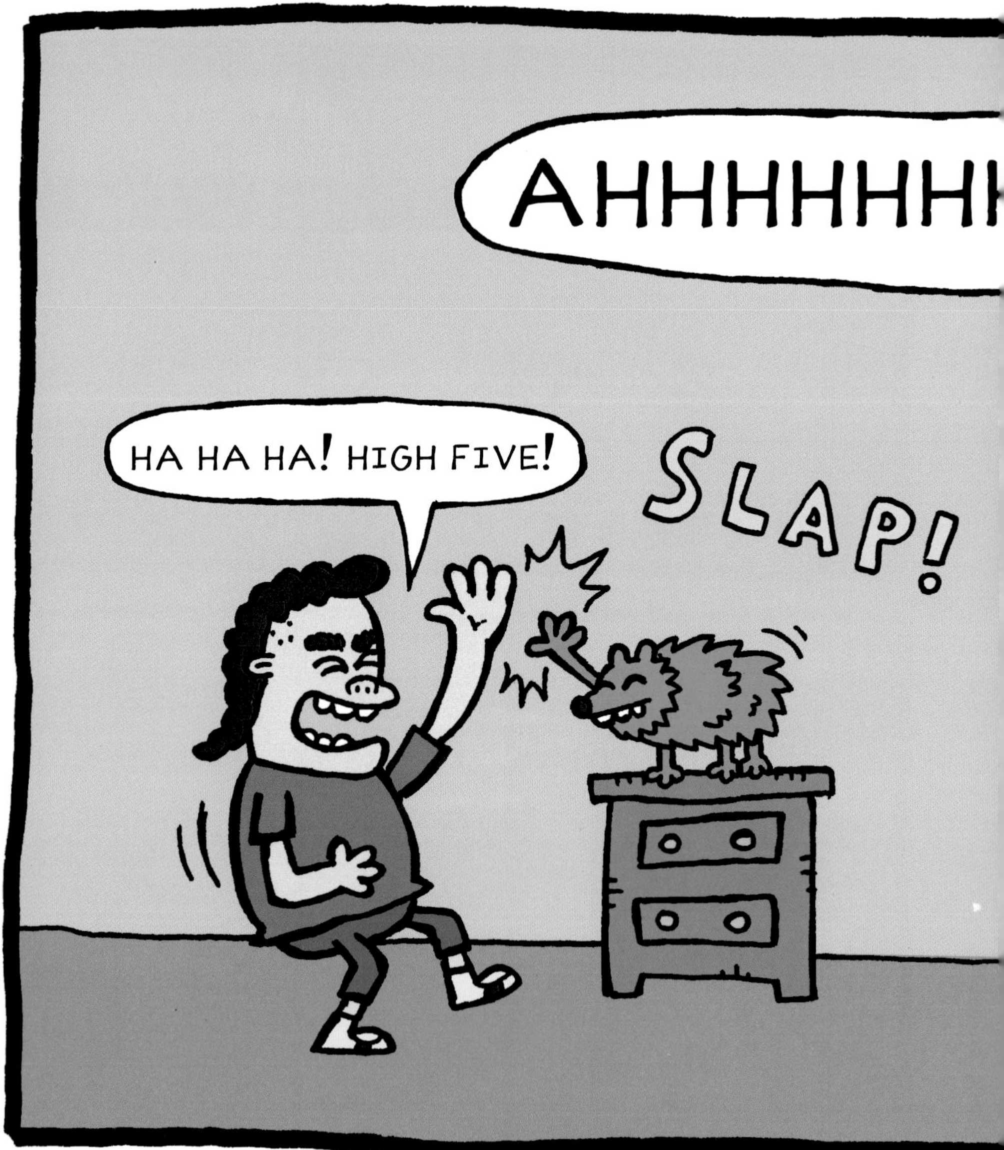
AHHHHHHH
HA HA HA! HIGH FIVE!
SLAP!

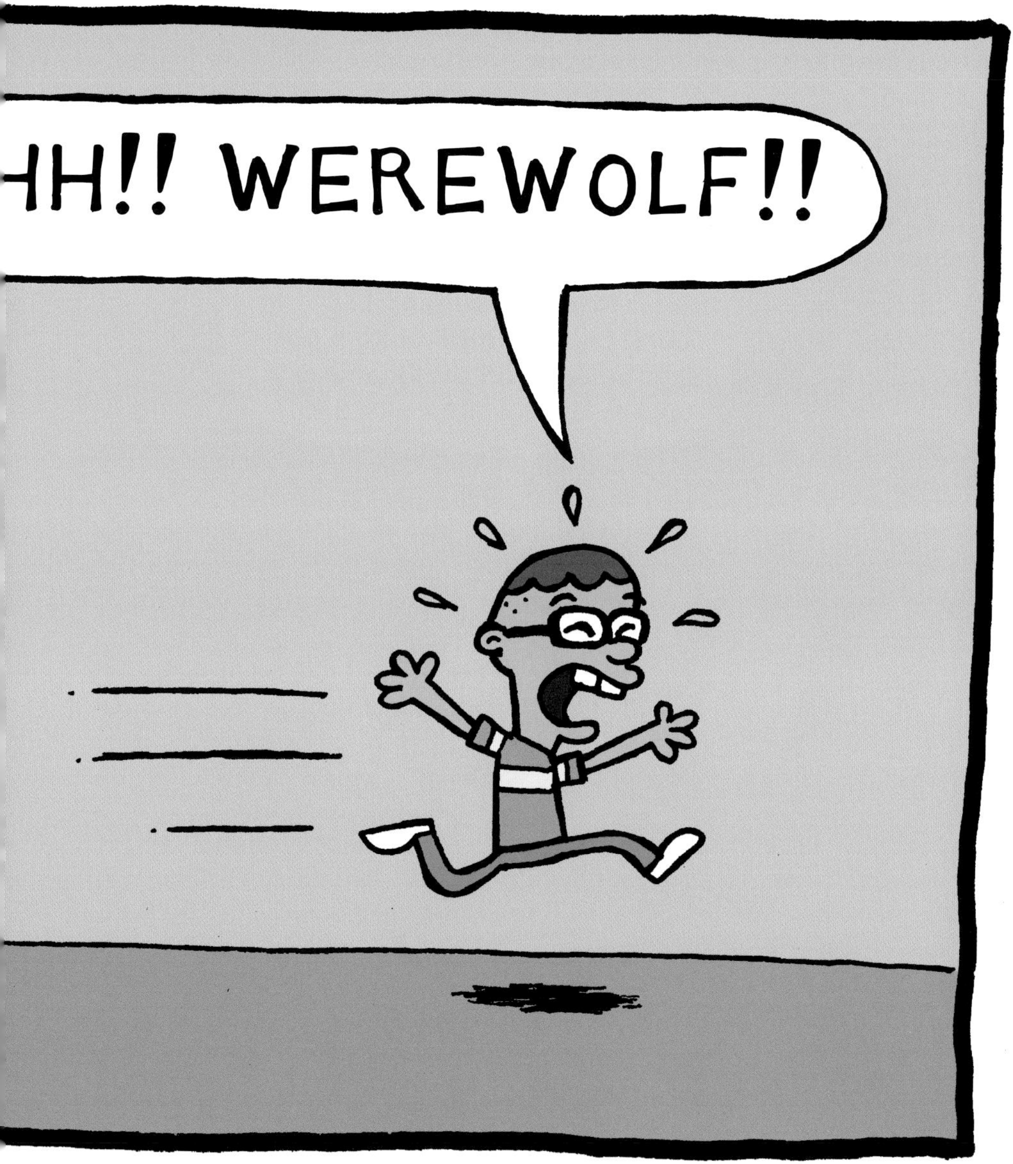
HH!! WEREWOLF!!

One day Carlton's older brother, Milt, got a brilliant, creepy older-brother-style idea...

Hey, I know, I'll dress up in horrible monster costumes and chase my younger brother, Carlton, around and he'll get scared and run away and cry and it will be SO AWESOME!

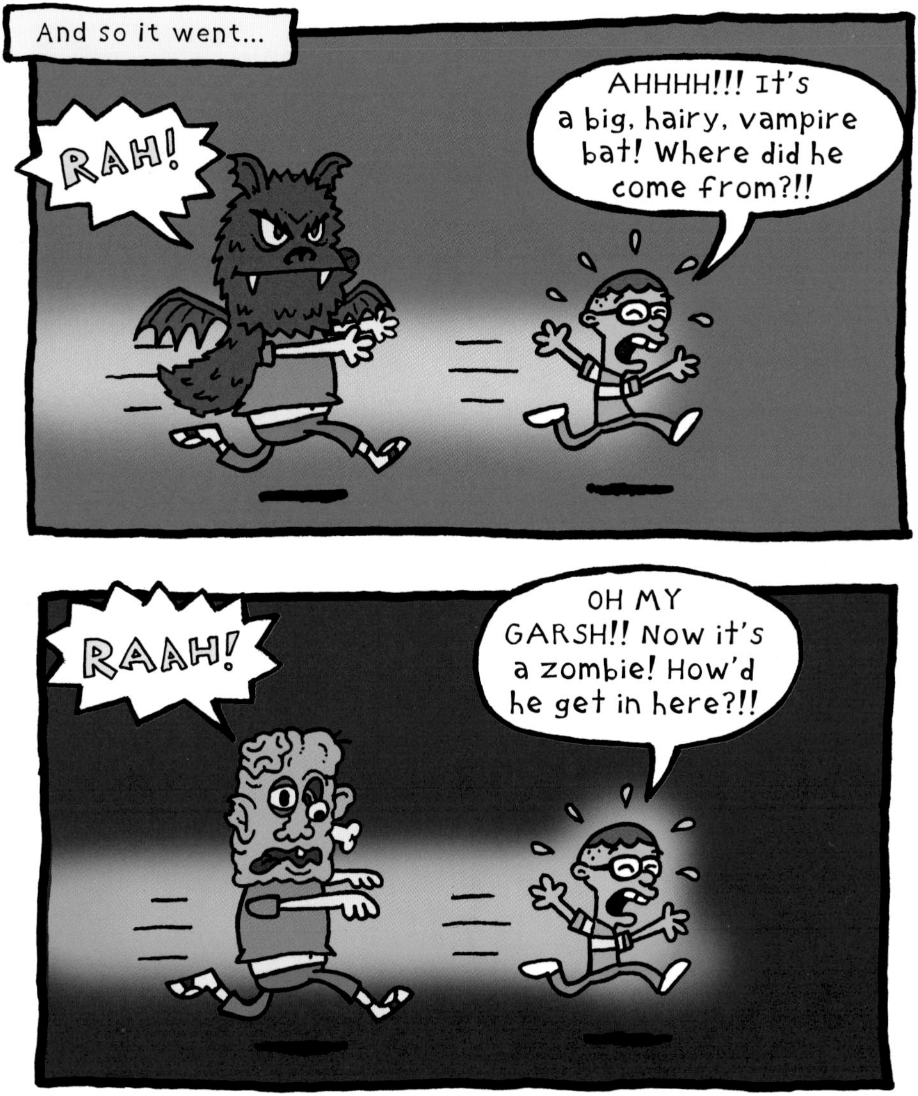
And so it went...
RAH!
AHHHH!!! It's a big, hairy, vampire bat! Where did he come from?!!
RAAH!
OH MY GARSH!! Now it's a zombie! How'd he get in here?!!

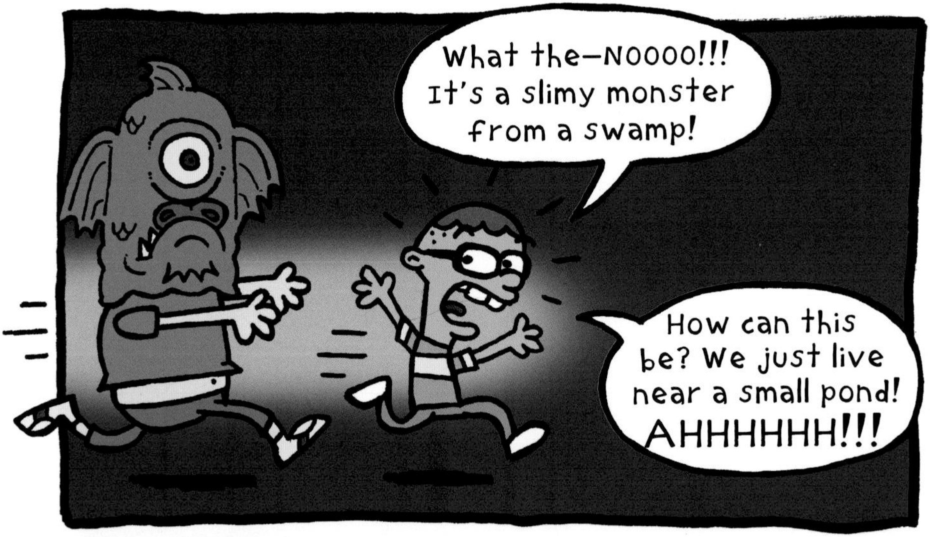
What the—NOOOO!!! It's a slimy monster from a swamp!
How can this be? We just live near a small pond! AHHHHHH!!!

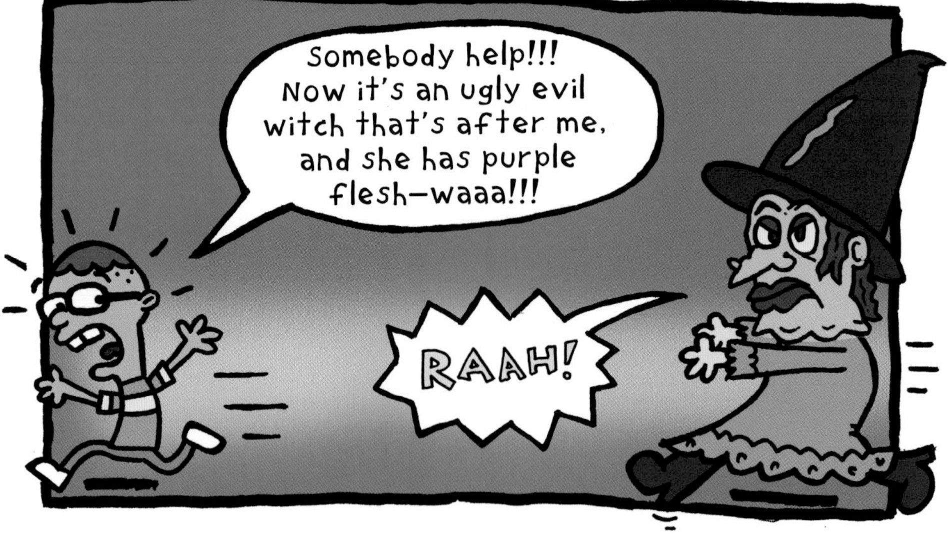
Somebody help!!! Now it's an ugly evil witch that's after me, and she has purple flesh—waaa!!!
RAAH!

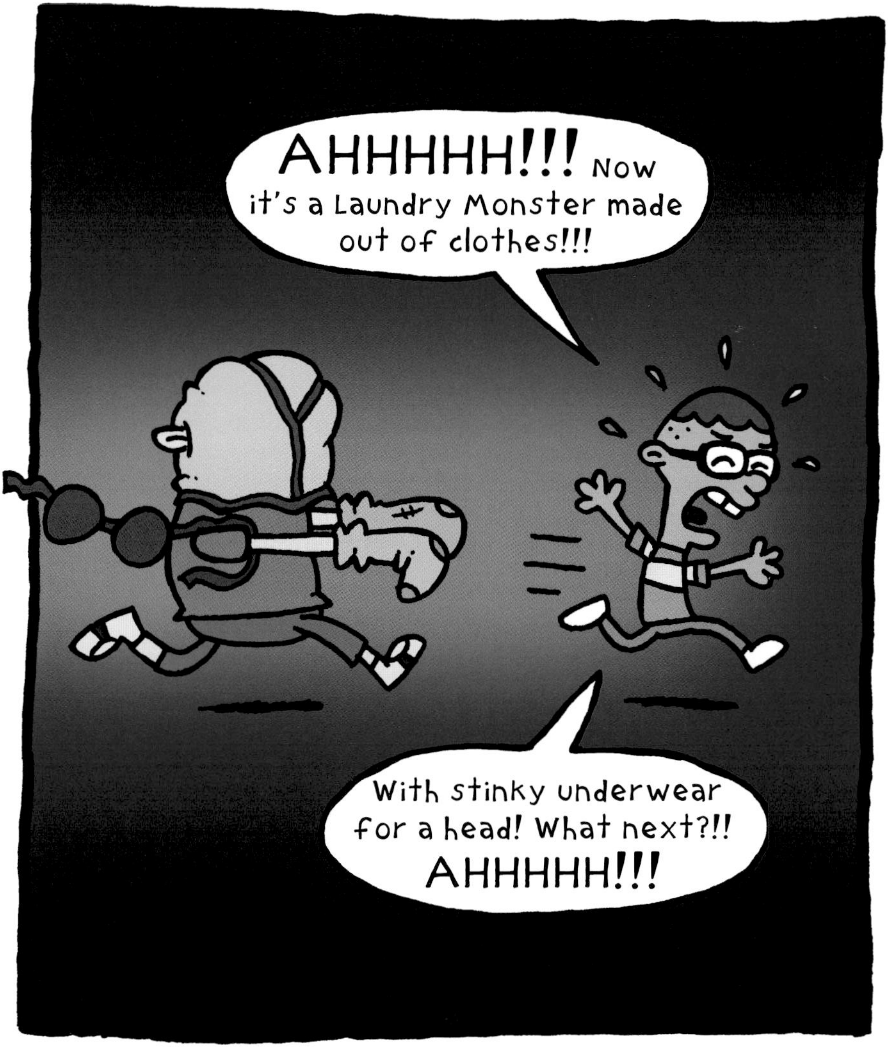
AHHHHH!!! Now it's a Laundry Monster made out of clothes!!!
With stinky underwear for a head! What next?!! AHHHHH!!!

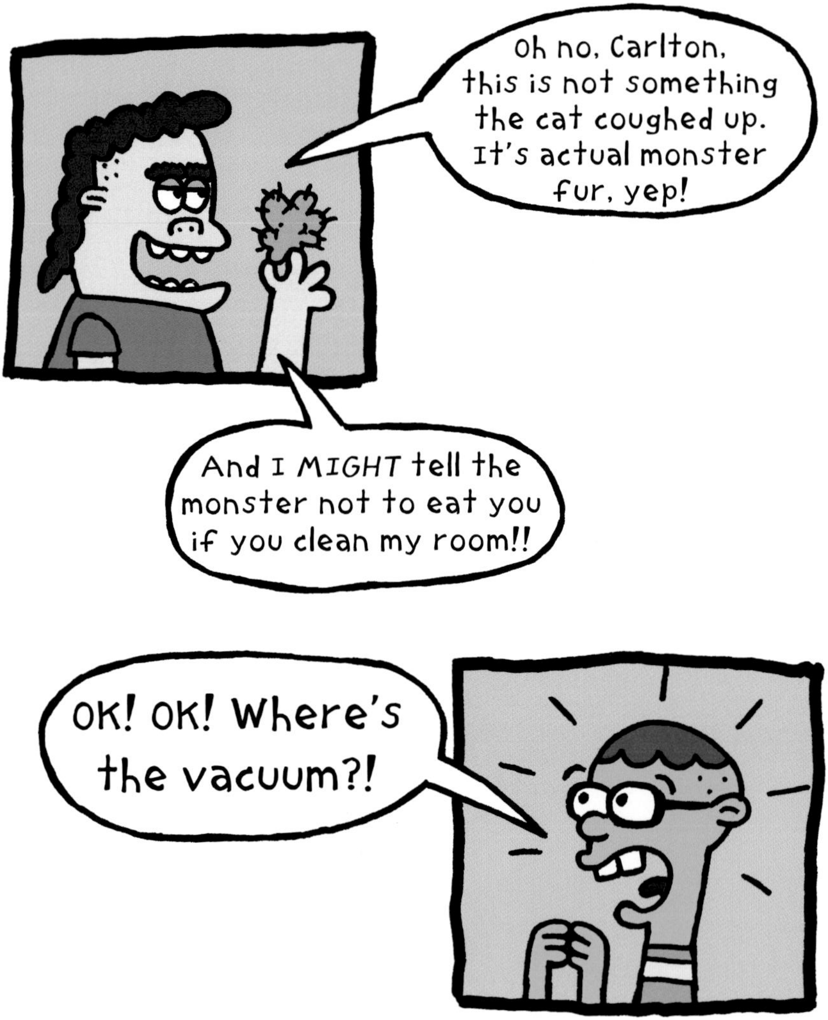
Oh no, Carlton, this is not something the cat coughed up. It's actual monster fur, yep!
And I MIGHT tell the monster not to eat you if you clean my room!!
OK! OK! Where's the vacuum?!

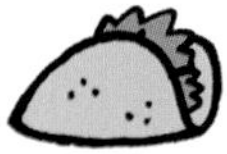

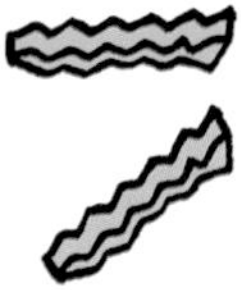

CHAPTER 2

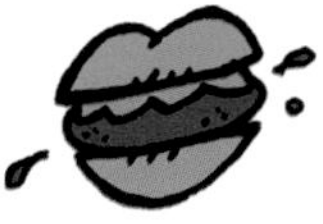

Carlton began to fear everything.

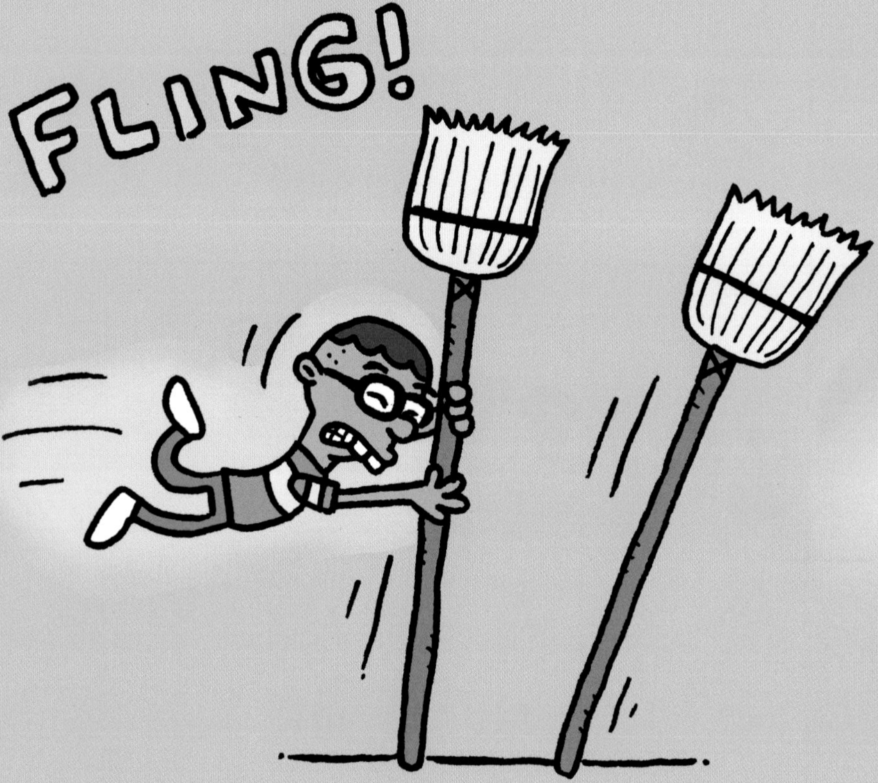
FLING!

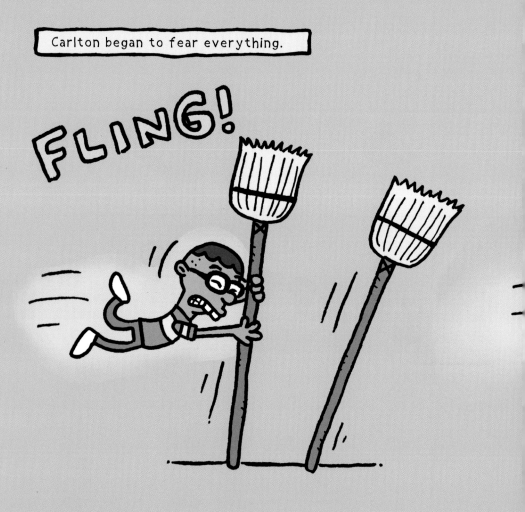

He was afraid of what might be under the bed...

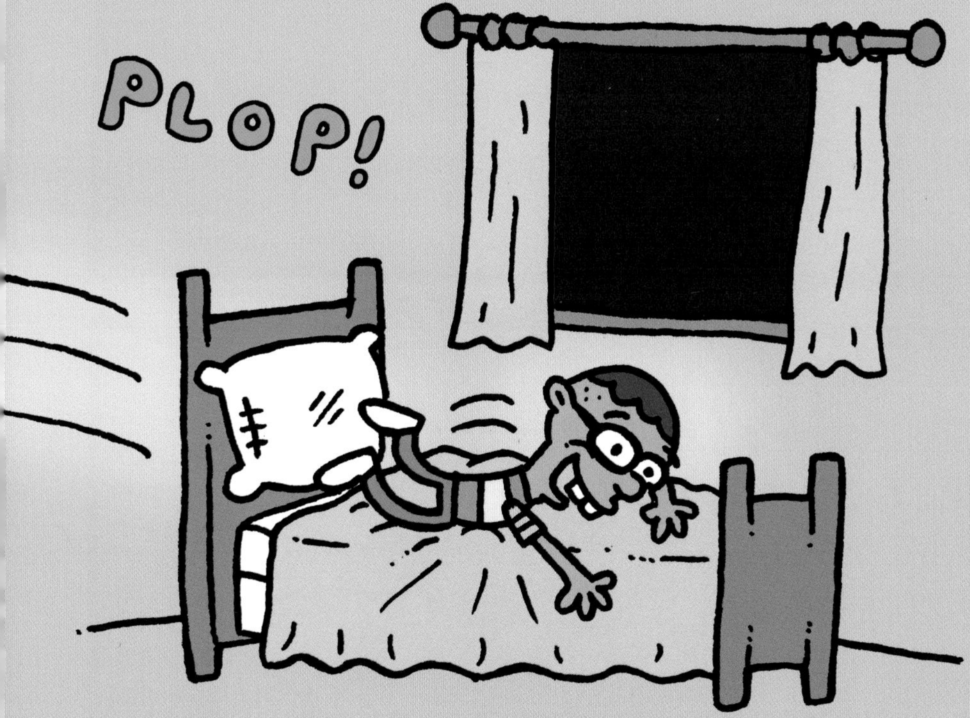
PLOP!

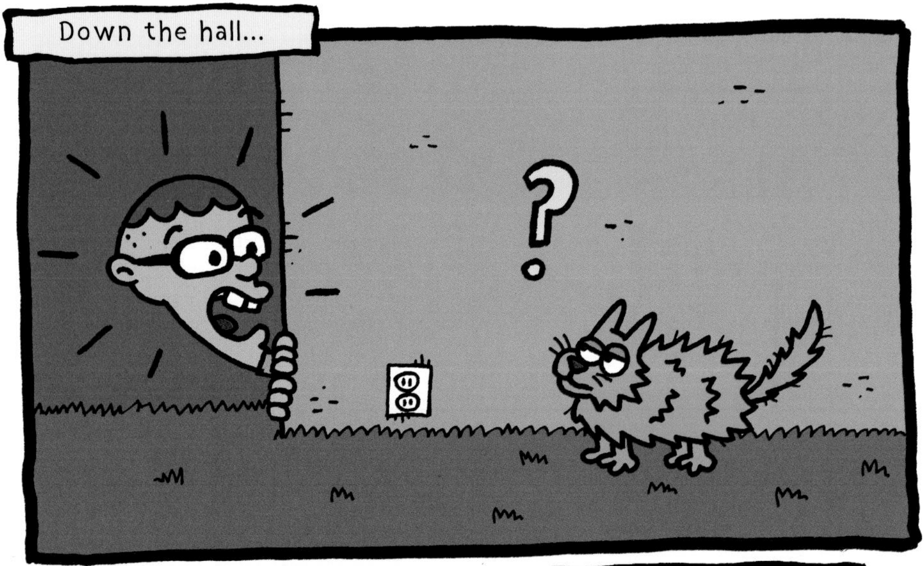
Down the hall...
?

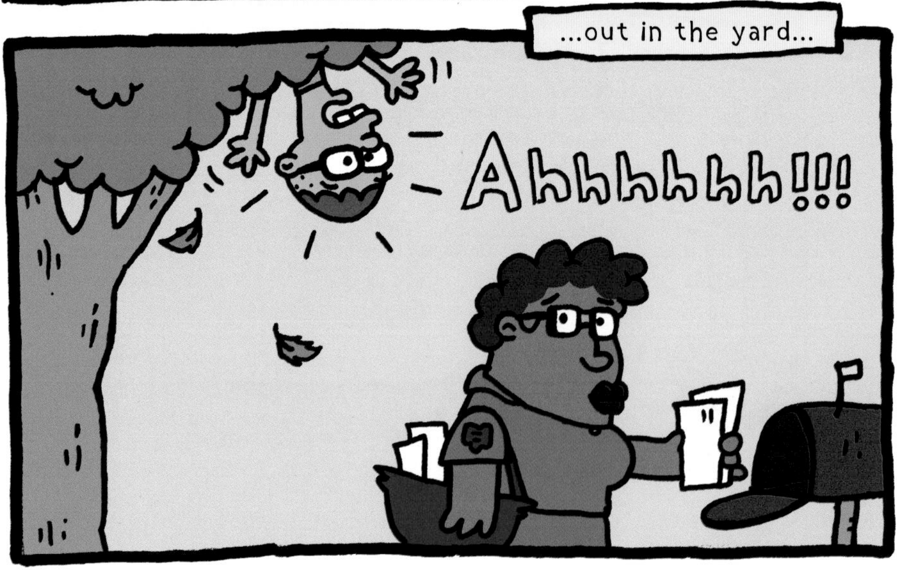
...out in the yard...
Ahhhhhh!!!

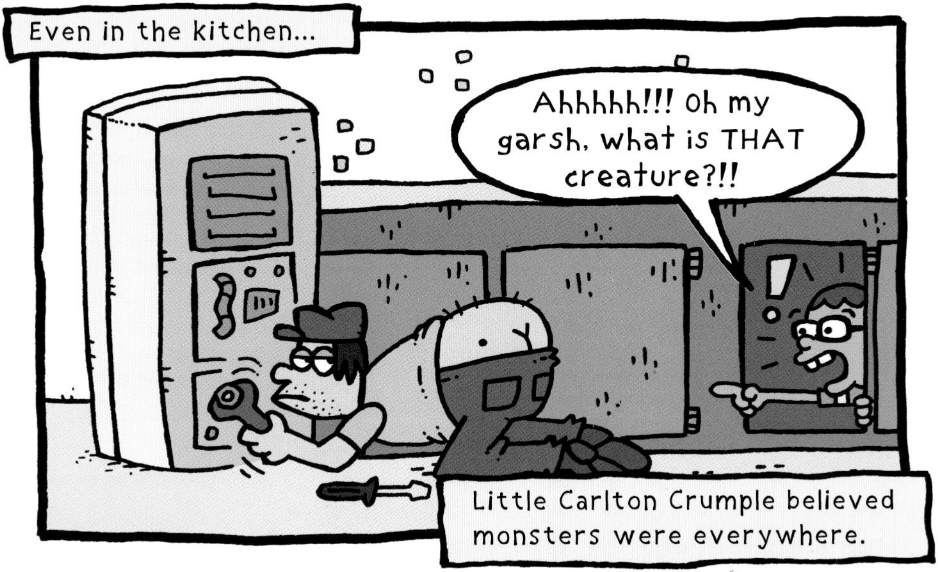
Even in the kitchen...
Ahhhhh!!! Oh my garsh, what is THAT creature?!!
Little Carlton Crumple believed monsters were everywhere.

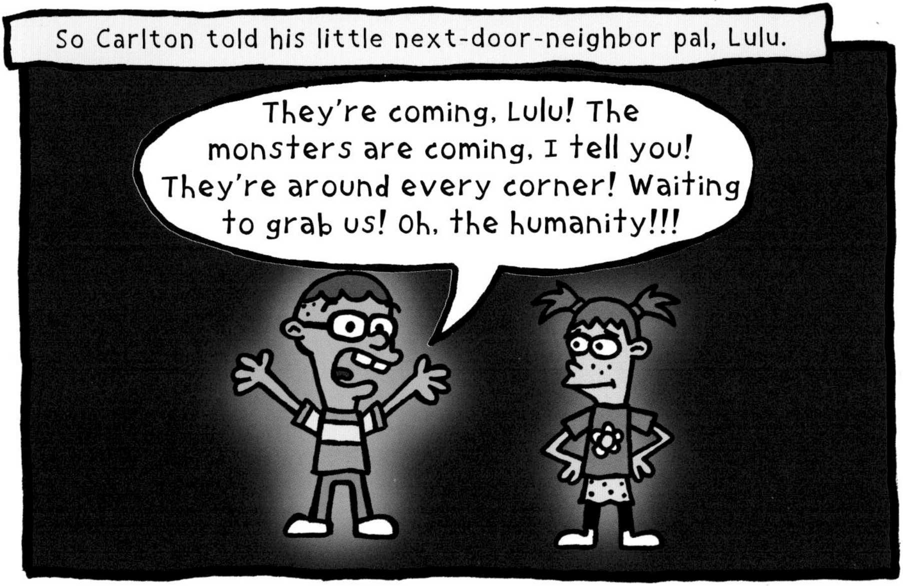
So Carlton told his little next-door-neighbor pal, Lulu.
They're coming, Lulu! The monsters are coming, I tell you! They're around every corner! Waiting to grab us! Oh, the humanity!!!

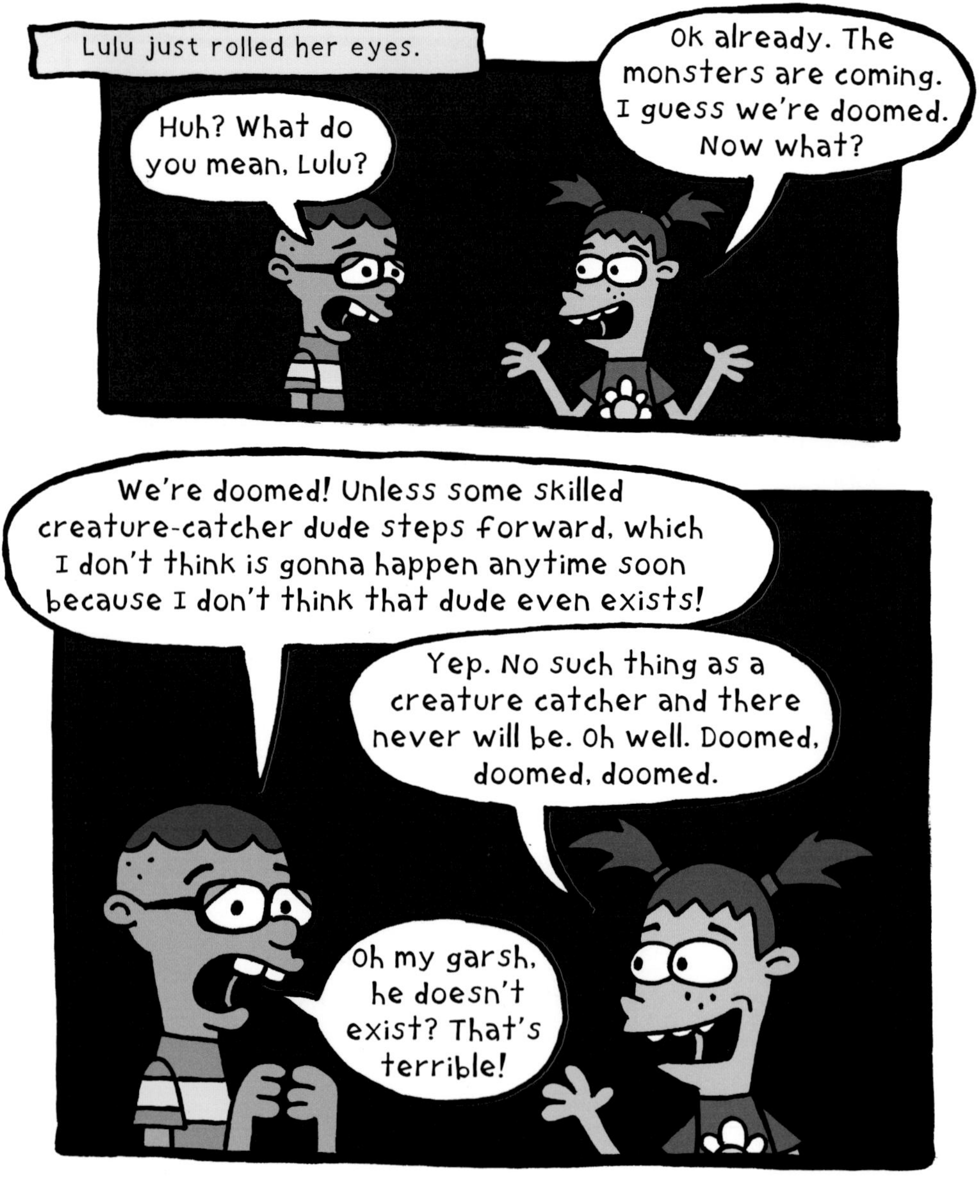
Lulu just rolled her eyes.
Huh? What do you mean, Lulu?
OK already. The monsters are coming. I guess we're doomed. Now what?
We're doomed! Unless some skilled creature-catcher dude steps forward, which I don't think is gonna happen anytime soon because I don't think that dude even exists!
Yep. No such thing as a creature catcher and there never will be. Oh well. Doomed, doomed, doomed.
Oh my garsh, he doesn't exist? That's terrible!

Then Carlton had an epiphany, which is like a great idea that you've been waiting for your whole life that suddenly explodes inside your head.

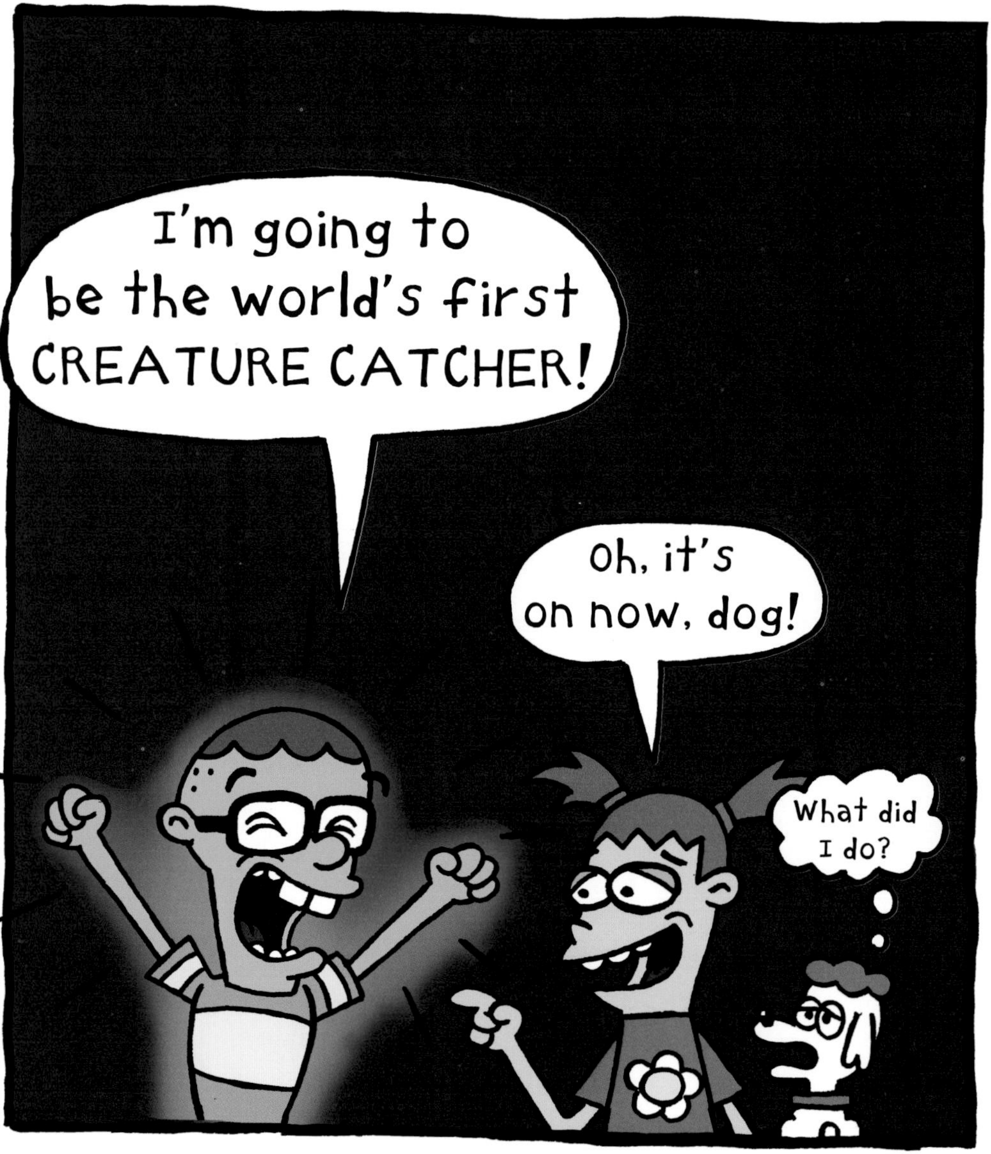
I'm going to
be the world's first
CREATURE CATCHER!
Oh, it's
on now, dog!
What did
I do?

CHAPTER 3

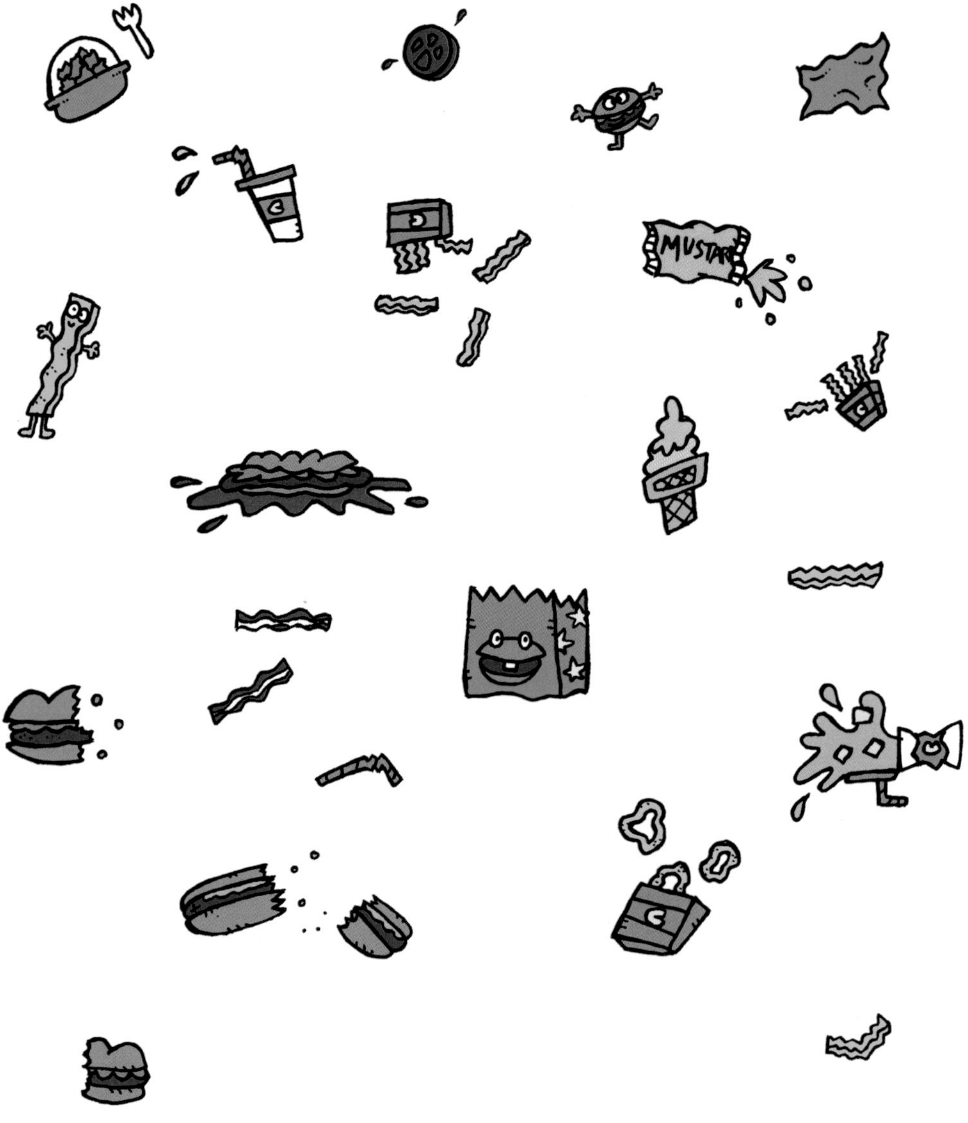
MUSTAR

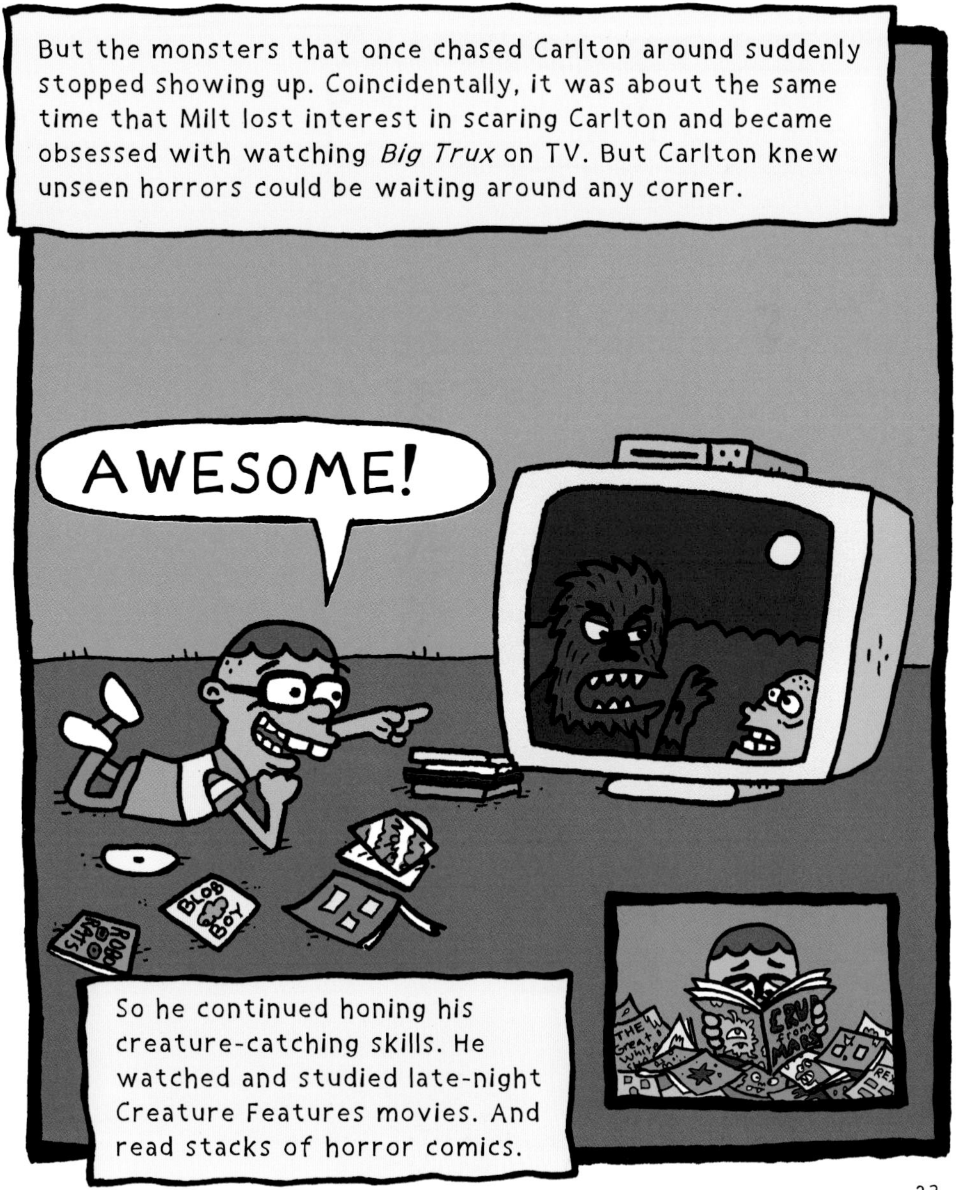
But the monsters that once chased Carlton around suddenly stopped showing up. Coincidentally, it was about the same time that Milt lost interest in scaring Carlton and became obsessed with watching *Big Trux* on TV. But Carlton knew unseen horrors could be waiting around any corner.
AWESOME!
BLOB BOY
So he continued honing his creature-catching skills. He watched and studied late-night Creature Features movies. And read stacks of horror comics.

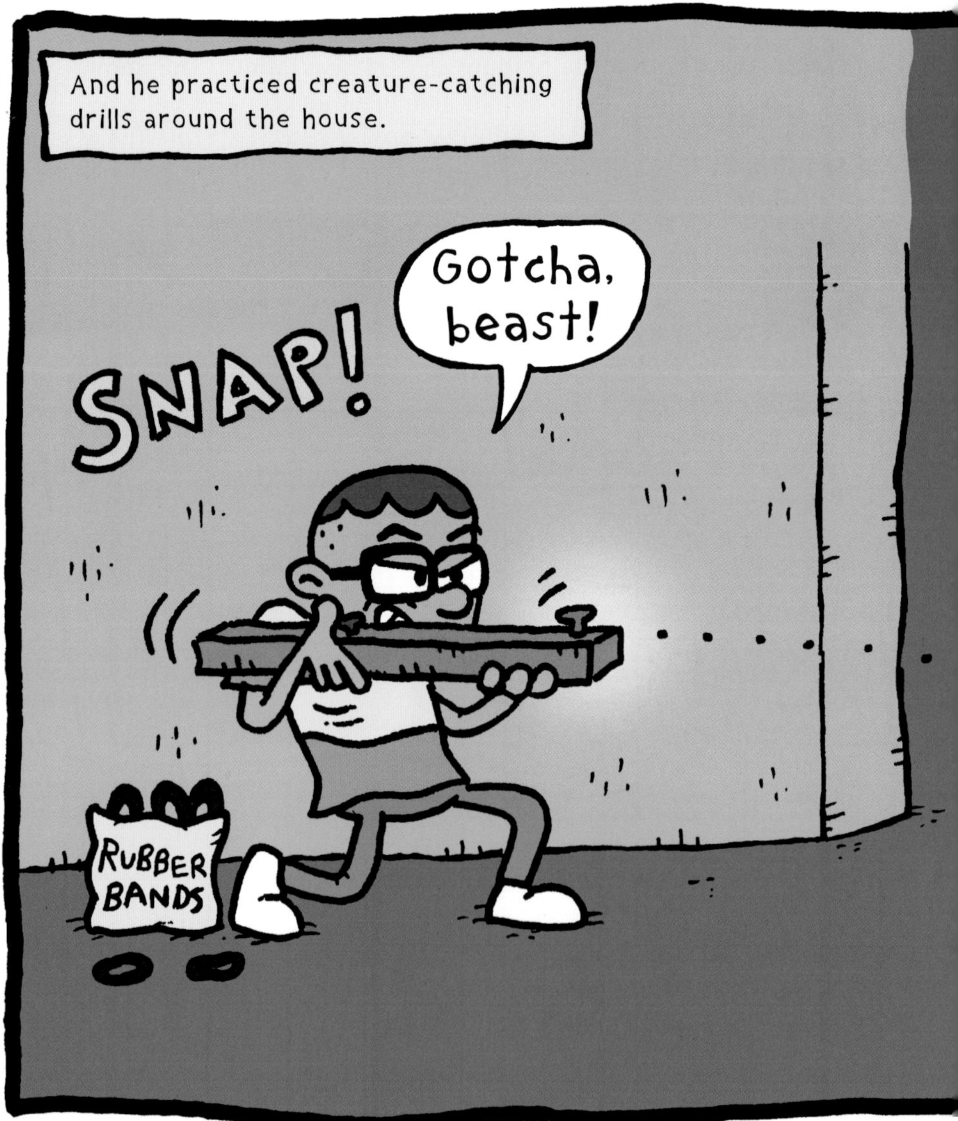
And he practiced creature-catching drills around the house.
SNAP!
Gotcha, beast!
RUBBER BANDS

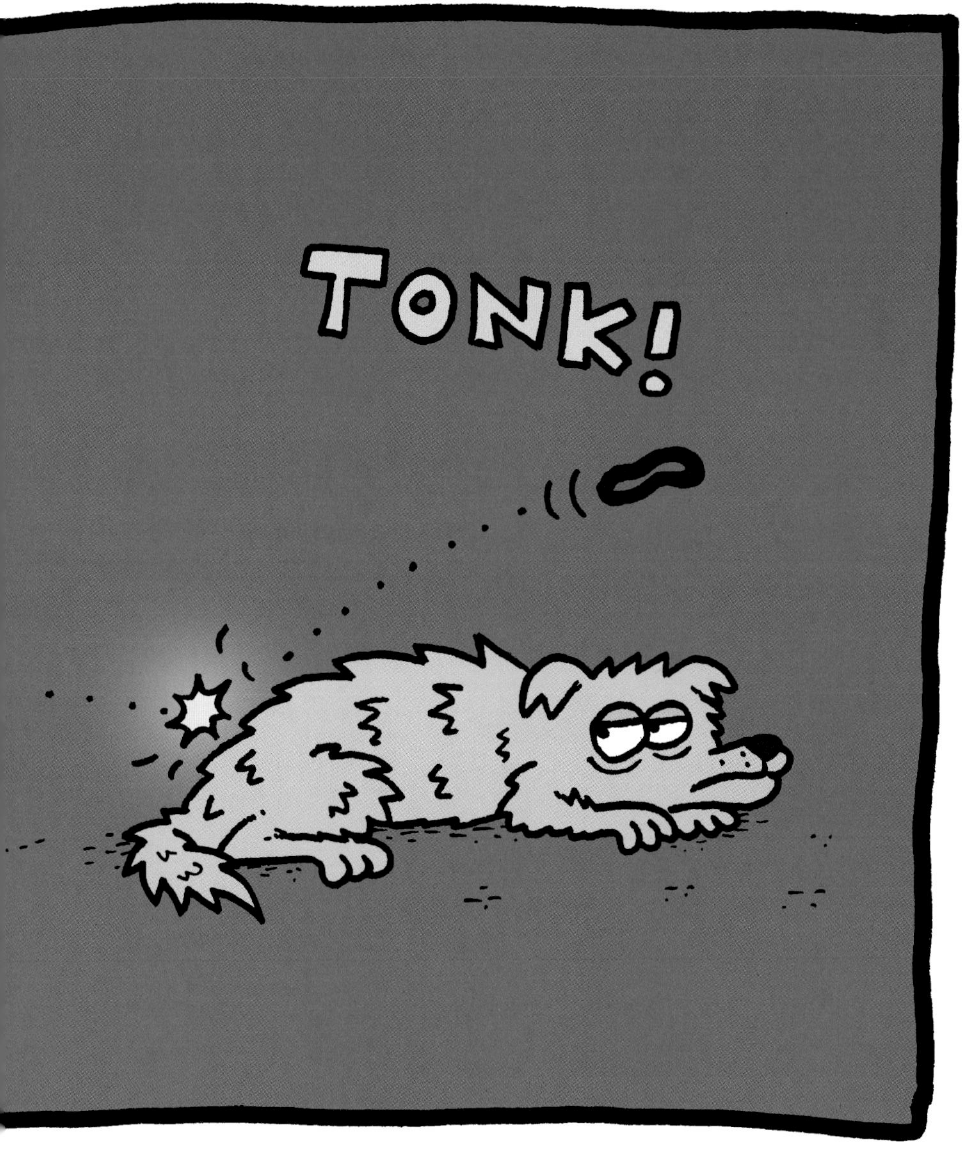
TONK!

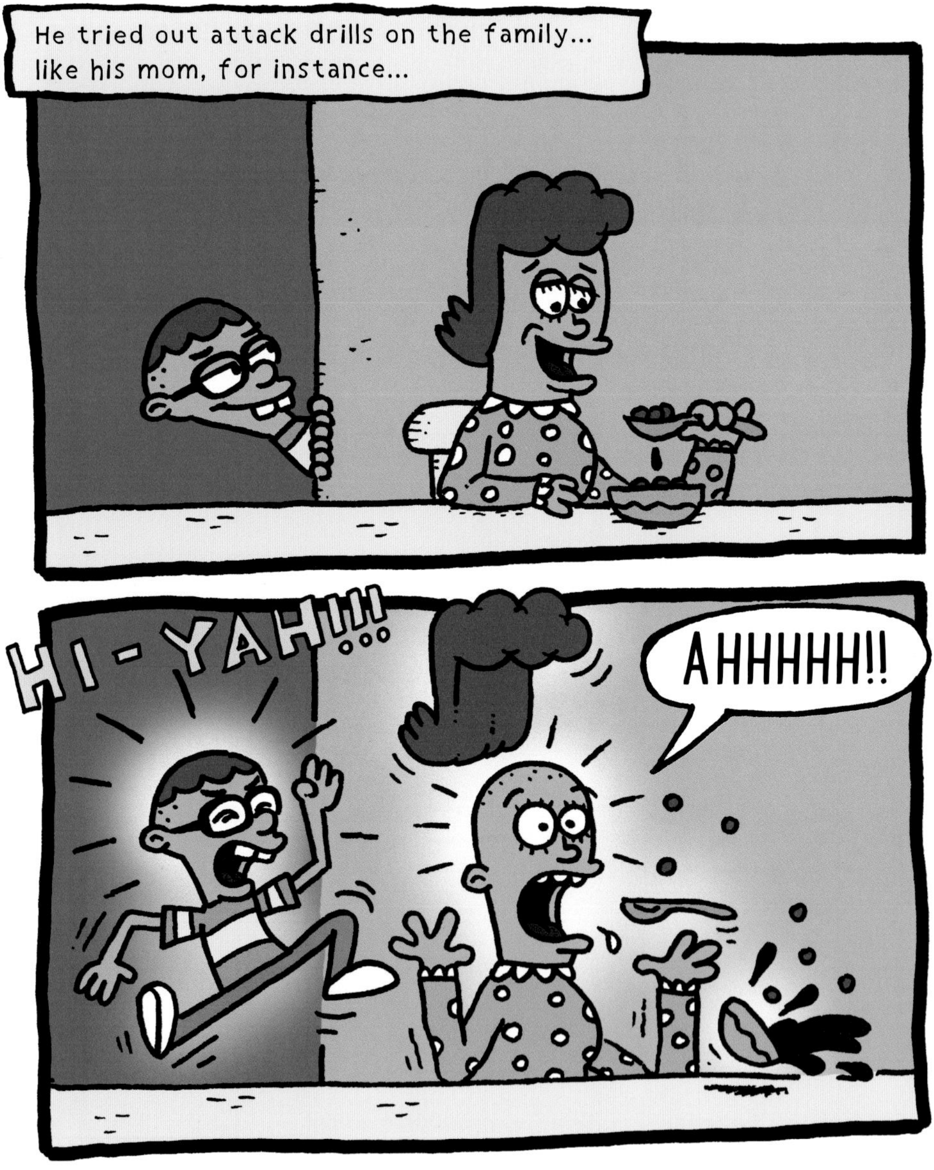
He tried out attack drills on the family... like his mom, for instance...
HI-YAH!!!
AHHHHH!!

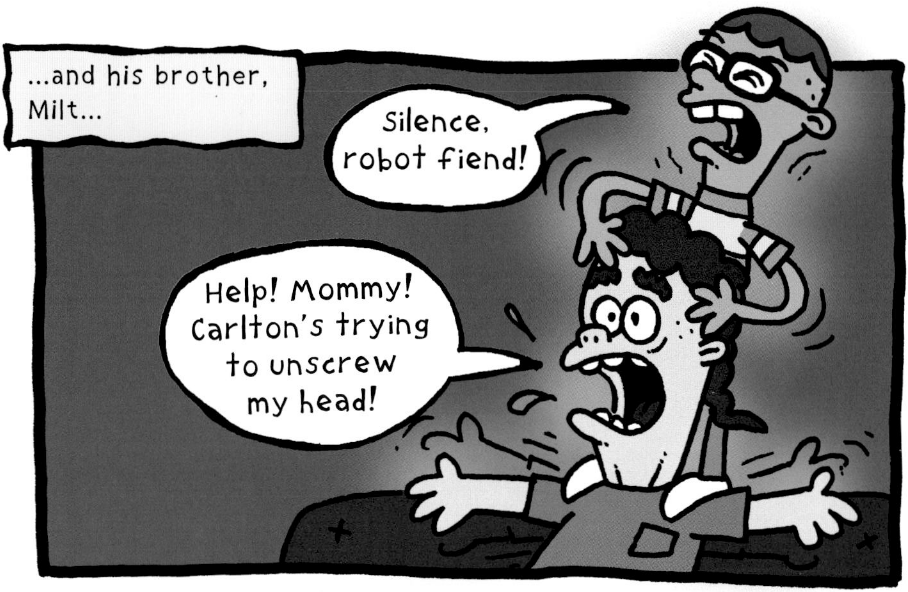
...and his brother, Milt...
Silence, robot fiend!
Help! Mommy! Carlton's trying to unscrew my head!

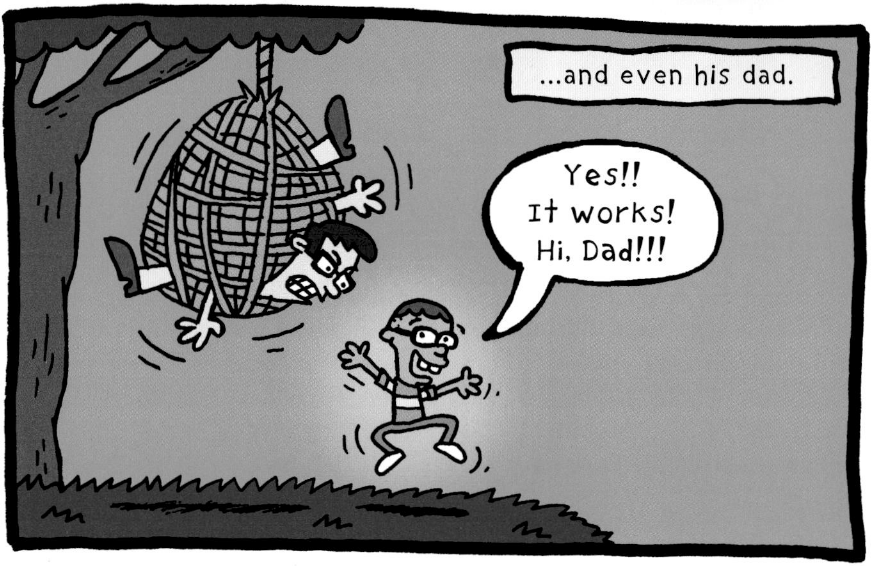
...and even his dad.
Yes!! It works! Hi, Dad!!!

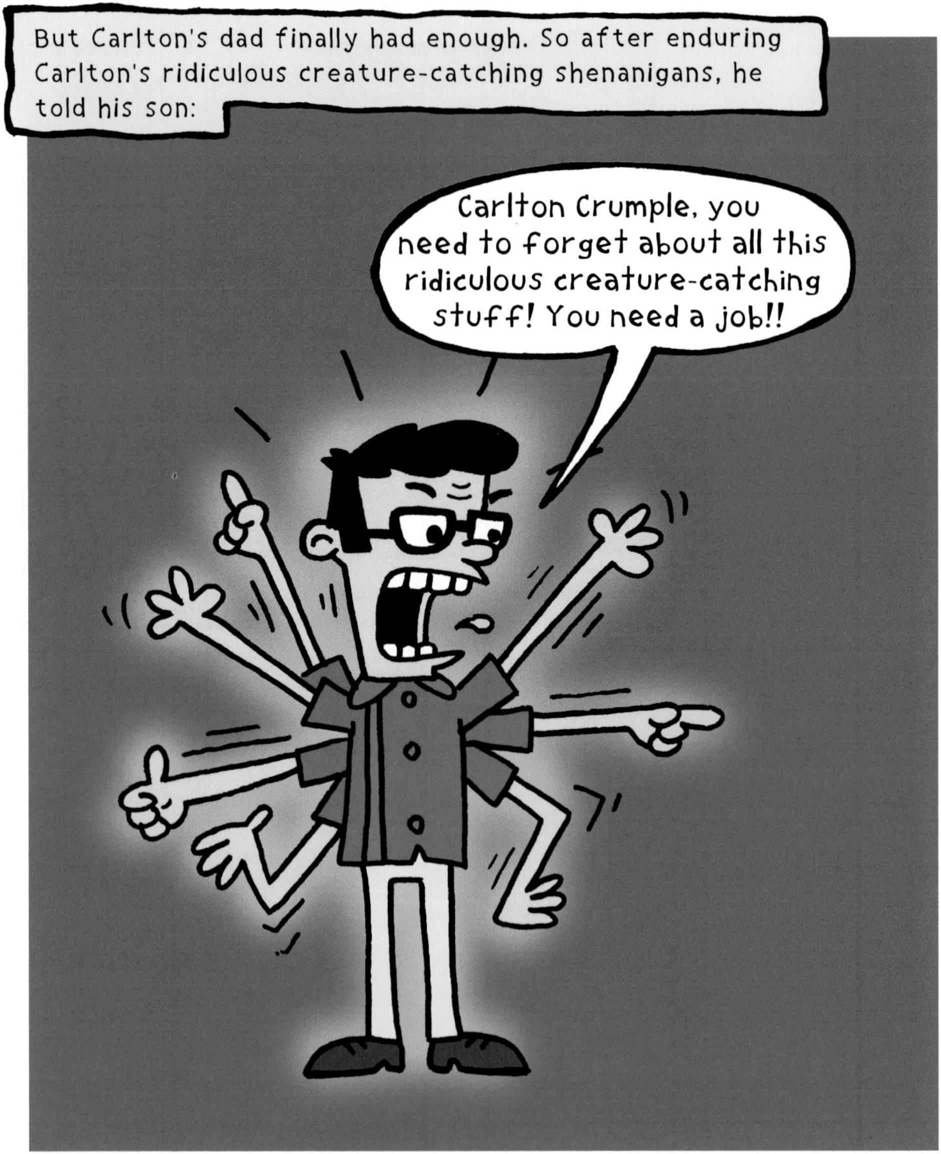
But Carlton's dad finally had enough. So after enduring Carlton's ridiculous creature-catching shenanigans, he told his son:
Carlton Crumple, you need to forget about all this ridiculous creature-catching stuff! You need a job!!

Carlton thought it wasn't a bad idea. Then he could save up his money to buy creature-catching gear, gizmos, helmet, body armor, and awesome stuff!

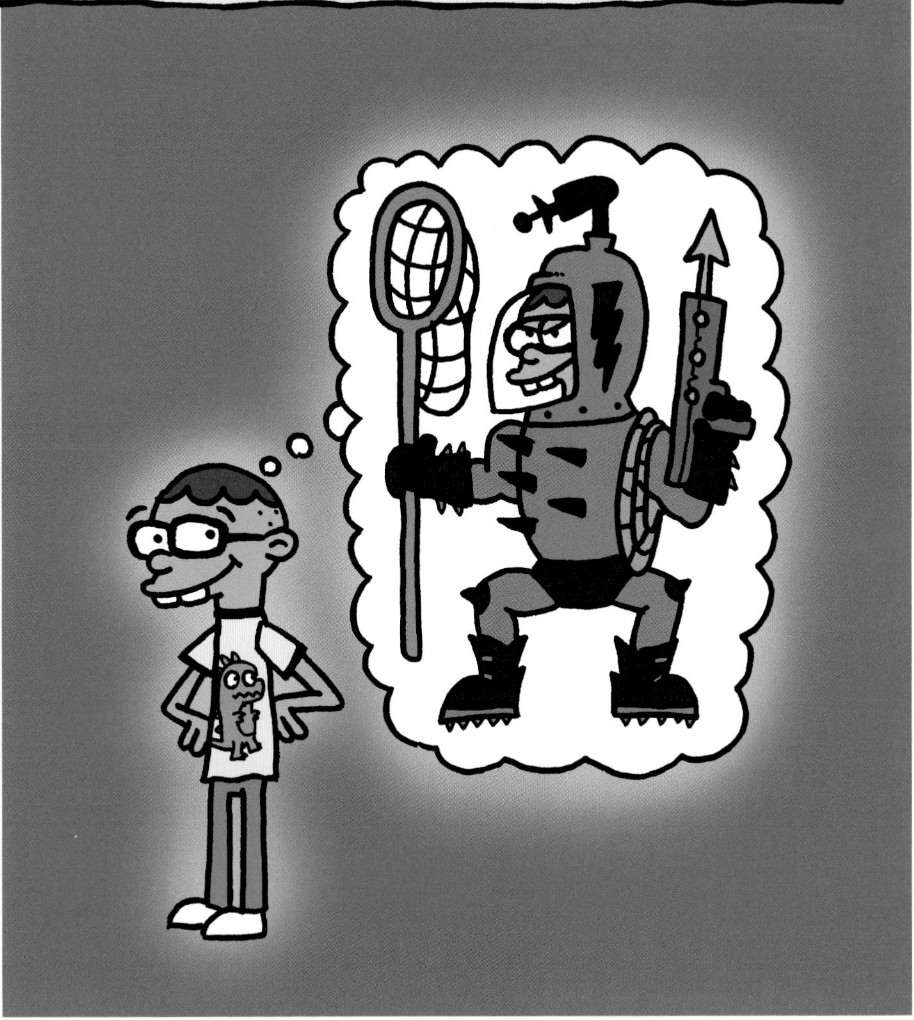

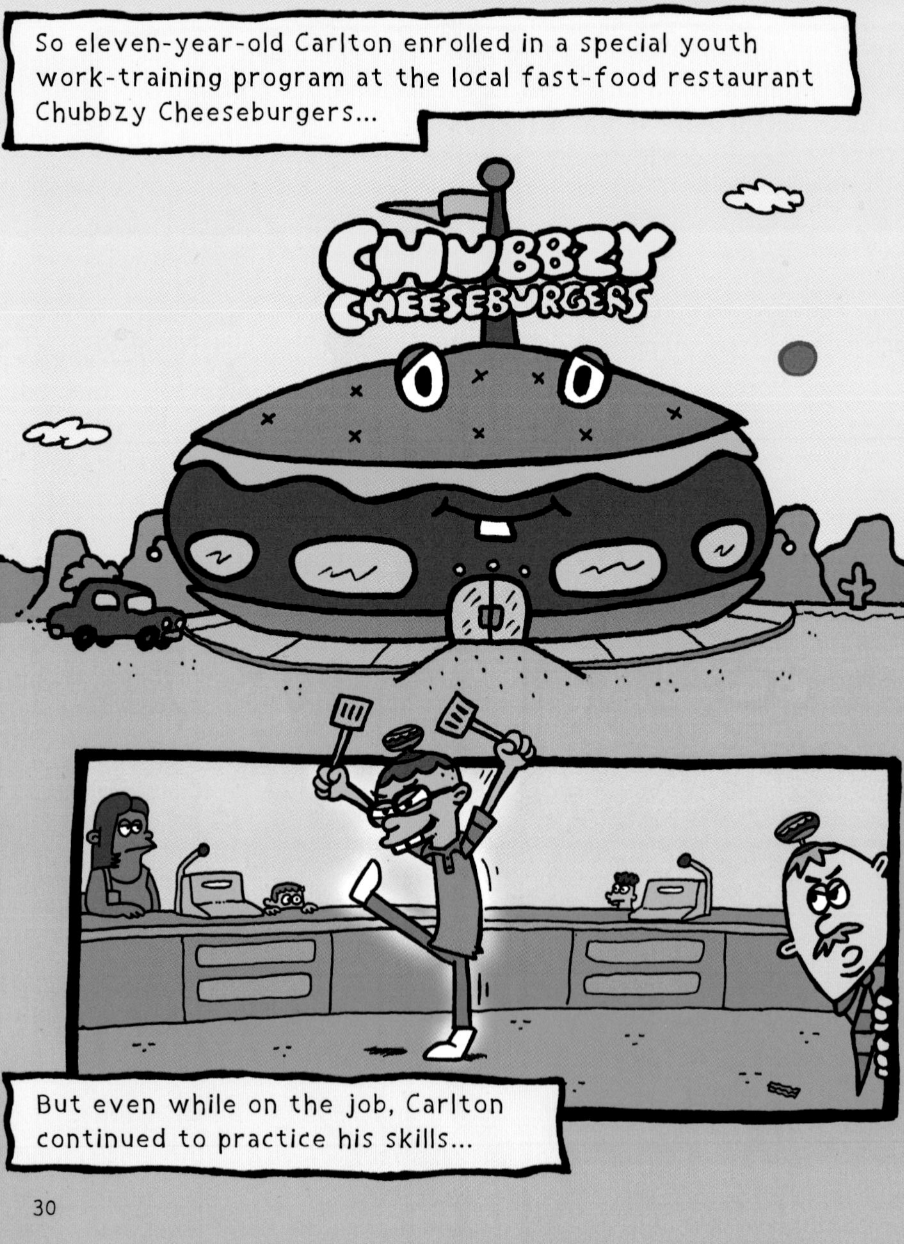
So eleven-year-old Carlton enrolled in a special youth work-training program at the local fast-food restaurant Chubbzy Cheeseburgers...
CHUBBZY CHEESEBURGERS
But even while on the job, Carlton continued to practice his skills...

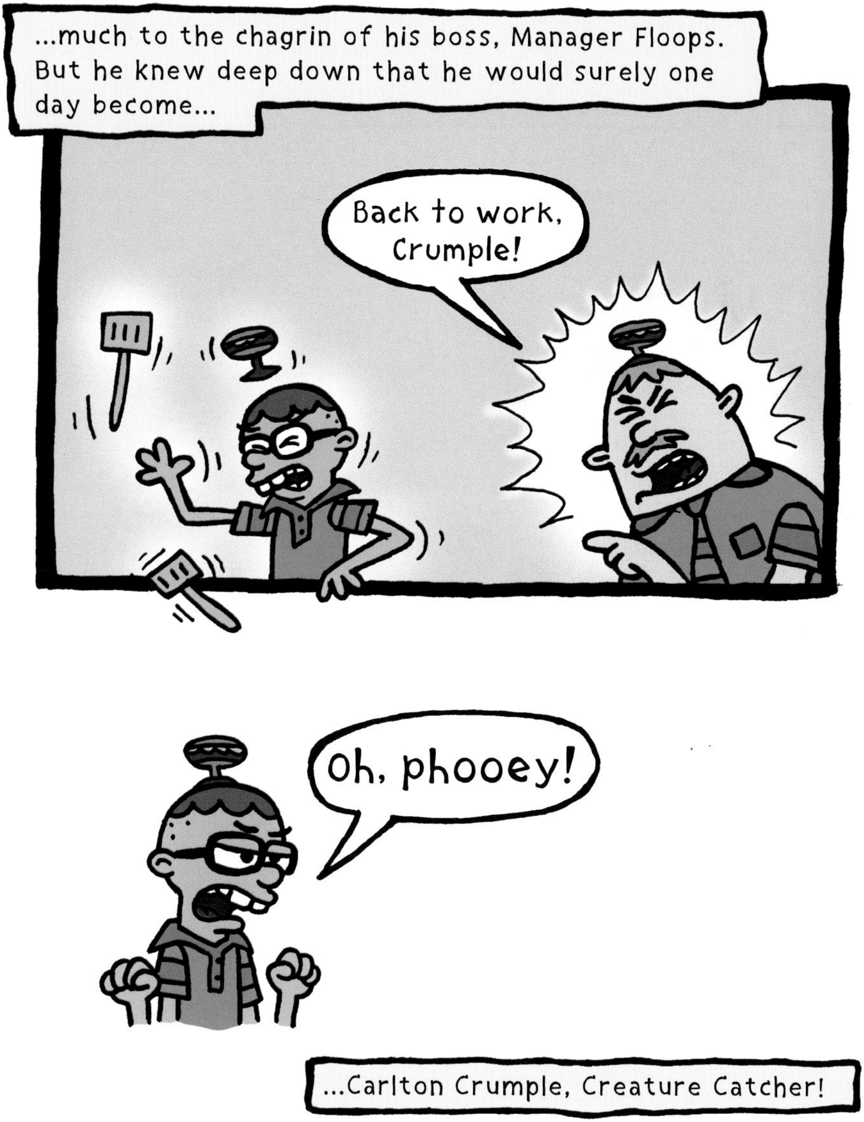
...much to the chagrin of his boss, Manager Floops. But he knew deep down that he would surely one day become...
Back to work, Crumple!
Oh, phooey!
...Carlton Crumple, Creature Catcher!

CHAPTER 4

MEANWHILE...A few miles up the road,
modern society was about to collapse.
And it all started with a french fry.

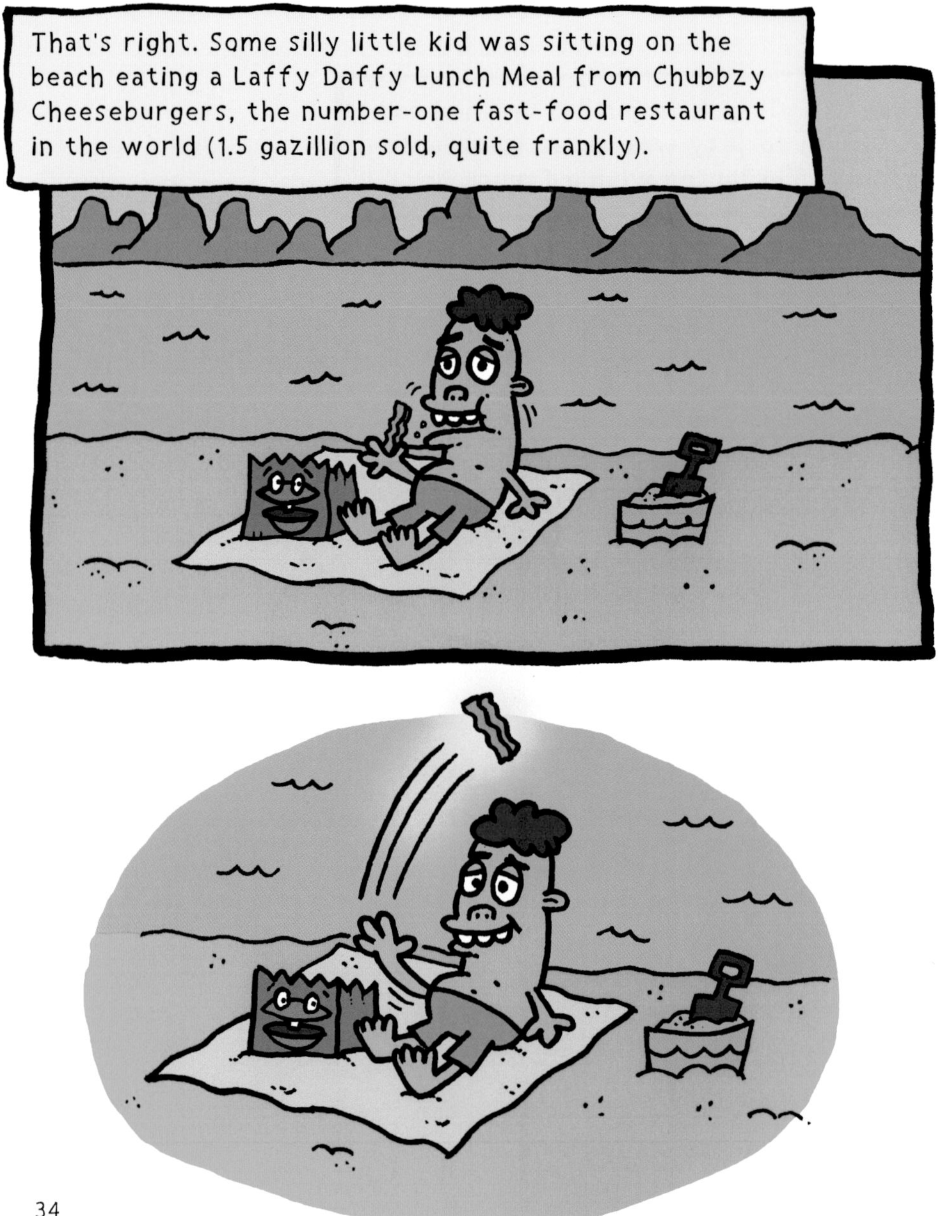
That's right. Some silly little kid was sitting on the beach eating a Laffy Daffy Lunch Meal from Chubbzy Cheeseburgers, the number-one fast-food restaurant in the world (1.5 gazillion sold, quite frankly).

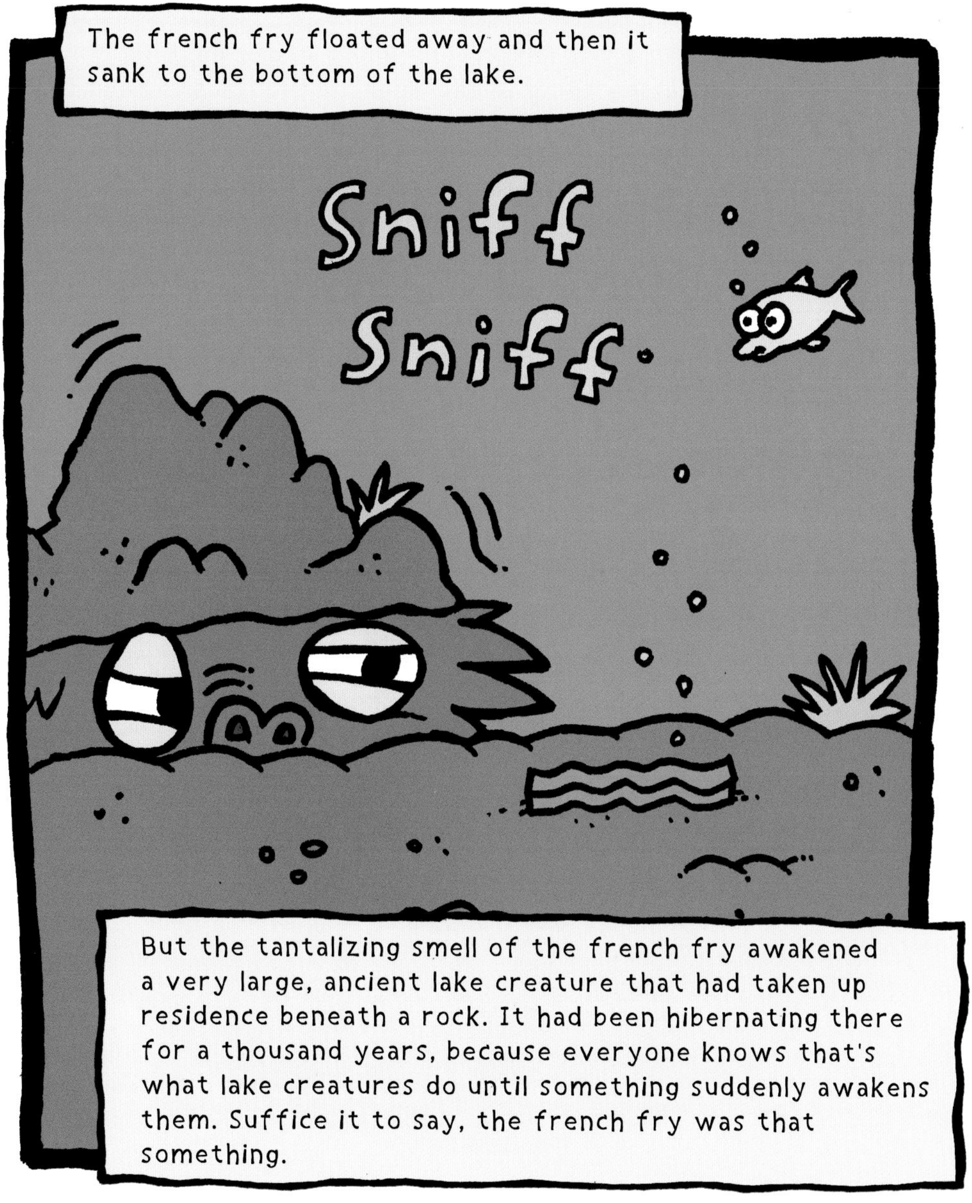
The french fry floated away and then it sank to the bottom of the lake.
Sniff
Sniff.
But the tantalizing smell of the french fry awakened a very large, ancient lake creature that had taken up residence beneath a rock. It had been hibernating there for a thousand years, because everyone knows that's what lake creatures do until something suddenly awakens them. Suffice it to say, the french fry was that something.

The creature gobbled the french fry down in one gulp. It was the most amazing thing it had ever tasted (plus it hadn't eaten anything in a really, really, really long time). So it woke up its ancient-lake-creature family and informed them in creature-speak that they must journey forth and find more of this food!

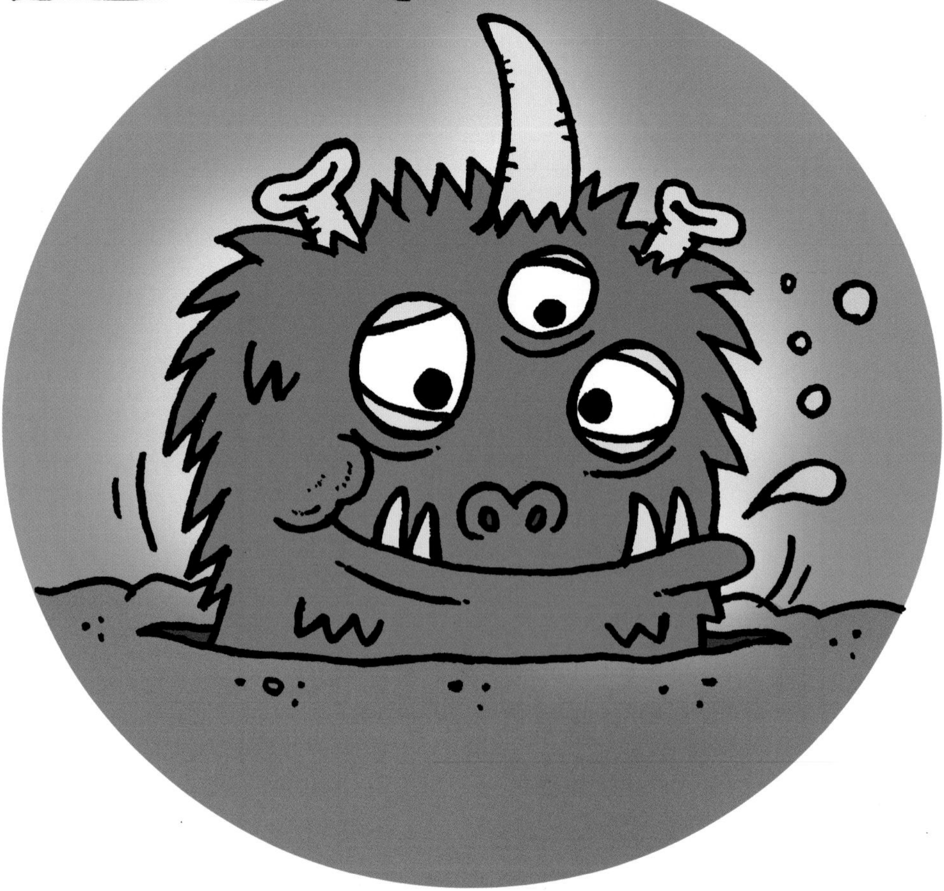

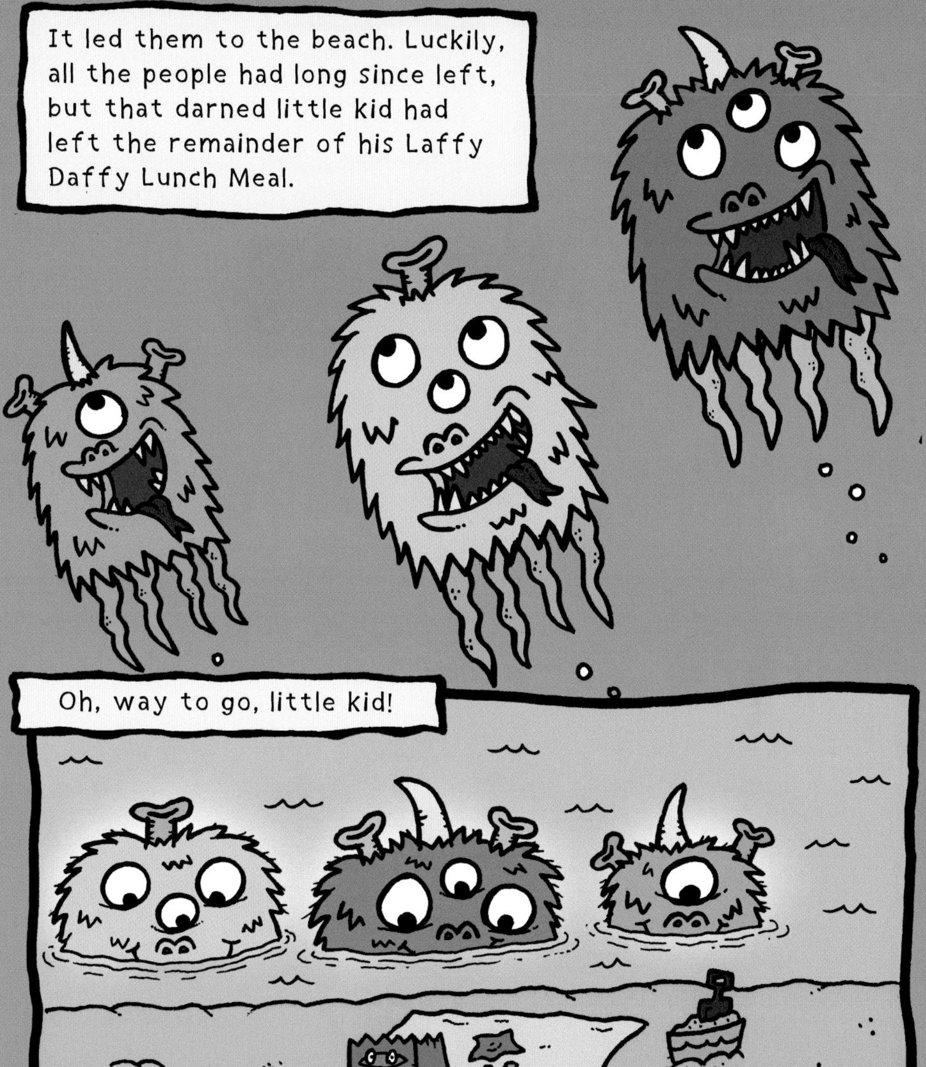
It led them to the beach. Luckily, all the people had long since left, but that darned little kid had left the remainder of his Laffy Daffy Lunch Meal.
Oh, way to go, little kid!

The creatures went wild and gobbled it down, including the free toy prize inside. But that wasn't enough. They were still hungry. They needed MORE!

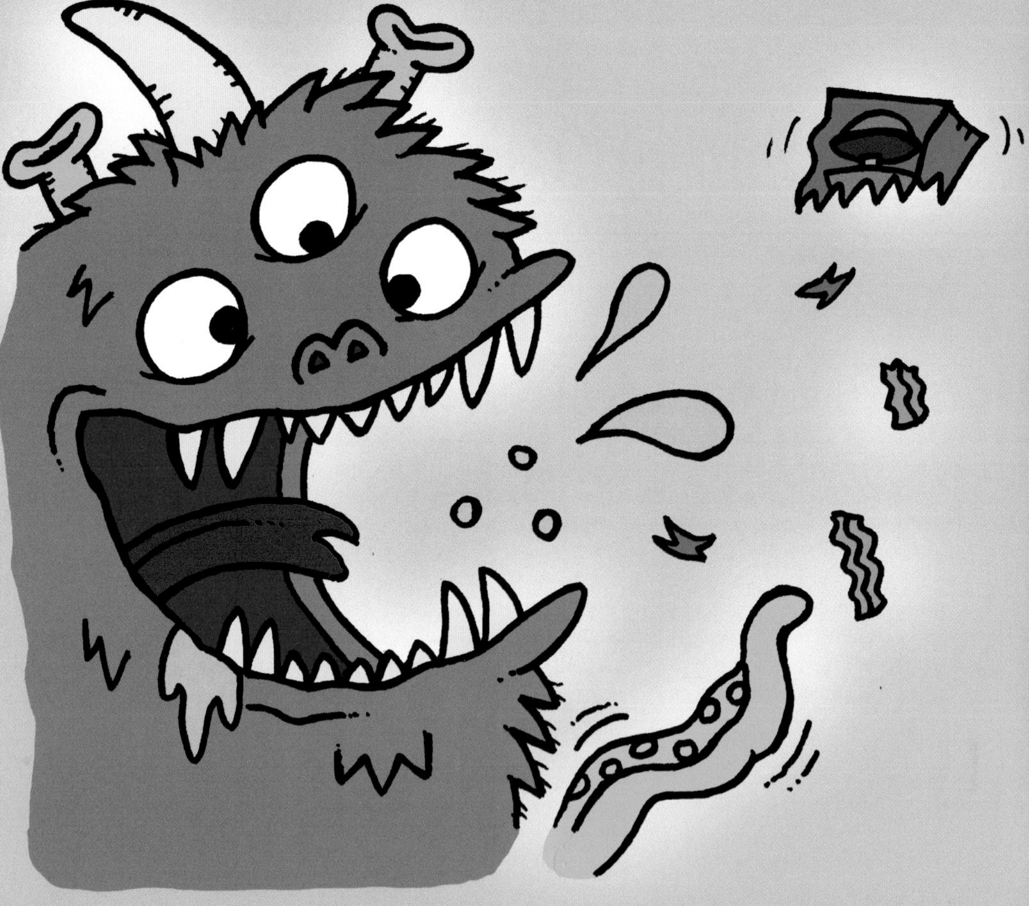

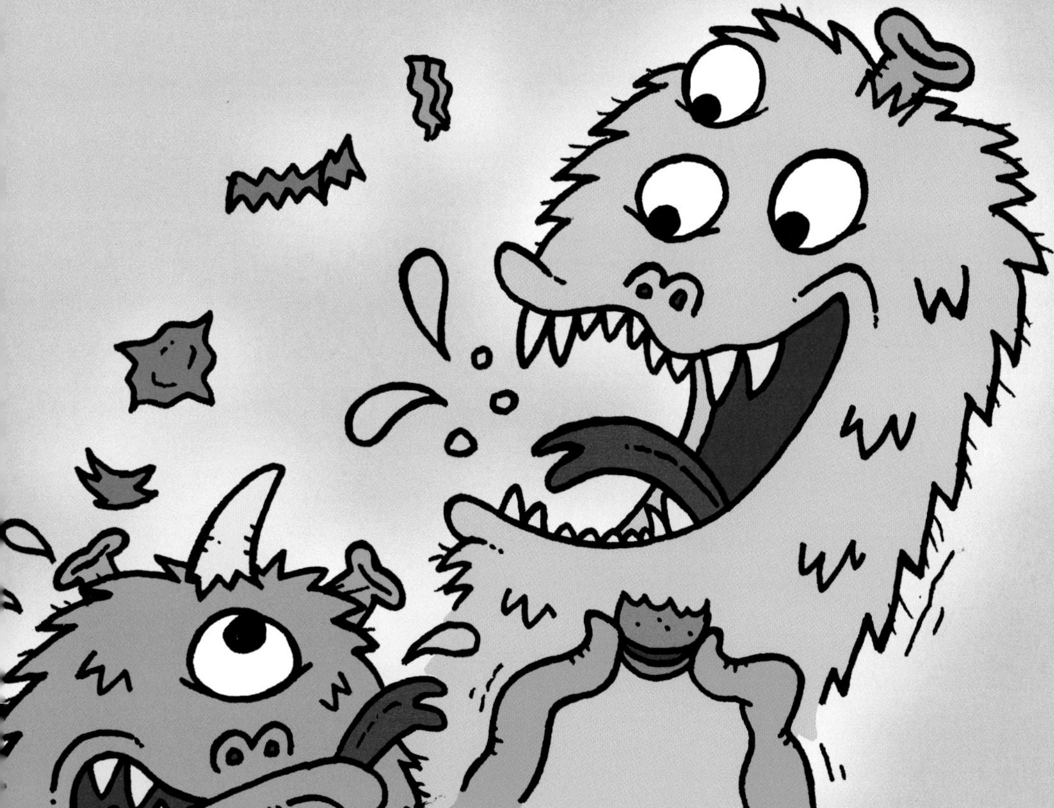

After scaring some stinky, hairy hippies out of their van, the even stinkier, hairier lake creatures hopped in and headed down the highway in search of more delicious fast food.

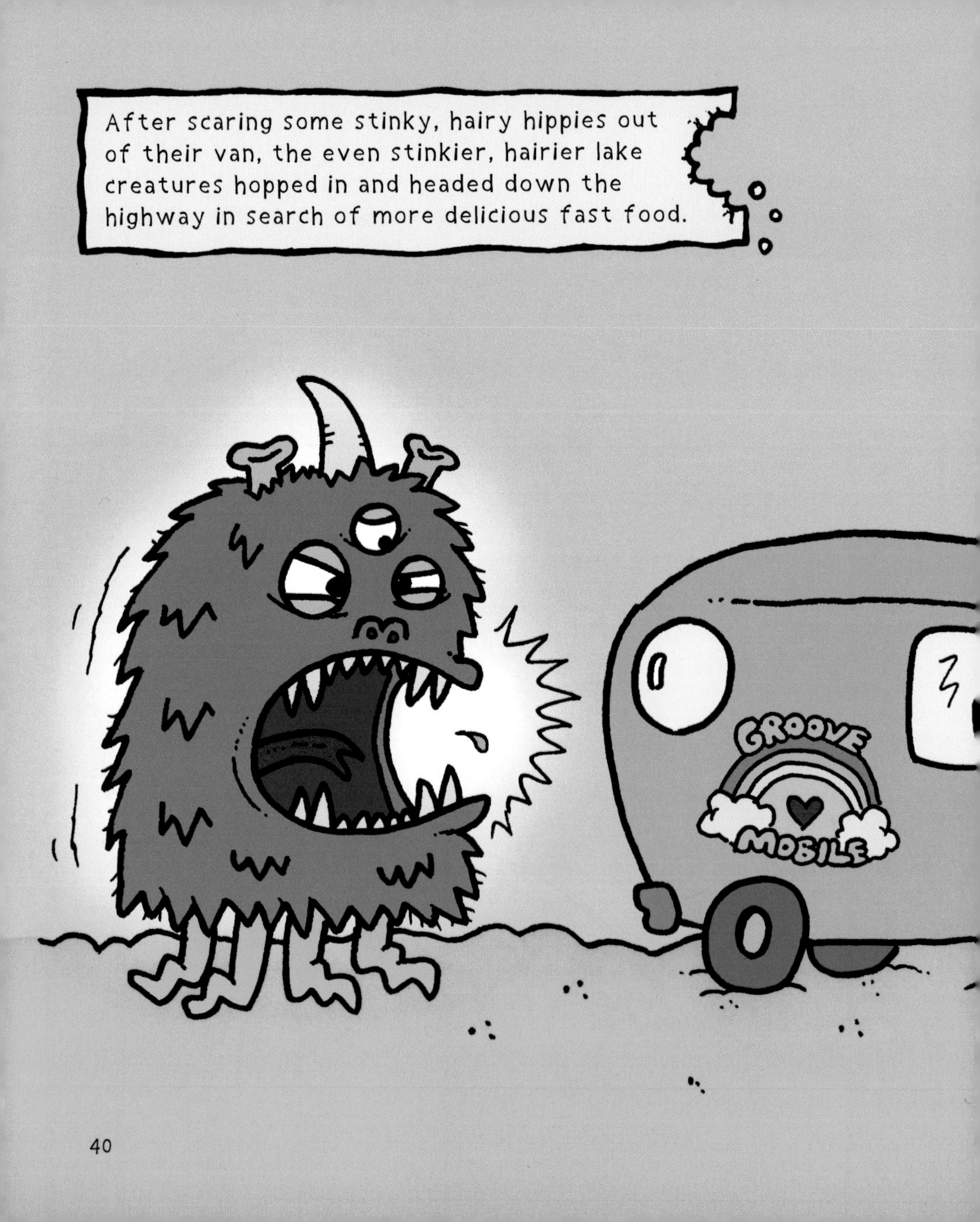
GROOVE
MOBILE

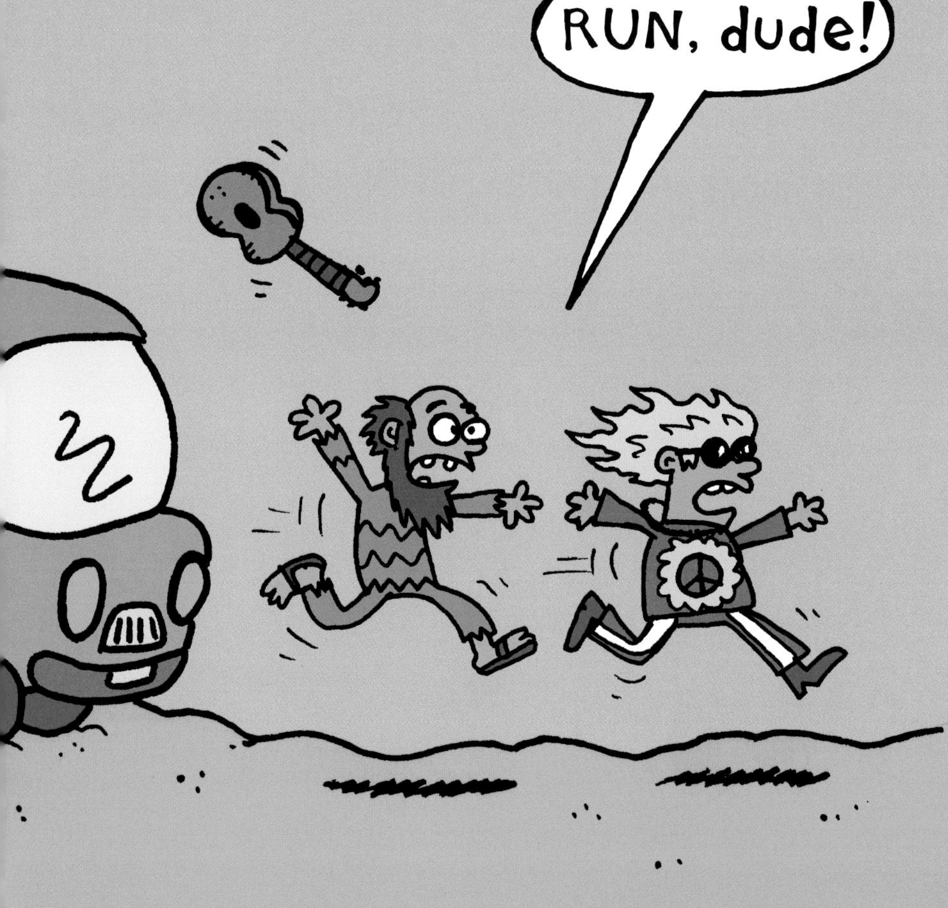
RUN, dude!

Luckily for the creatures, the highway had lots of Chubbzy Cheeseburgers signs. So the creatures just followed them. There was a Chubbzy sign about every ten feet.

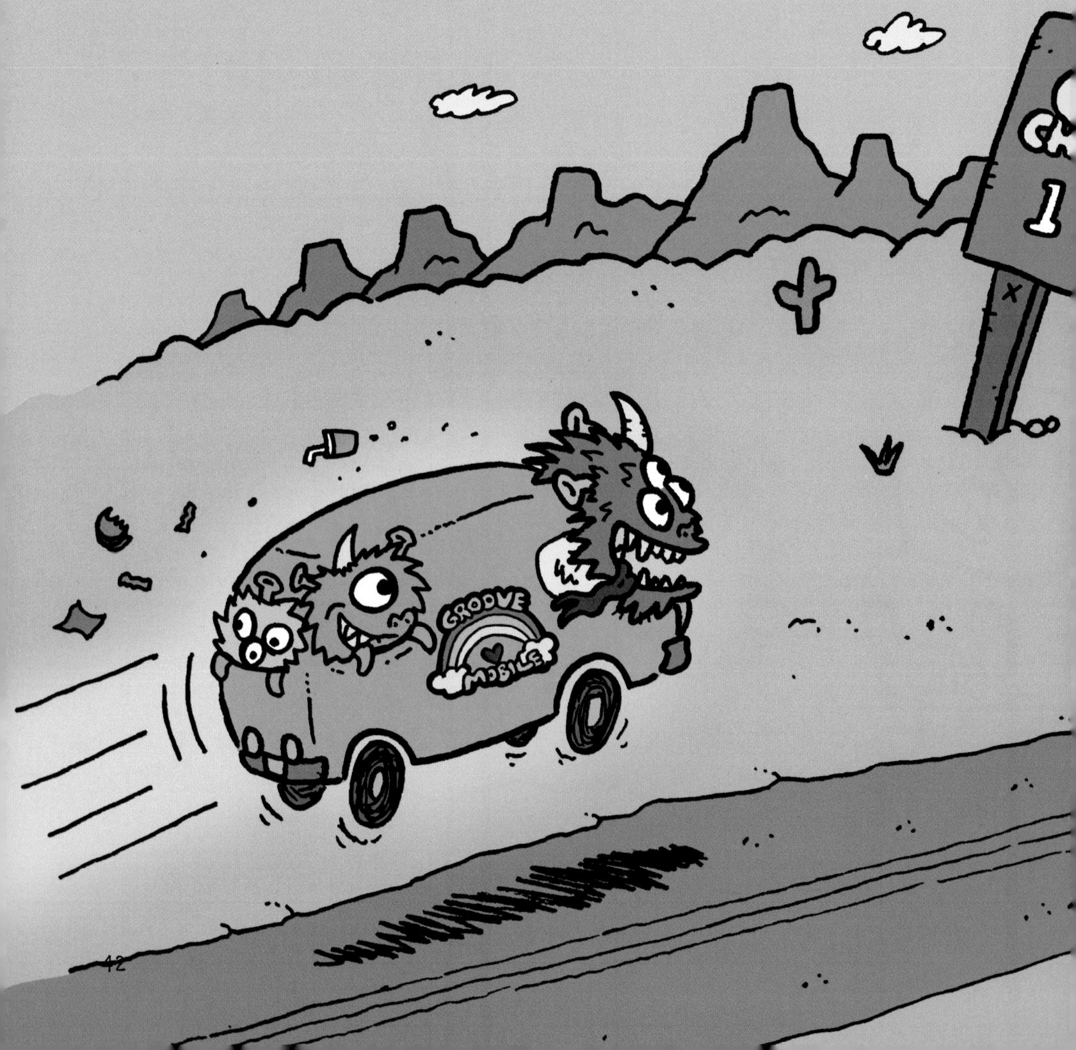
GROOVE
MOBILE

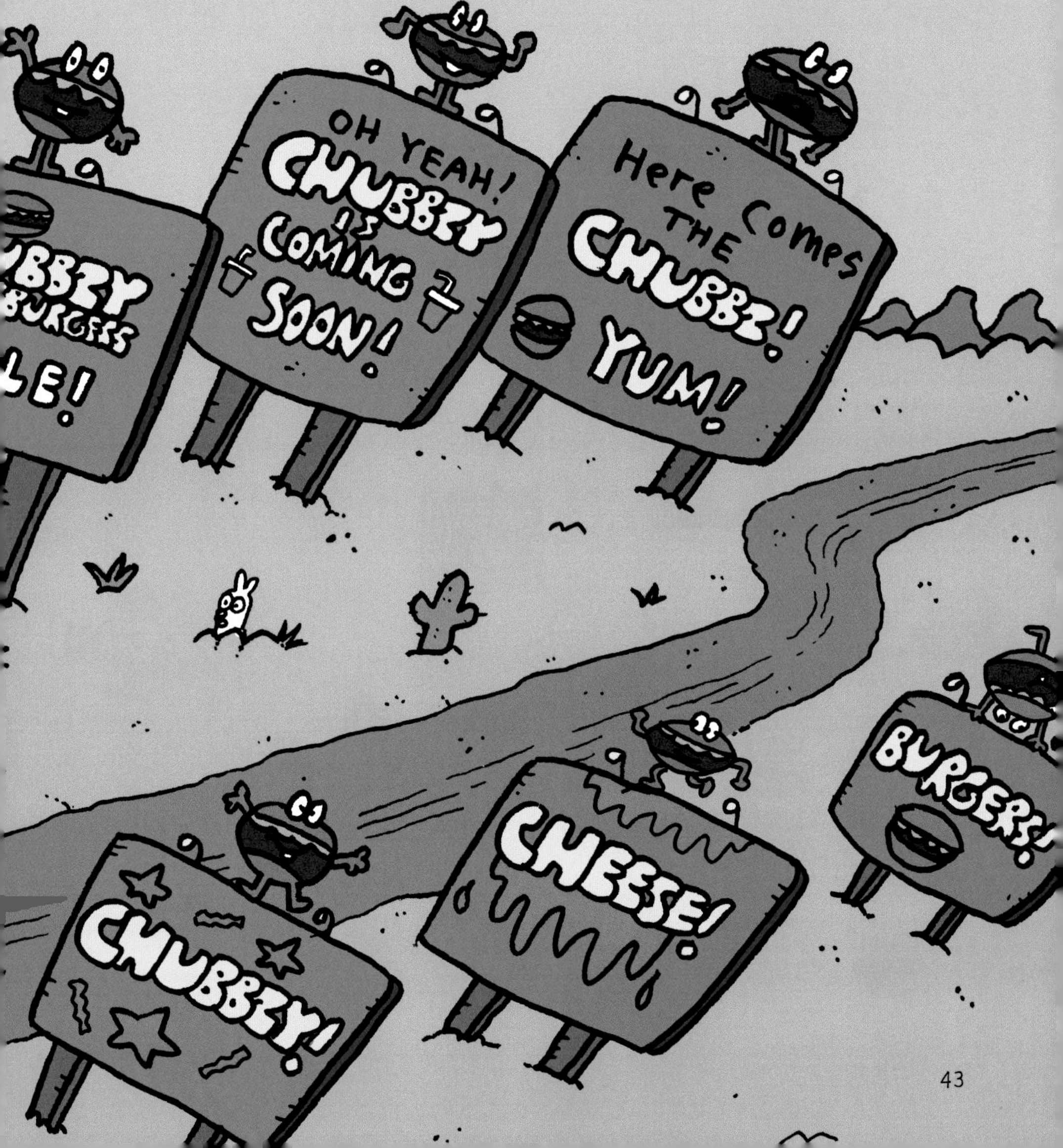
OH YEAH!
CHUBBZY IS COMING SOON!
Here Comes THE CHUBBZ!
YUM!
CHUBBZY!
CHEESE!
BURGERS!

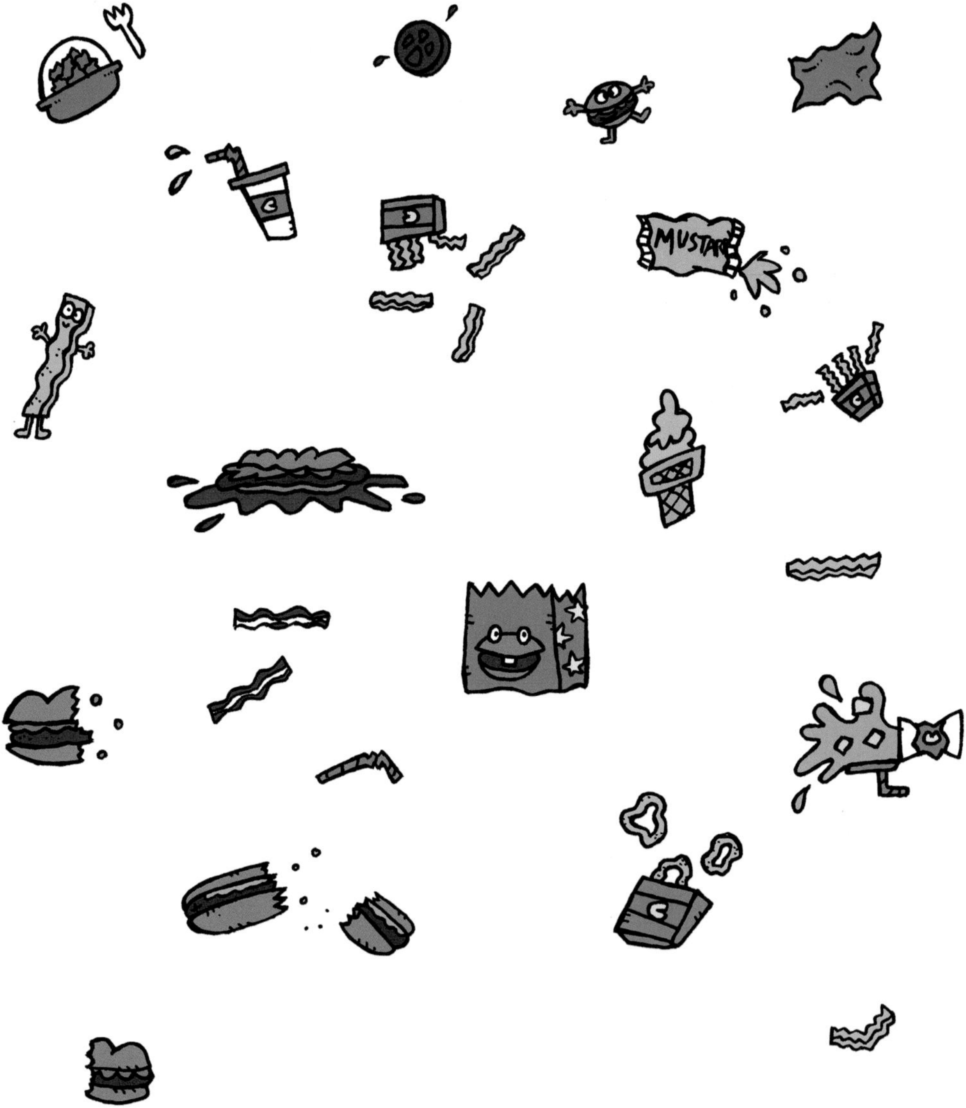
MUSTAR

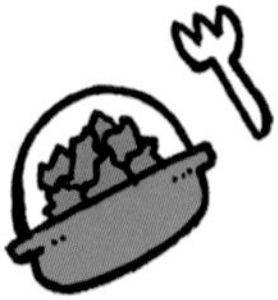

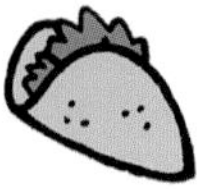

CHAPTER 5

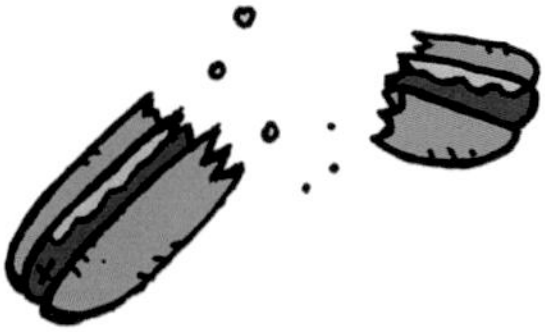

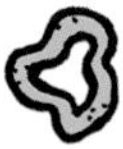

MEANWHILE...up the highway a few miles at a Chubbzy Cheeseburgers restaurant...
And the next time you decide to put chili sauce on a burger instead of ketchup, you're FIRED!
CHUBBZY CHEESEBURGERS
...mild-mannered fast-food worker Carlton Crumple was being reprimanded by his boss, Manager Floops...

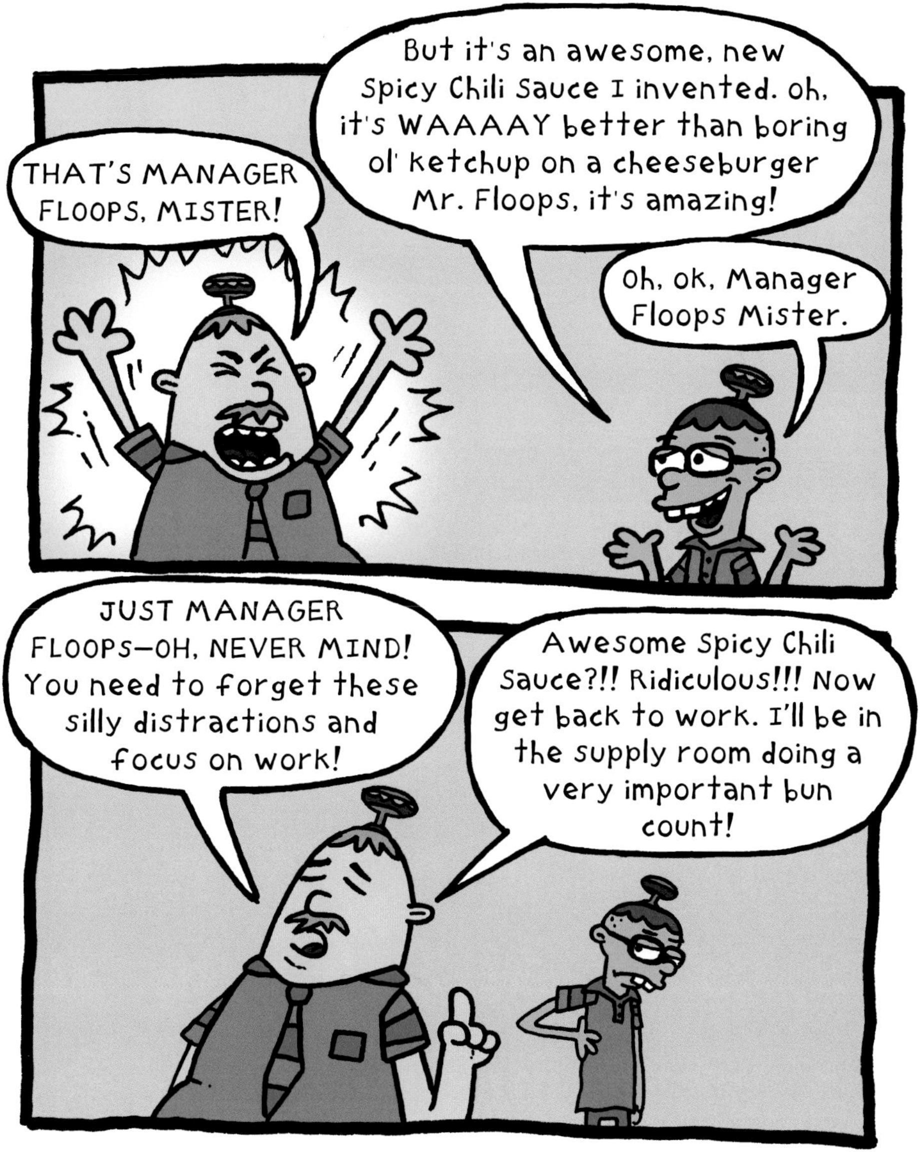
THAT'S MANAGER FLOOPS, MISTER!
But it's an awesome, new Spicy Chili Sauce I invented. oh, it's WAAAAY better than boring ol' ketchup on a cheeseburger Mr. Floops, it's amazing!
Oh, ok, Manager Floops Mister.
JUST MANAGER FLOOPS—OH, NEVER MIND! You need to forget these silly distractions and focus on work!
Awesome Spicy Chili Sauce?!! Ridiculous!!! Now get back to work. I'll be in the supply room doing a very important bun count!

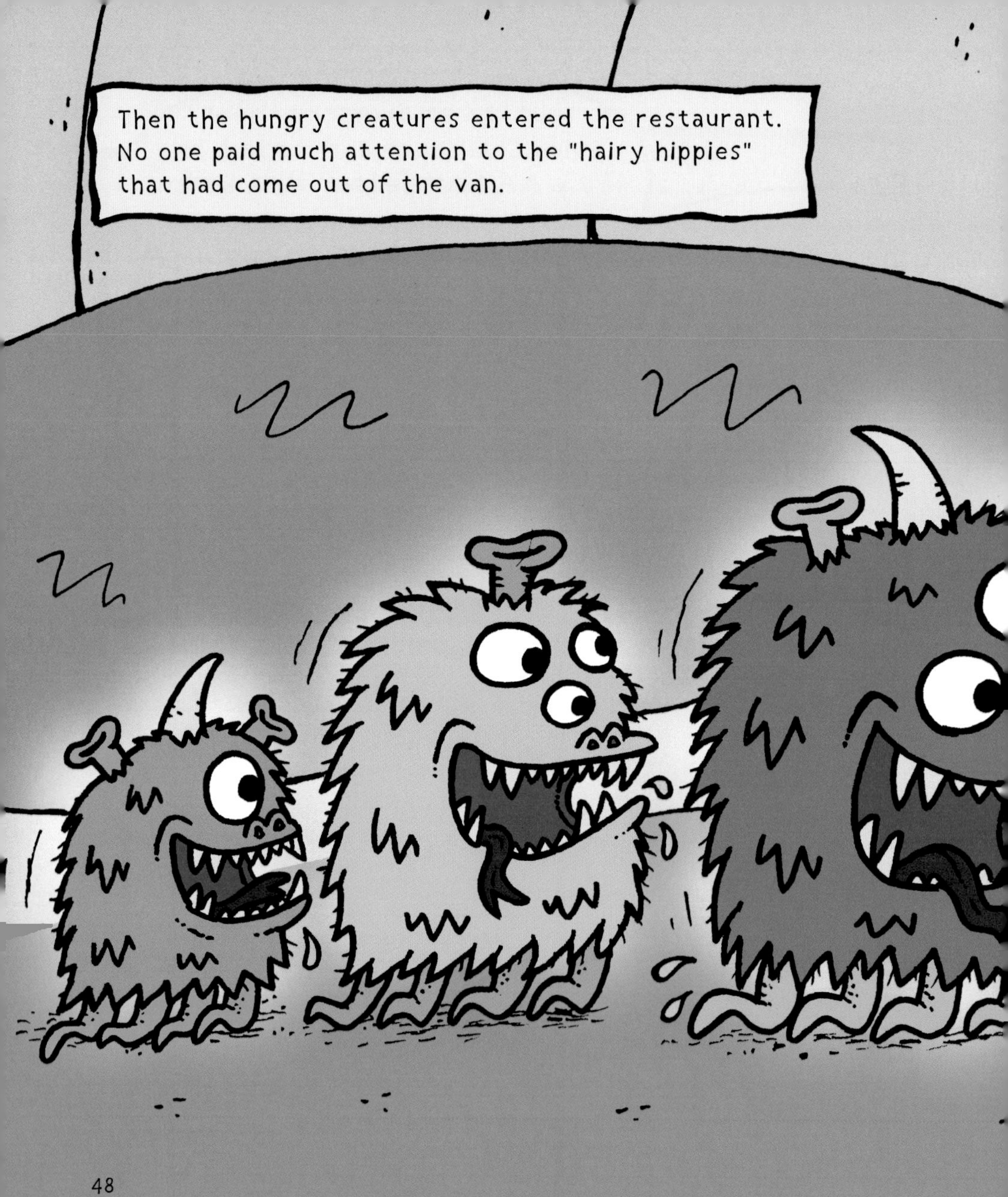
Then the hungry creatures entered the restaurant. No one paid much attention to the "hairy hippies" that had come out of the van.

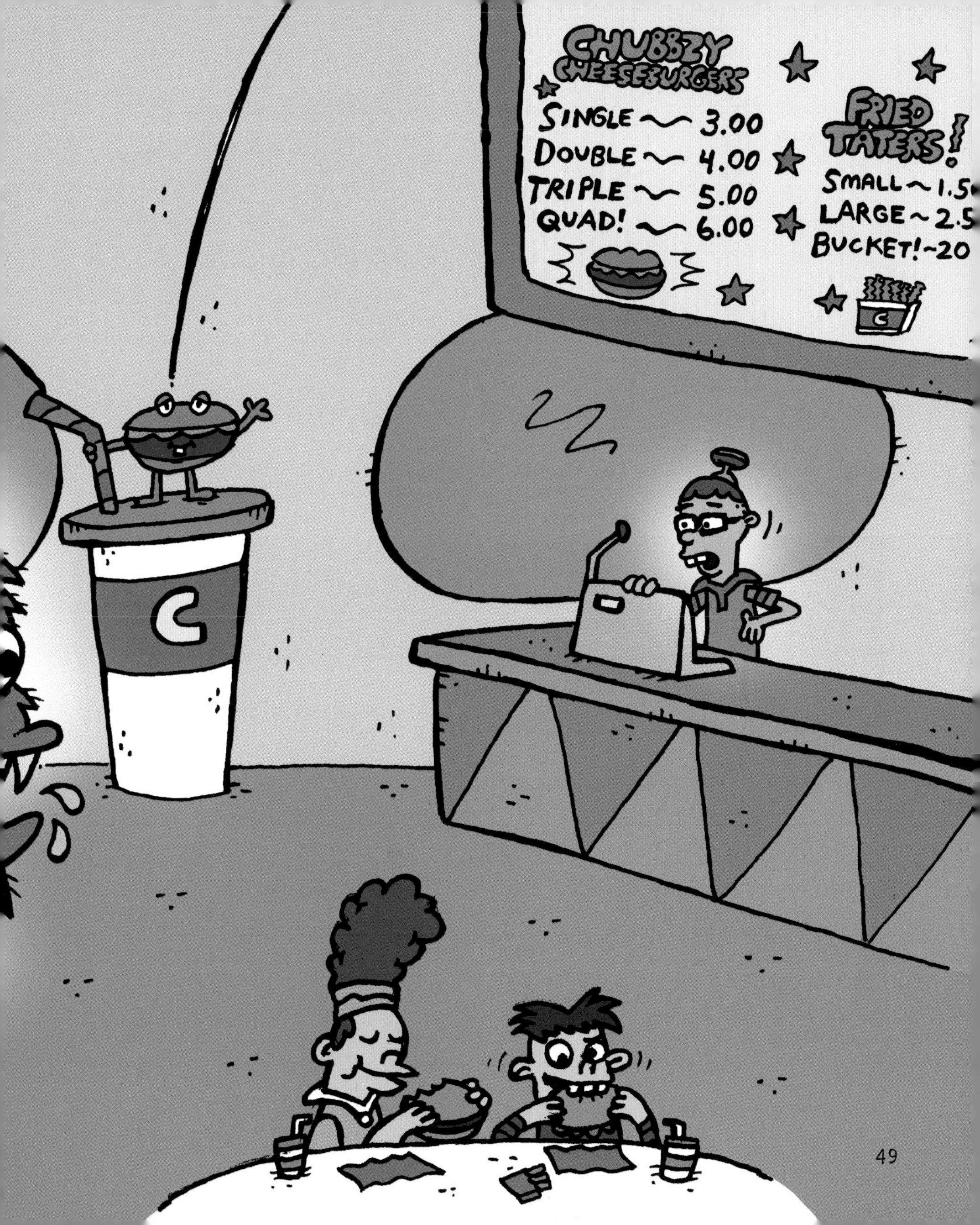
CHUBBZY CHEESEBURGERS
SINGLE ~ 3.00
DOUBLE ~ 4.00
TRIPLE ~ 5.00
QUAD! ~ 6.00
FRIED TATERS!
SMALL ~ 1.5
LARGE ~ 2.5
BUCKET! ~ 20
C
C
C

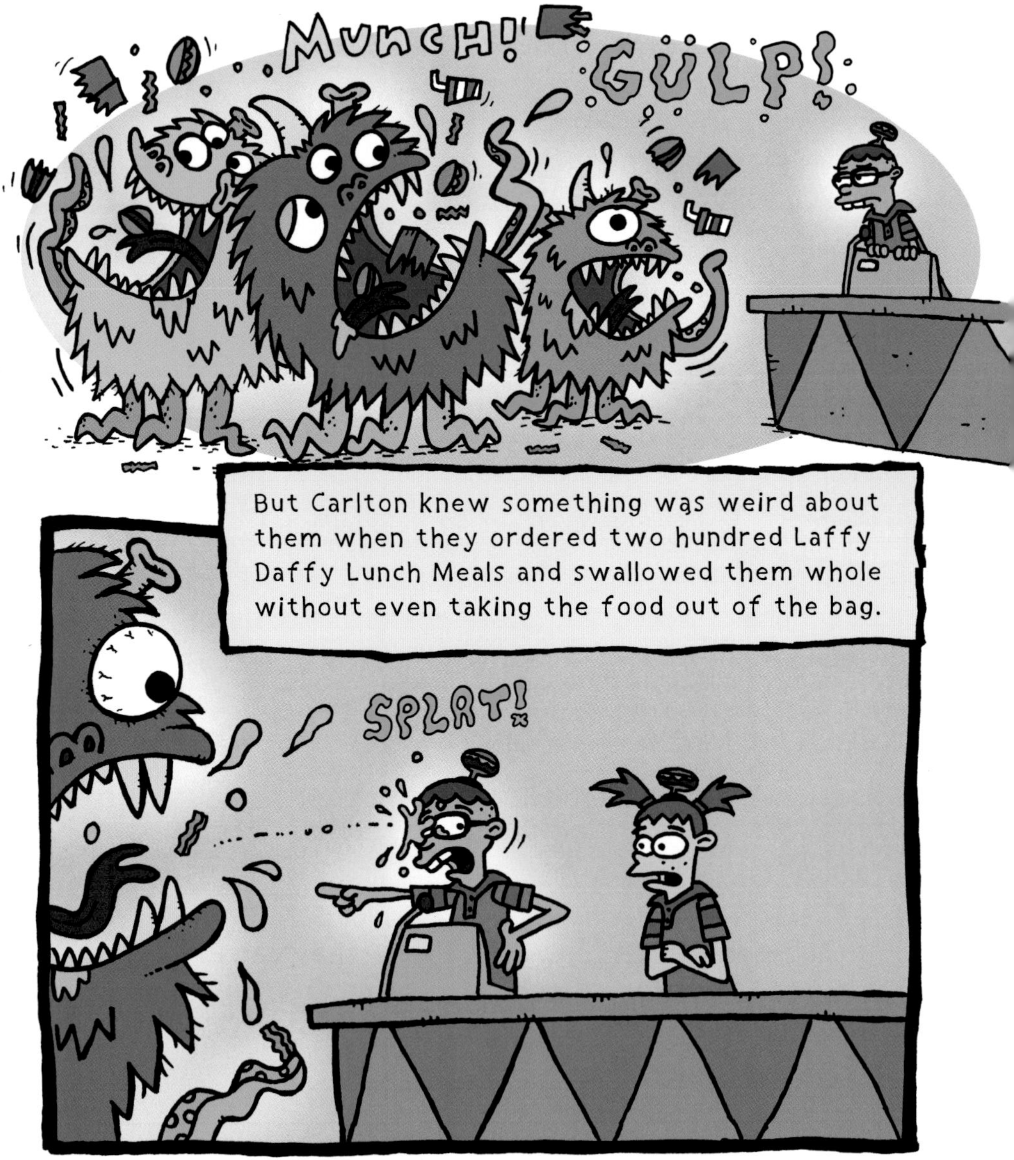
MUNCH!
GULP!
But Carlton knew something was weird about them when they ordered two hundred Laffy Daffy Lunch Meals and swallowed them whole without even taking the food out of the bag.
SPLAT!

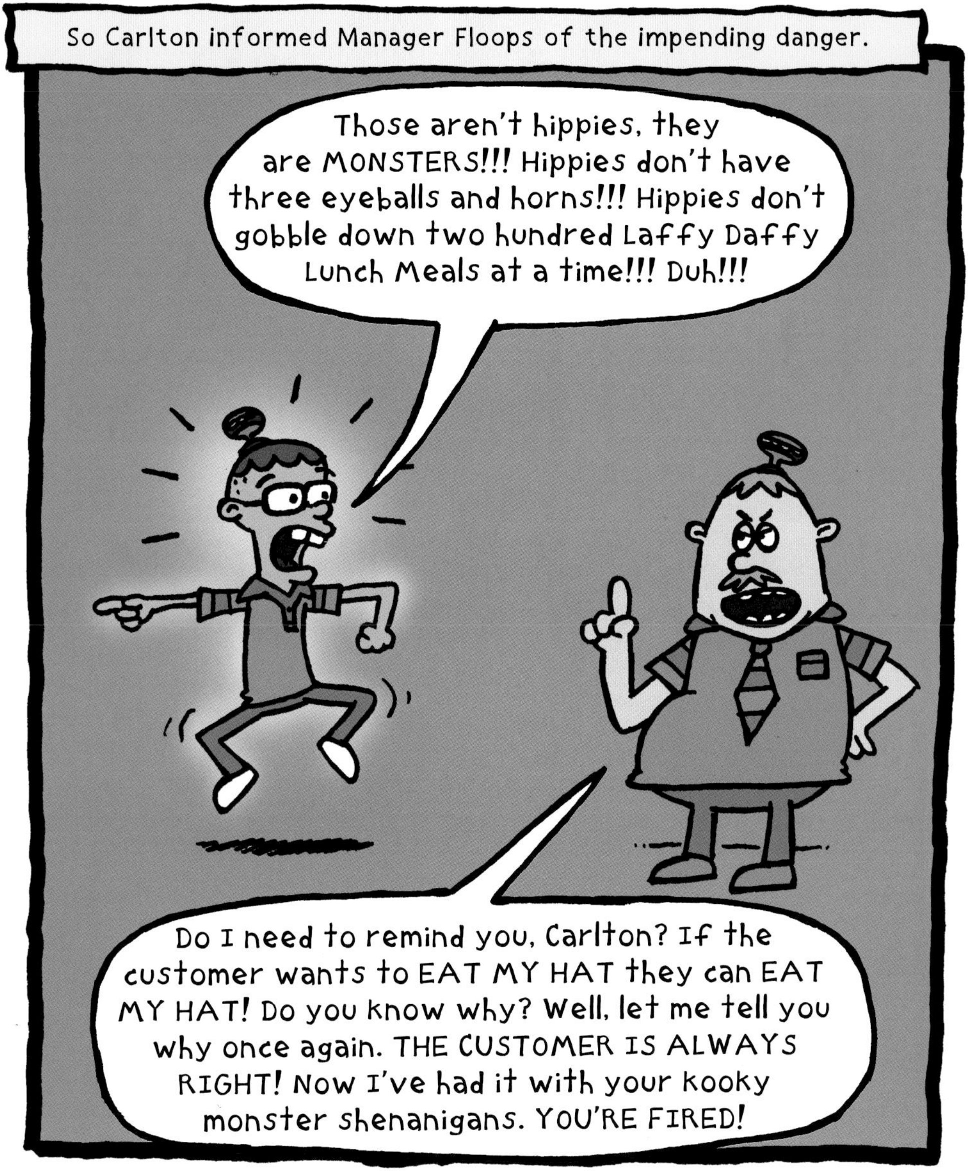
So Carlton informed Manager Floops of the impending danger.
Those aren't hippies, they are MONSTERS!!! Hippies don't have three eyeballs and horns!!! Hippies don't gobble down two hundred Laffy Daffy Lunch Meals at a time!!! Duh!!!
Do I need to remind you, Carlton? If the customer wants to EAT MY HAT they can EAT MY HAT! Do you know why? Well, let me tell you why once again. THE CUSTOMER IS ALWAYS RIGHT! Now I've had it with your kooky monster shenanigans. YOU'RE FIRED!

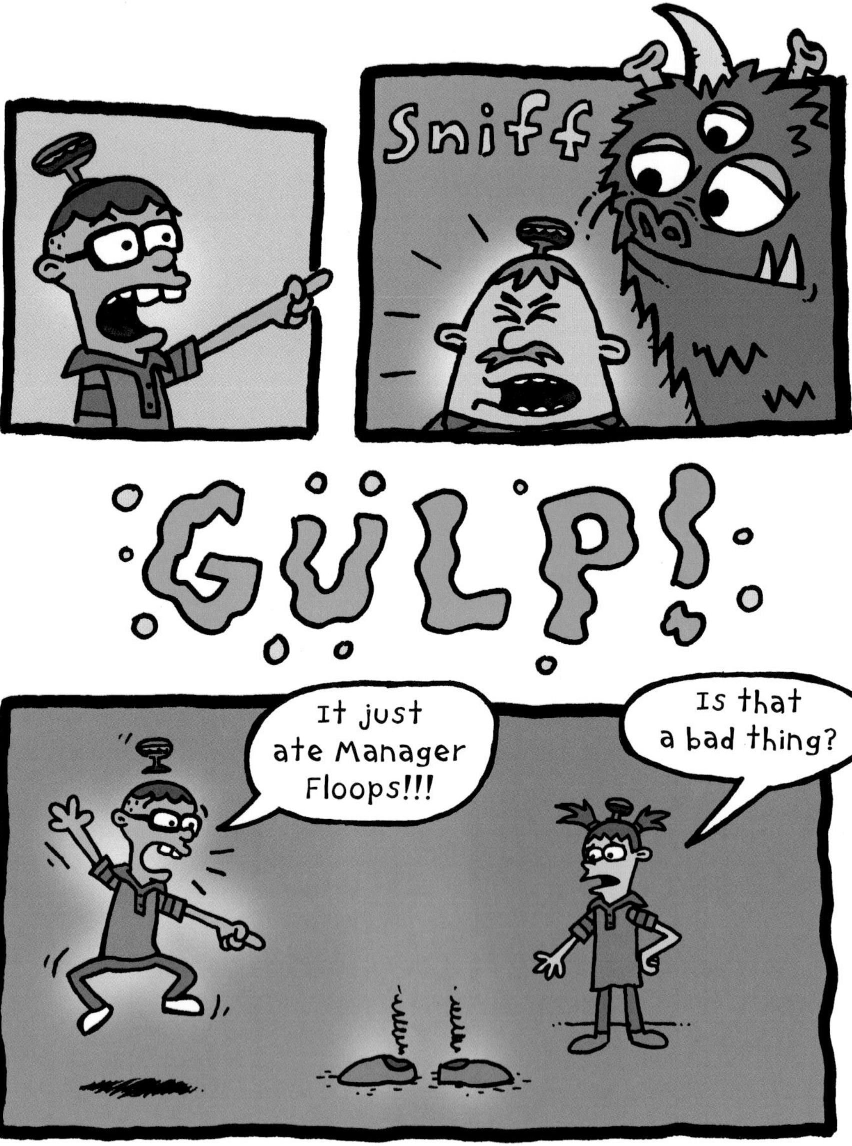
Sniff
GULP!
It just ate Manager Floops!!!
Is that a bad thing?

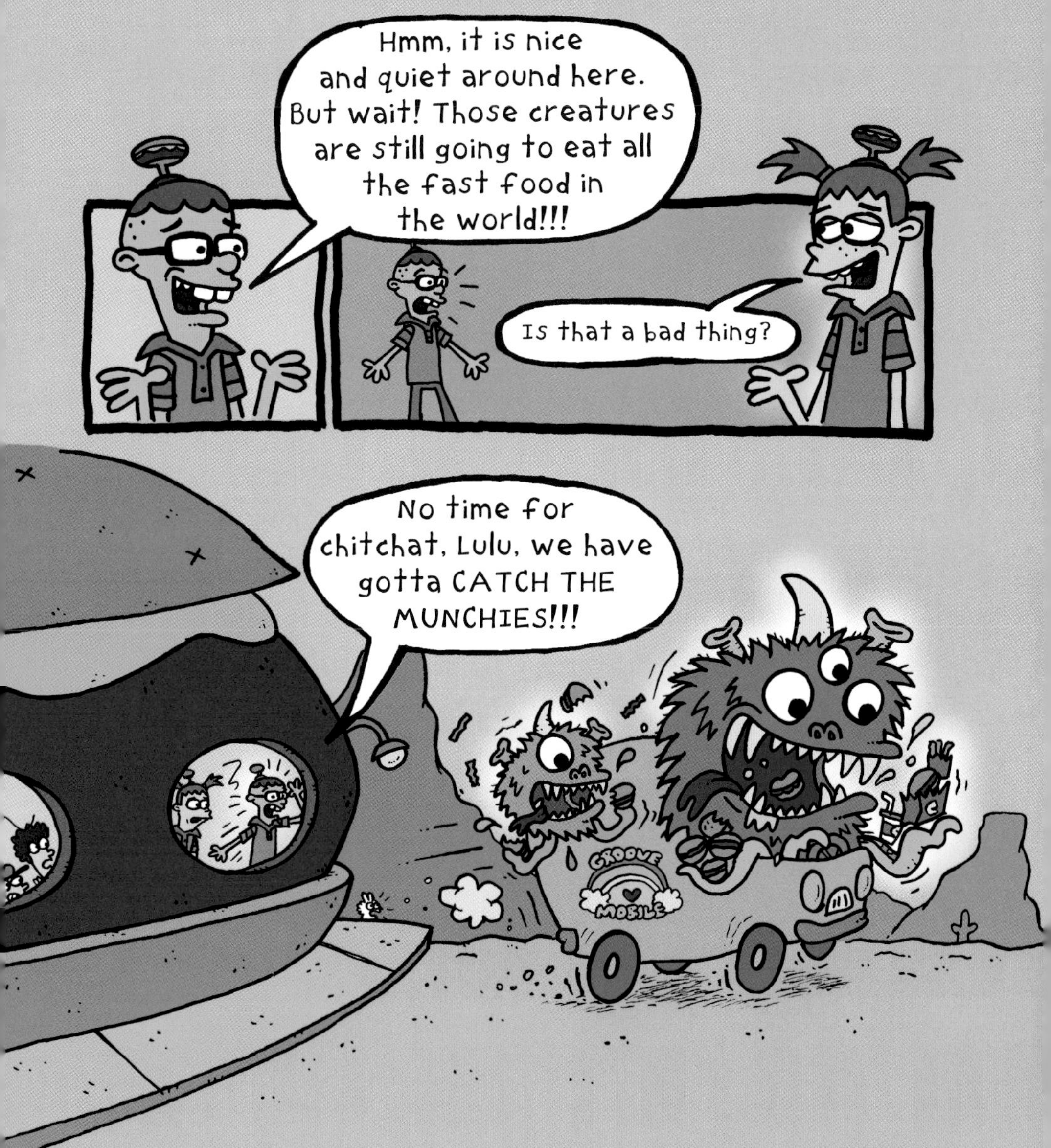
Hmm, it is nice and quiet around here. But wait! Those creatures are still going to eat all the fast food in the world!!!
Is that a bad thing?
No time for chitchat, Lulu, we have gotta CATCH THE MUNCHIES!!!
GROOVE MOBILE

CHAPTER 6

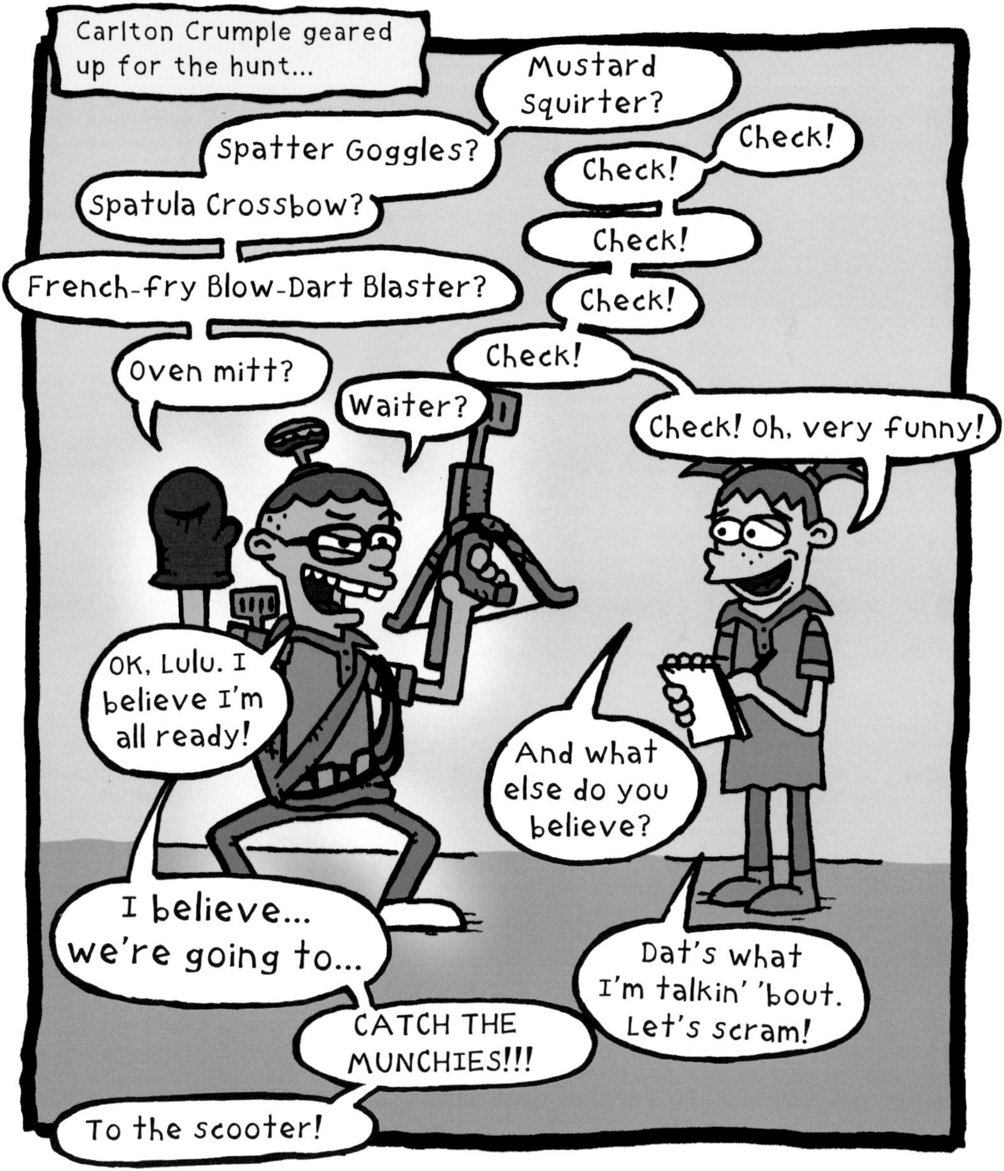
Carlton Crumple geared up for the hunt...
Mustard Squirter?
Check!
Spatter Goggles?
Check!
Spatula Crossbow?
Check!
French-fry Blow-Dart Blaster?
Check!
Oven mitt?
Check!
Waiter?
Check! Oh, very funny!
OK, Lulu. I believe I'm all ready!
And what else do you believe?
I believe... we're going to...
CATCH THE MUNCHIES!!!
Dat's what I'm talkin' 'bout. Let's scram!
To the scooter!

And then Carlton and his faithful sidekick, Lulu, her "attack poodle" Poof-Poof and Poof-Poof's best pal Iggy the Iguana all jumped onto Lulu's motorized scooter and hit the highway in hot pursuit of the terrible and horrific Munchies! All they had to do was follow the Chubbzy Cheeseburgers signs and the crumpled burger wrappers!!!

This is all too exciting! Let's take a commercial break, folks...

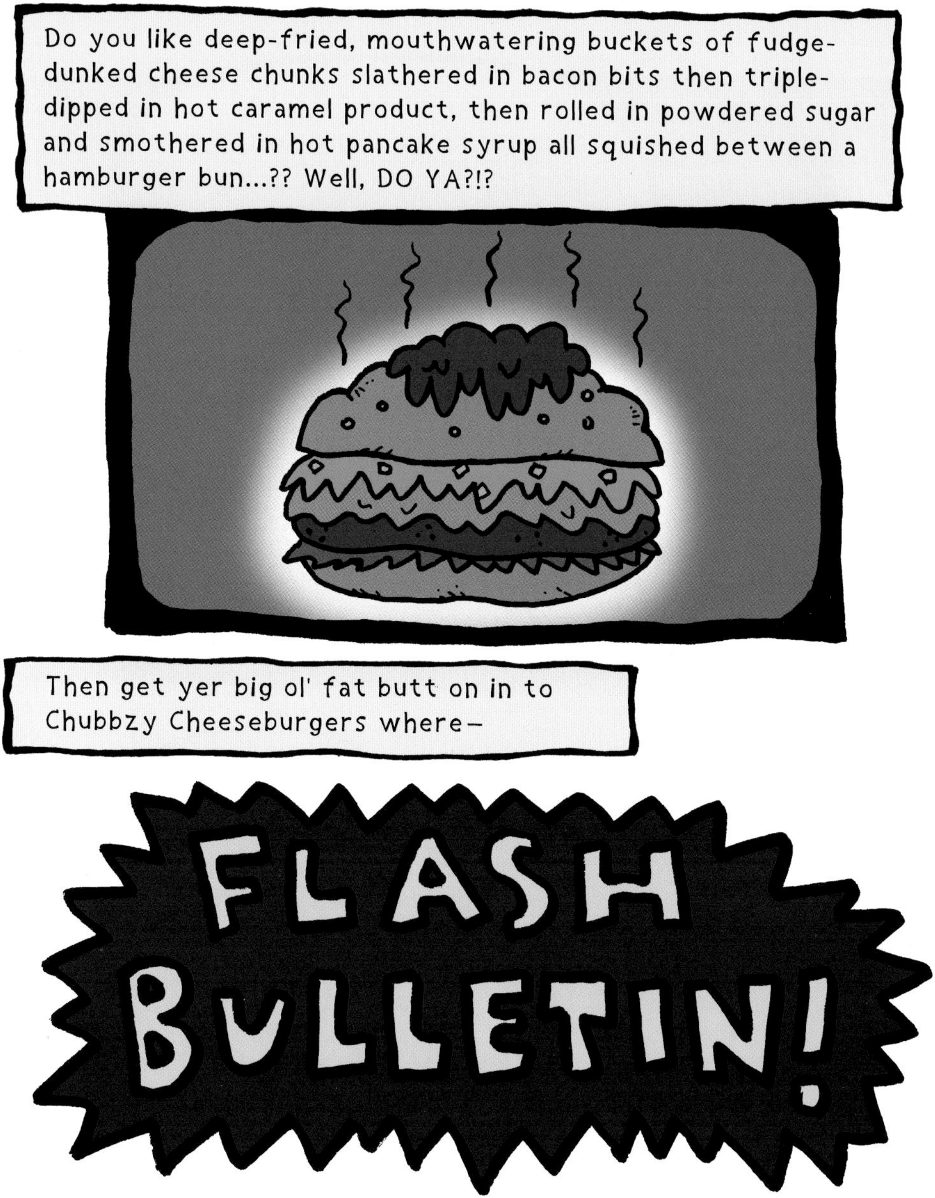
Do you like deep-fried, mouthwatering buckets of fudge-dunked cheese chunks slathered in bacon bits then triple-dipped in hot caramel product, then rolled in powdered sugar and smothered in hot pancake syrup all squished between a hamburger bun...?? Well, DO YA?!?
Then get yer big ol' fat butt on in to Chubbzy Cheeseburgers where—
FLASH BULLETIN!

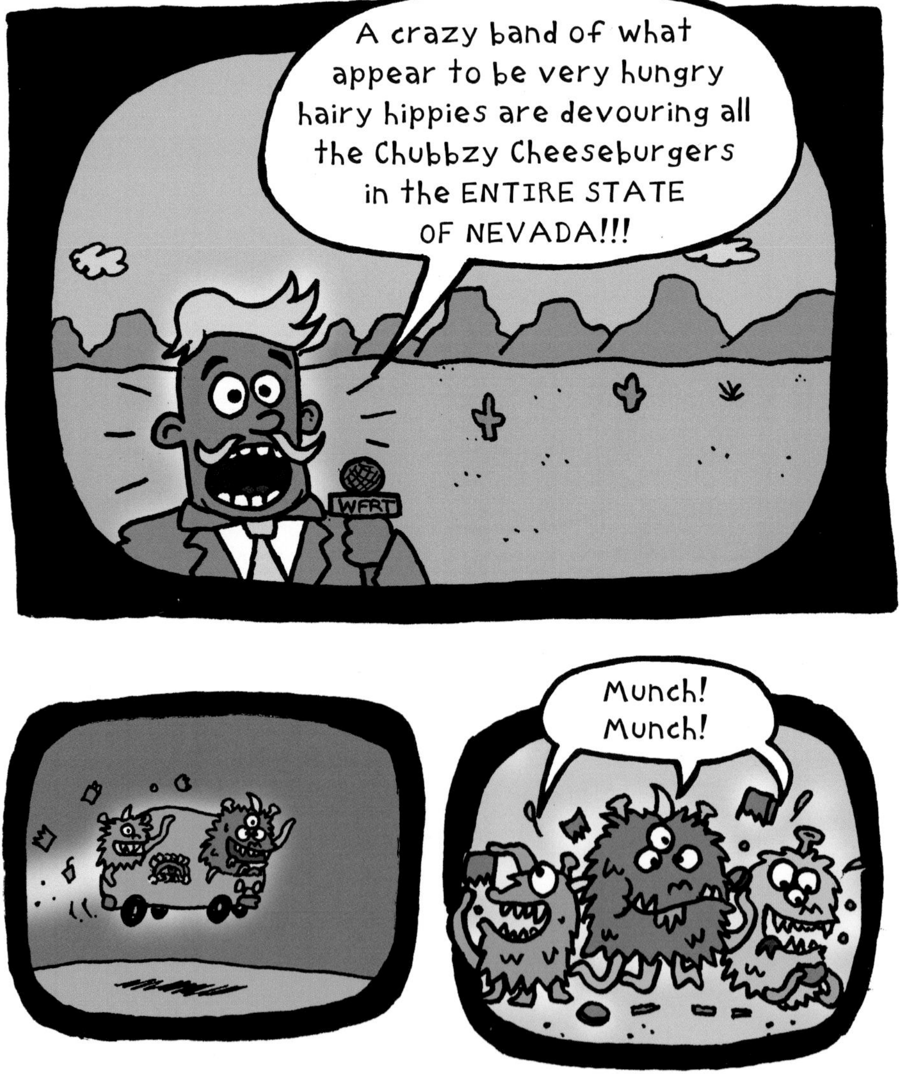
A crazy band of what appear to be very hungry hairy hippies are devouring all the Chubbzy Cheeseburgers in the ENTIRE STATE OF NEVADA!!!
WFRT
Munch! Munch!

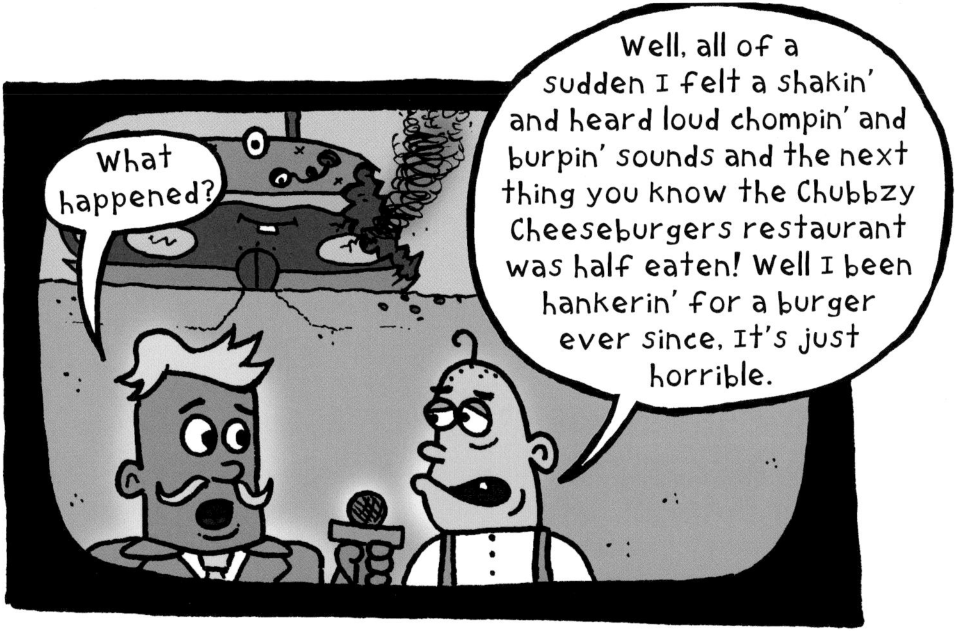
What happened?
Well, all of a sudden I felt a shakin' and heard loud chompin' and burpin' sounds and the next thing you know the Chubbzy Cheeseburgers restaurant was half eaten! Well I been hankerin' for a burger ever since. It's just horrible.

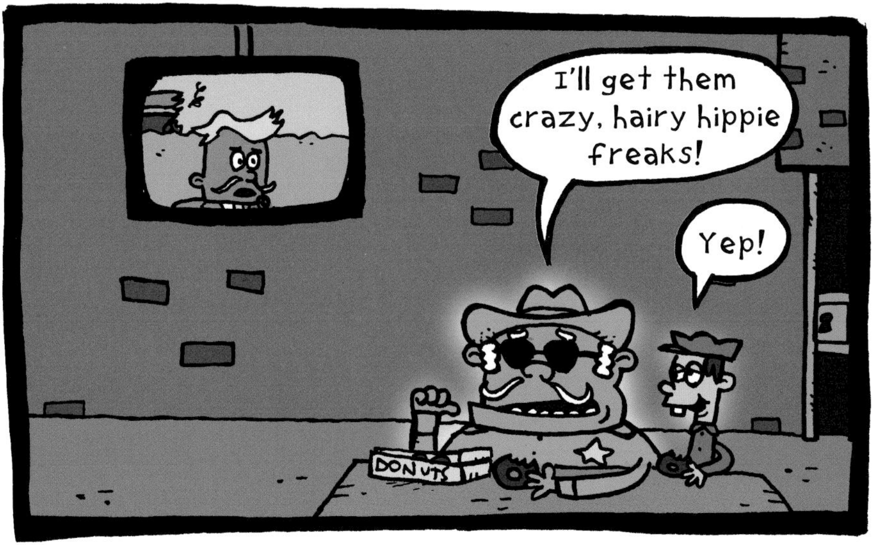
I'll get them crazy, hairy hippie freaks!
Yep!
DONUTS

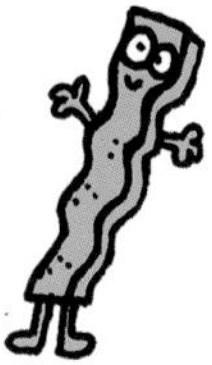
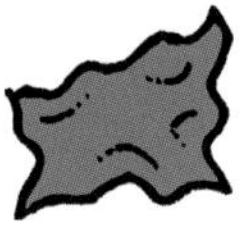
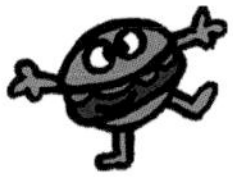

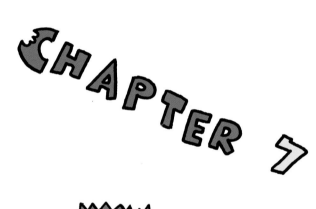

CHAPTER 7

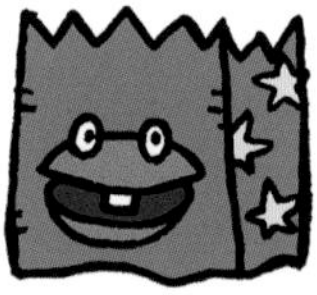
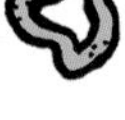

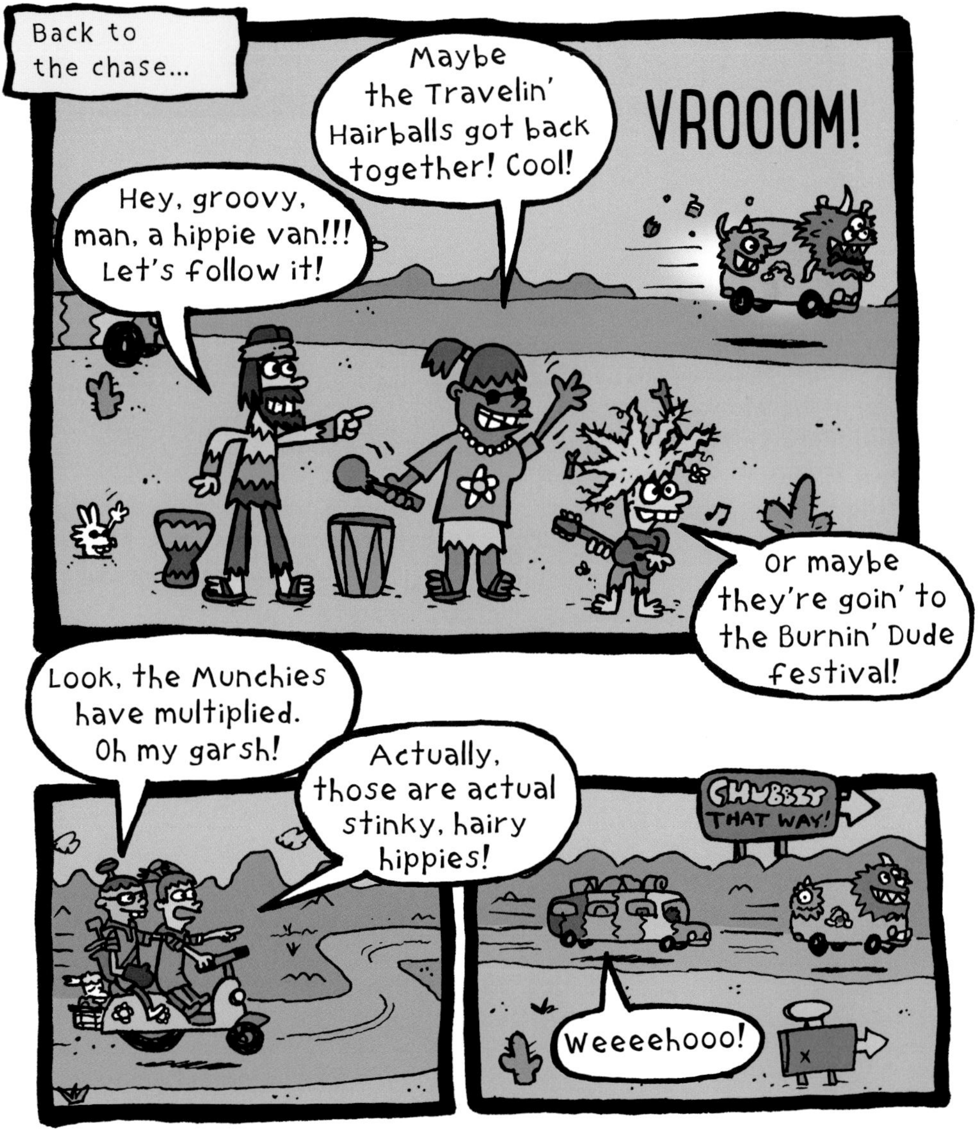
Back to the chase...
Hey, groovy, man, a hippie van!!! Let's follow it!
Maybe the Travelin' Hairballs got back together! Cool!
VROOOM!
Or maybe they're goin' to the Burnin' Dude festival!
Look, the Munchies have multiplied. Oh my garsh!
Actually, those are actual stinky, hairy hippies!
THAT WAY!
Weeeehooo!

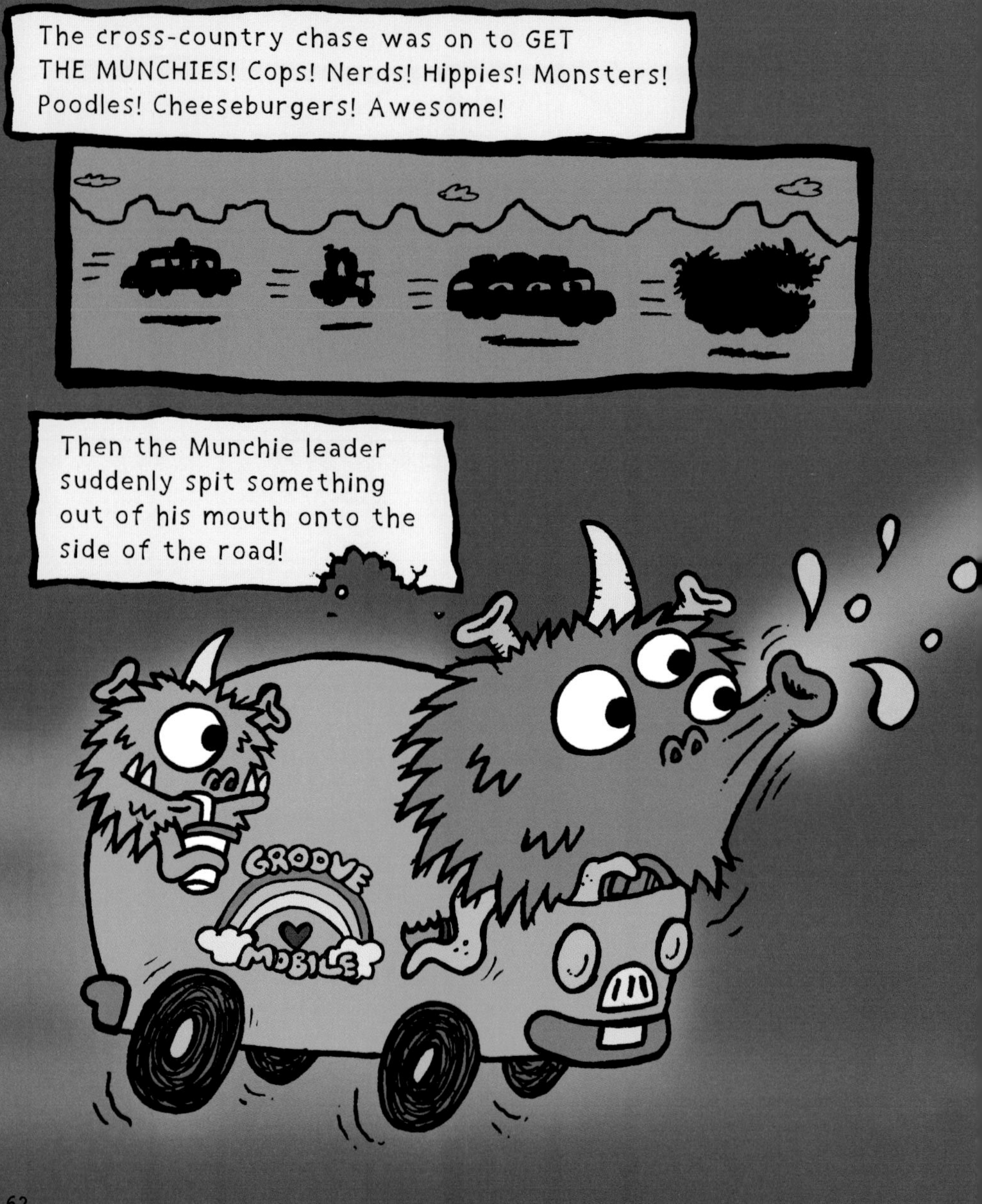
The cross-country chase was on to GET THE MUNCHIES! Cops! Nerds! Hippies! Monsters! Poodles! Cheeseburgers! Awesome!
Then the Munchie leader suddenly spit something out of his mouth onto the side of the road!
GROOVE
MOBILE

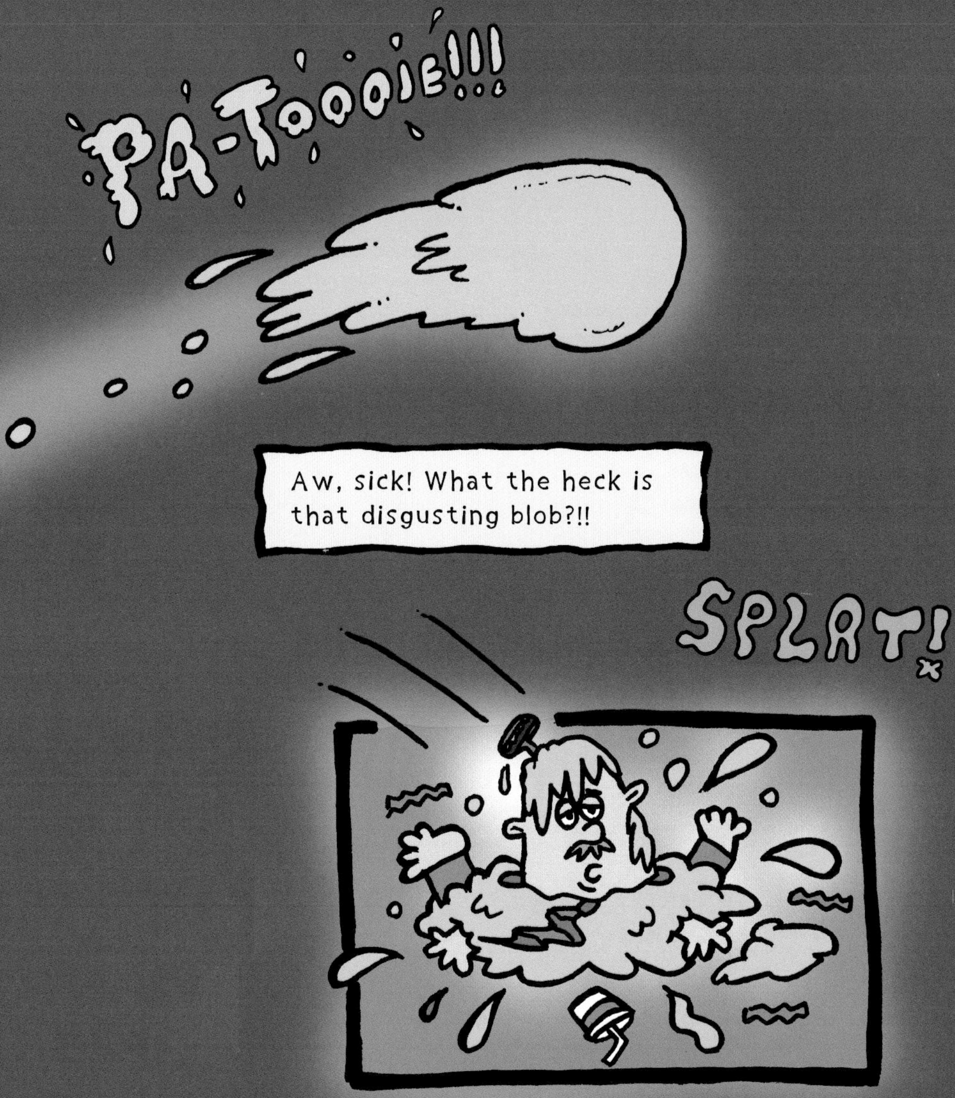
PA-TOOOIE!!!
Aw, sick! What the heck is that disgusting blob?!!
SPLAT!

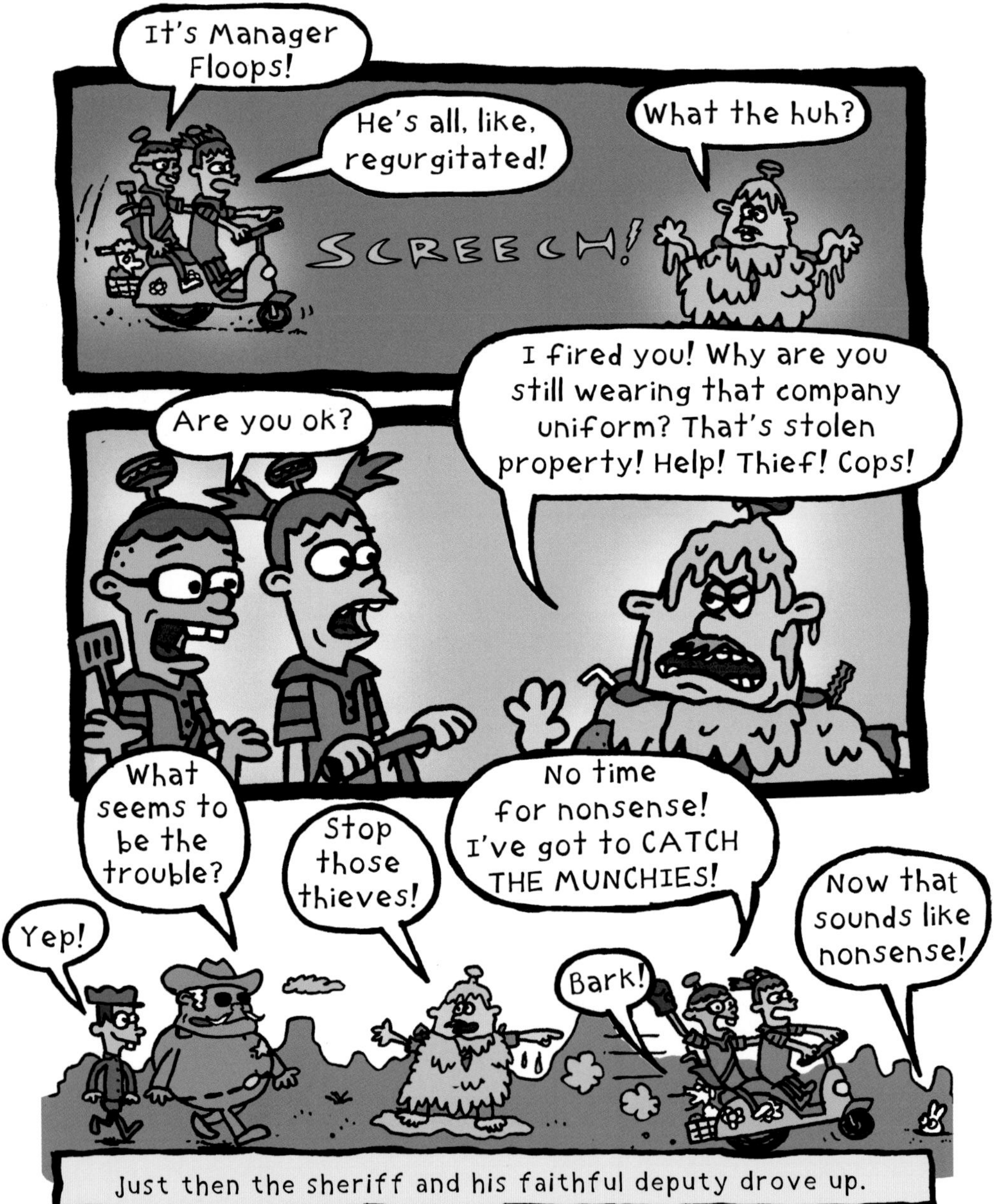
It's Manager Floops!
He's all, like, regurgitated!
SCREECH!
What the huh?
Are you ok?
I fired you! Why are you still wearing that company uniform? That's stolen property! Help! Thief! Cops!
Yep!
What seems to be the trouble?
Stop those thieves!
No time for nonsense! I've got to CATCH THE MUNCHIES!
Bark!
Now that sounds like nonsense!
Just then the sheriff and his faithful deputy drove up.

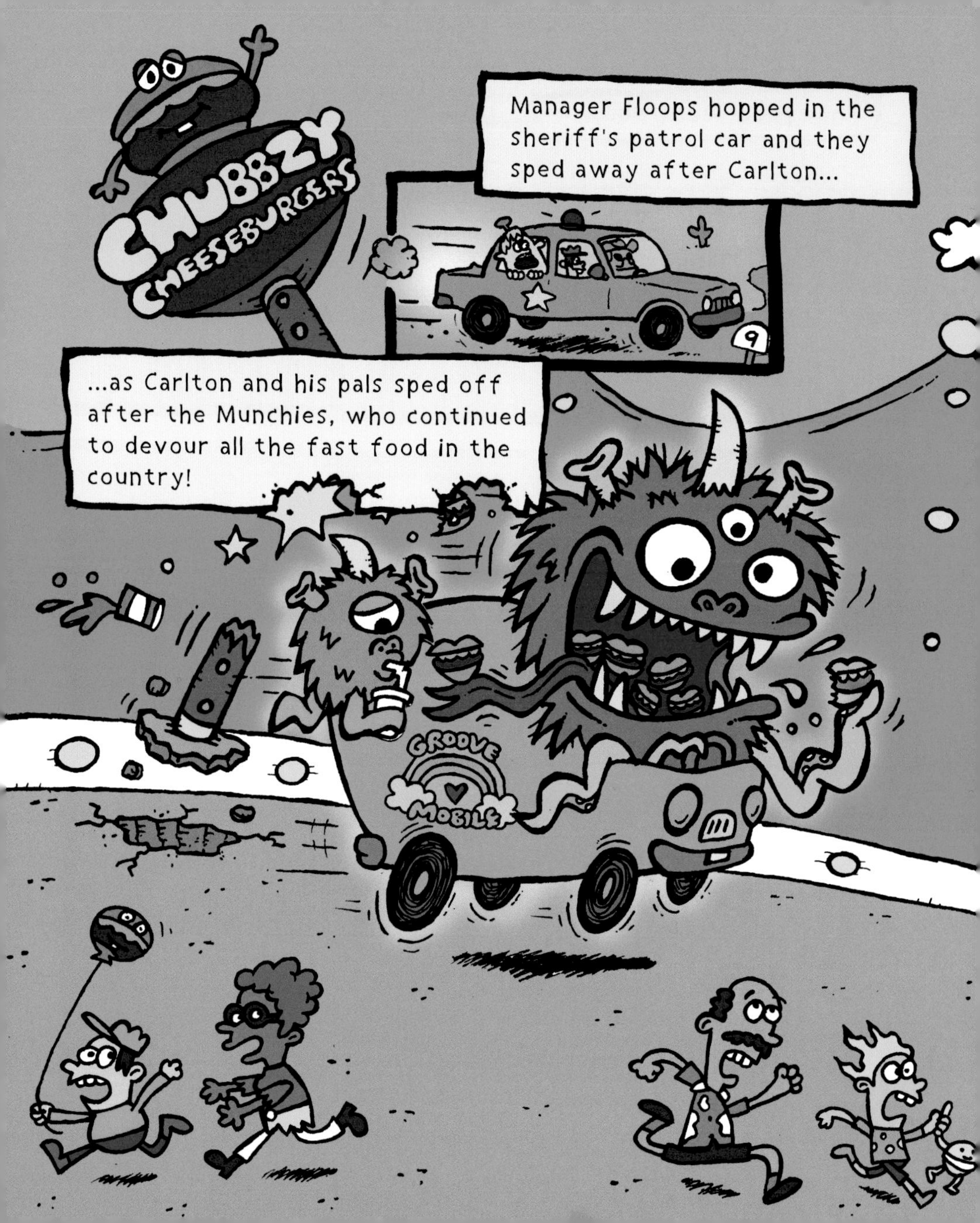
Manager Floops hopped in the sheriff's patrol car and they sped away after Carlton...
CHUBBZY CHEESEBURGERS
9
...as Carlton and his pals sped off after the Munchies, who continued to devour all the fast food in the country!
GROOVE MOBILE

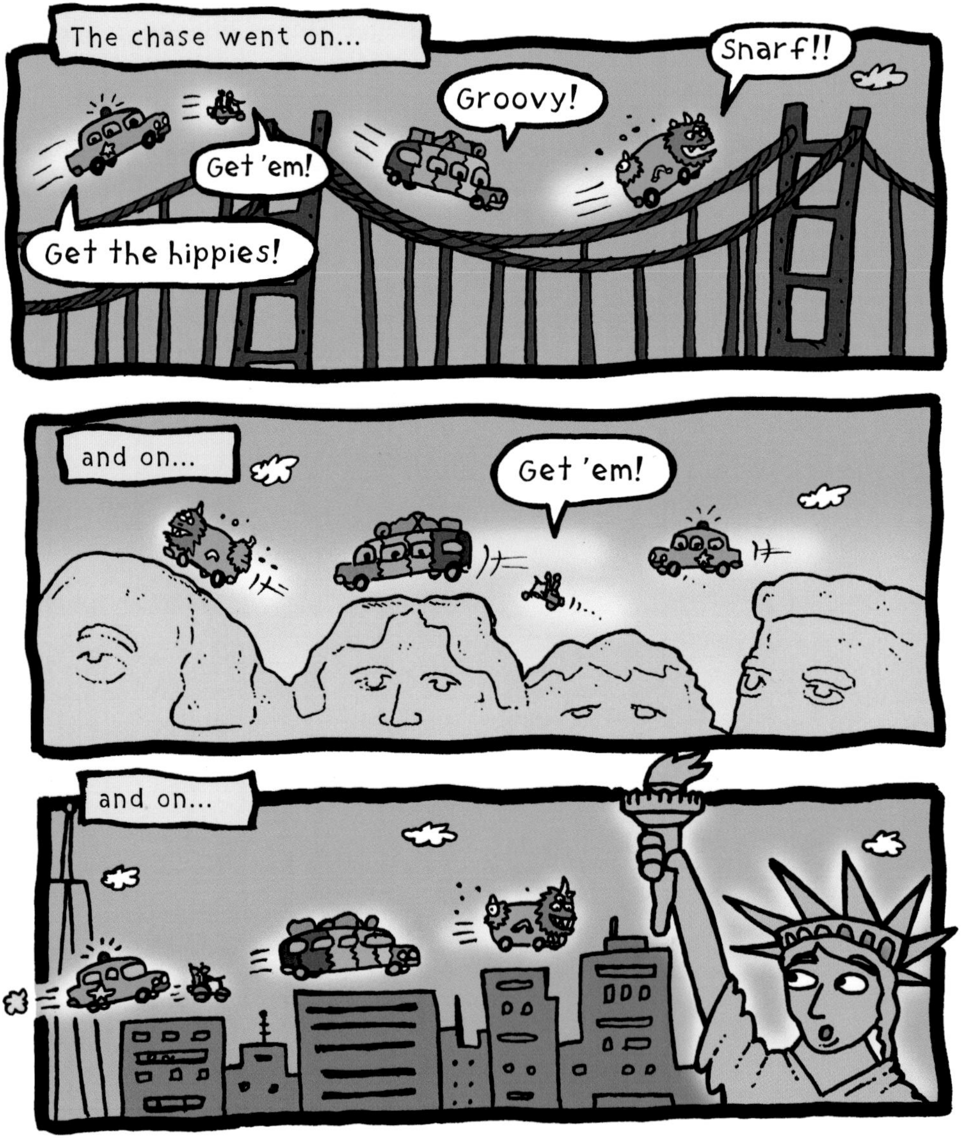
The chase went on...
Get the hippies!
Get 'em!
Groovy!
Snarf!!
and on...
Get 'em!
and on...

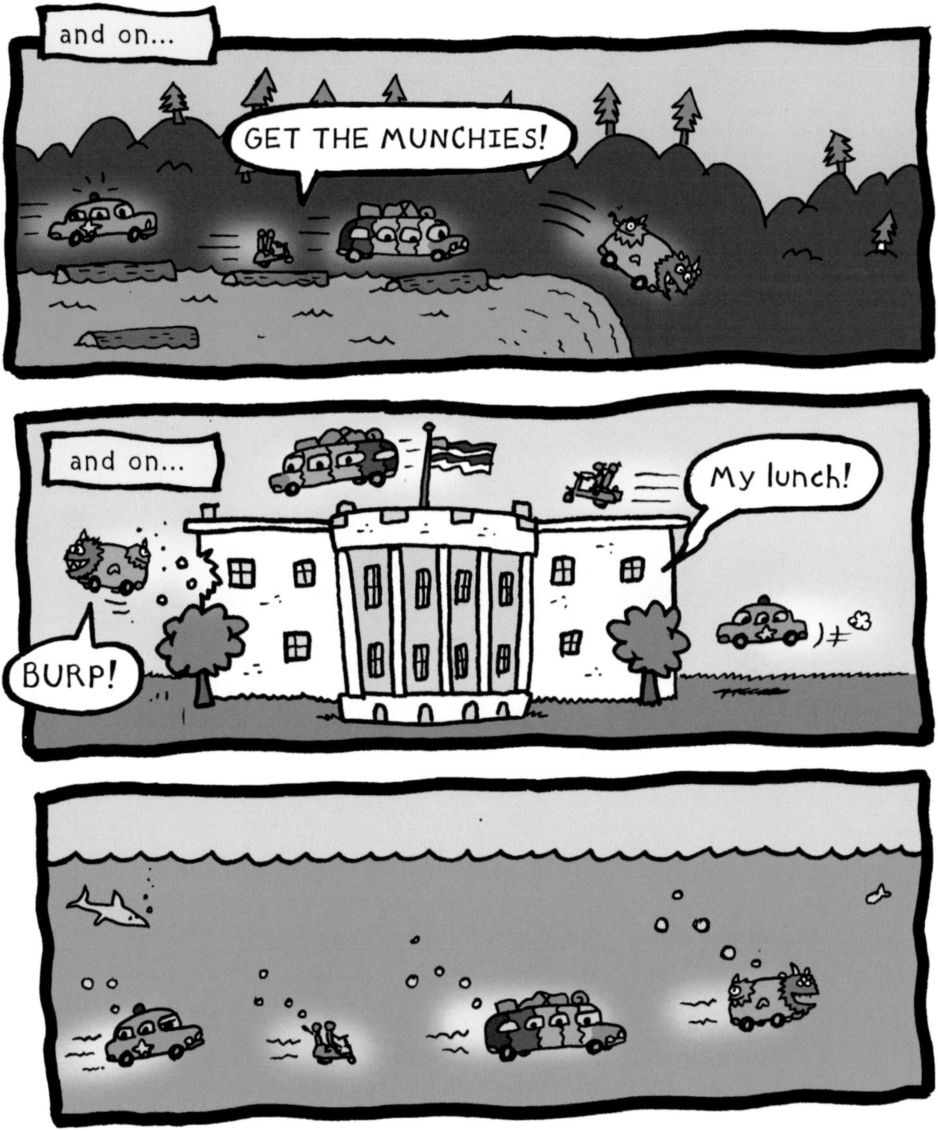
and on...
GET THE MUNCHIES!
and on...
My lunch!
BURP!

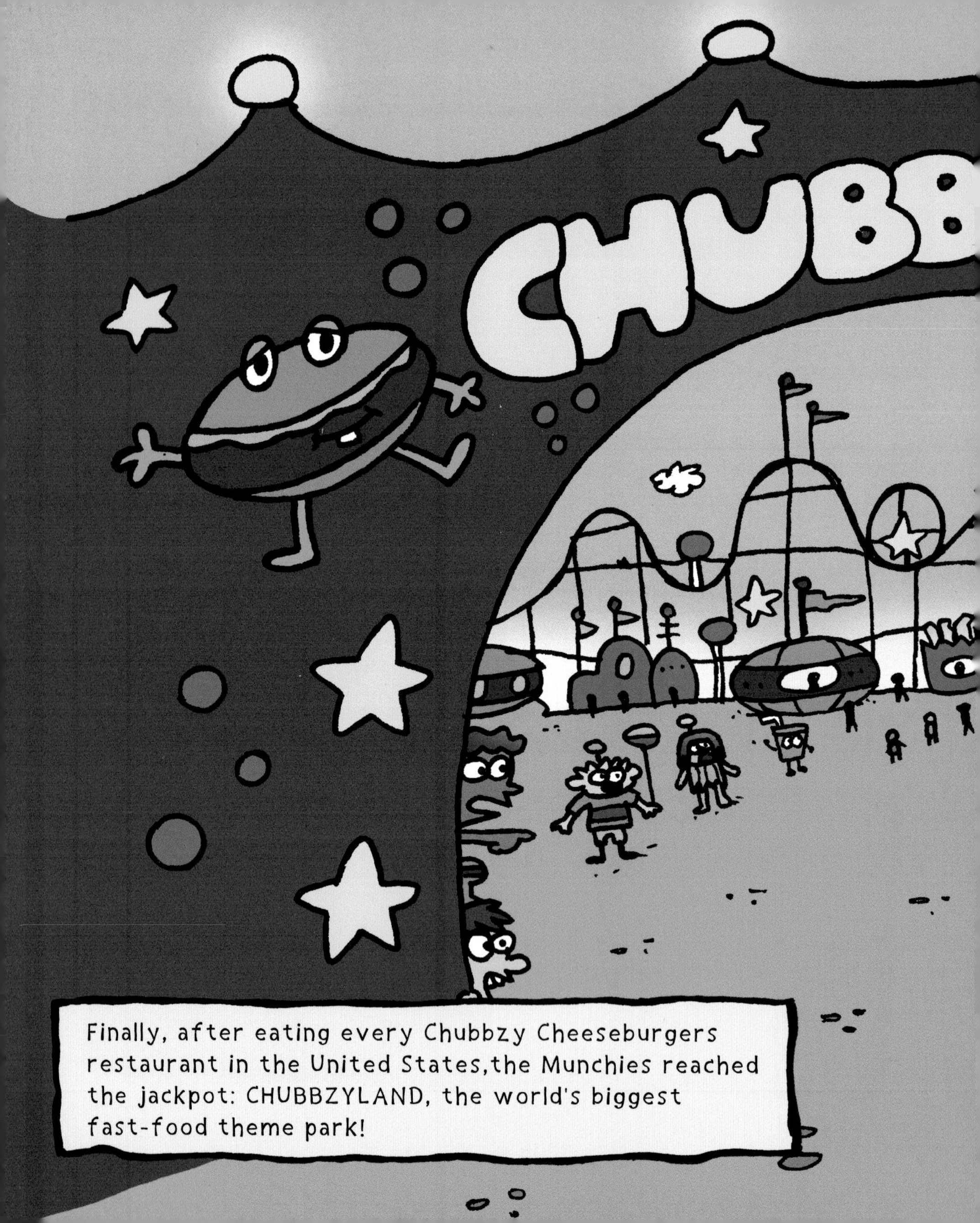
CHUBB
Finally, after eating every Chubbzy Cheeseburgers restaurant in the United States,the Munchies reached the jackpot: CHUBBZYLAND, the world's biggest fast-food theme park!

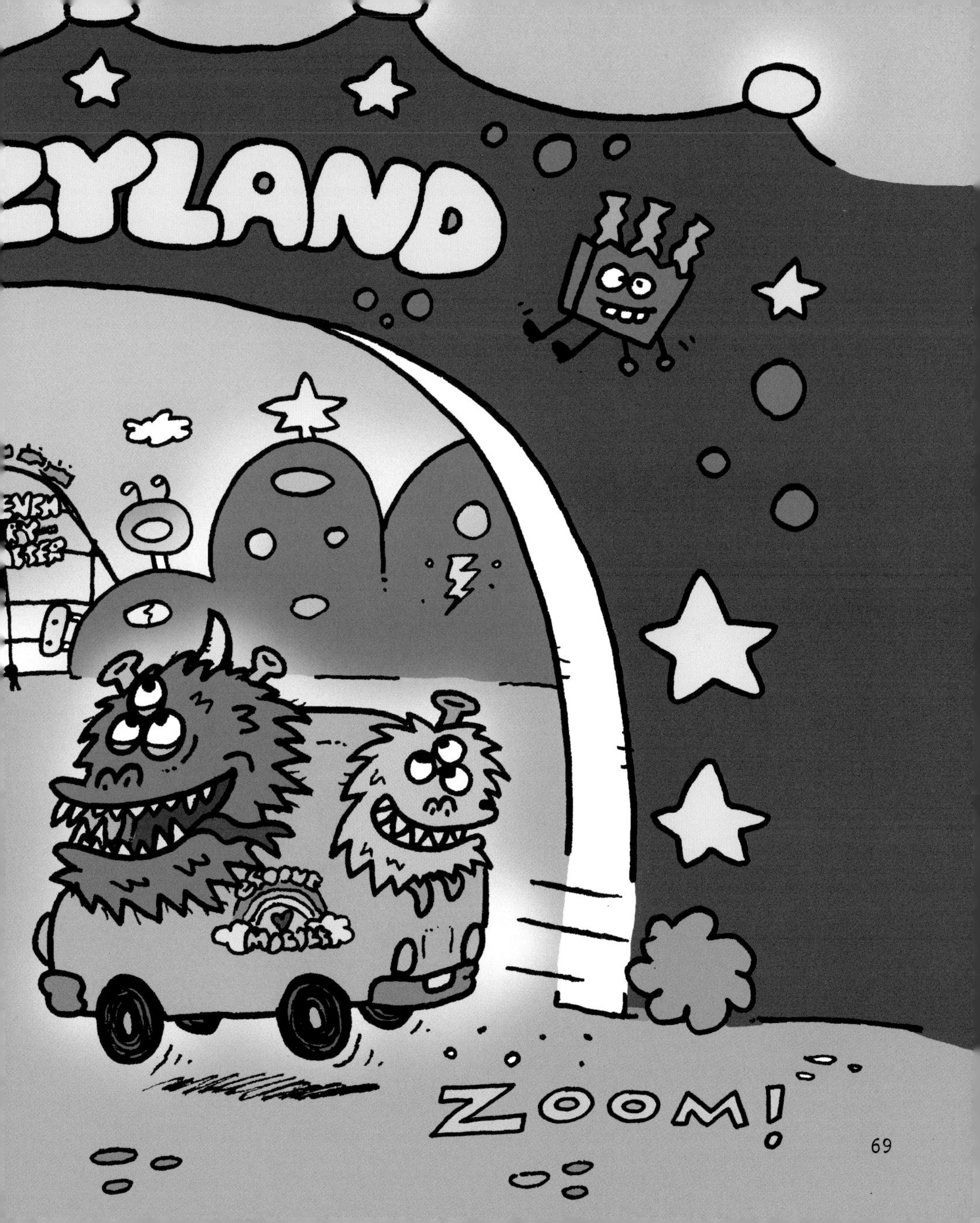
YLAND
ZOOM!

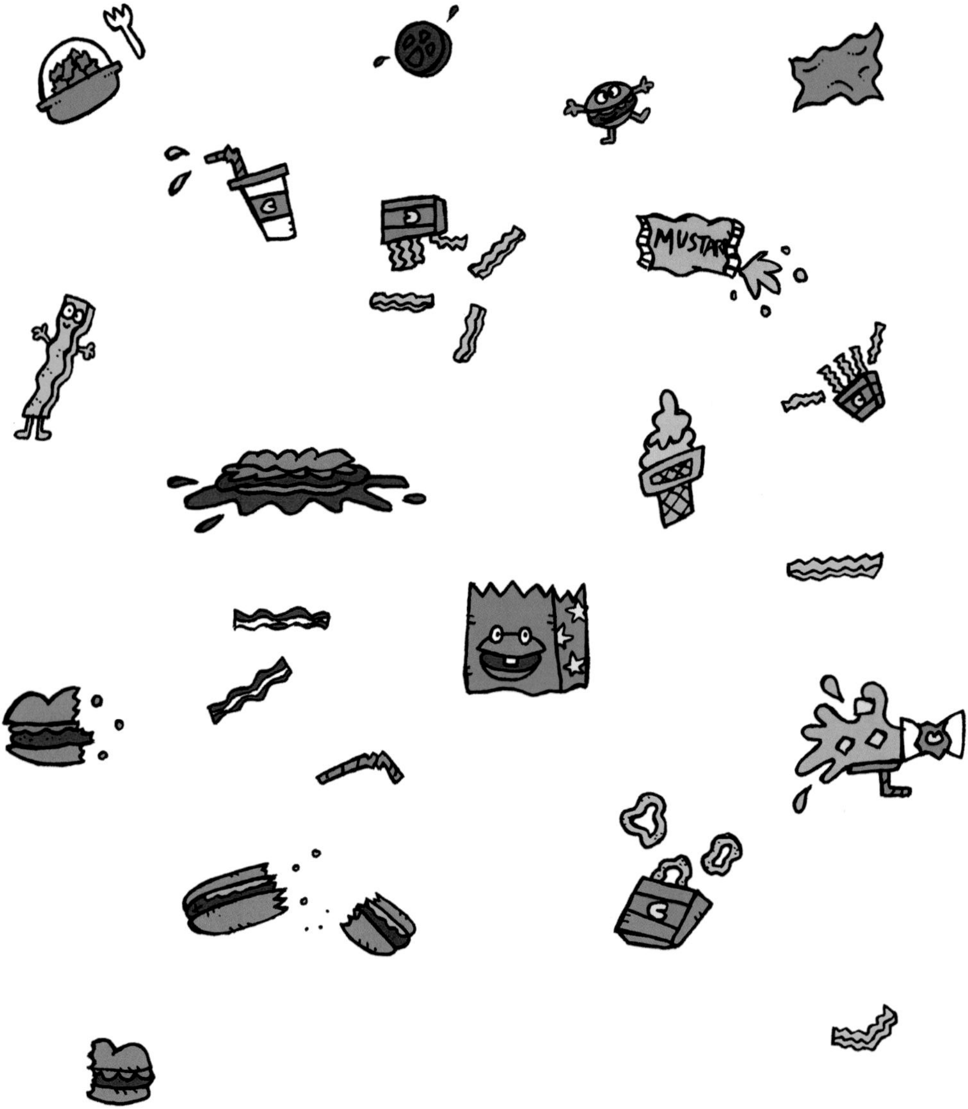
MUSTAR

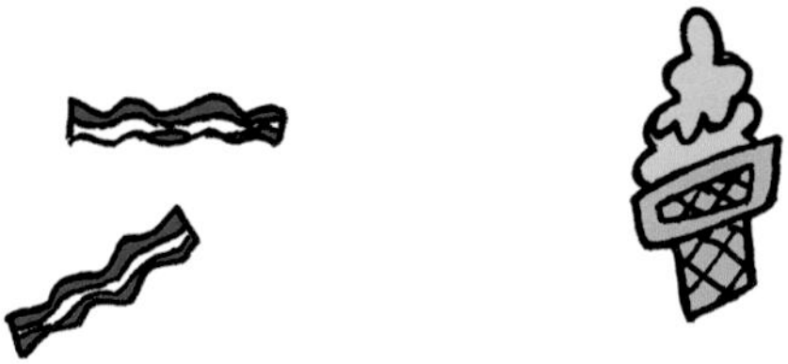

CHAPTER 8

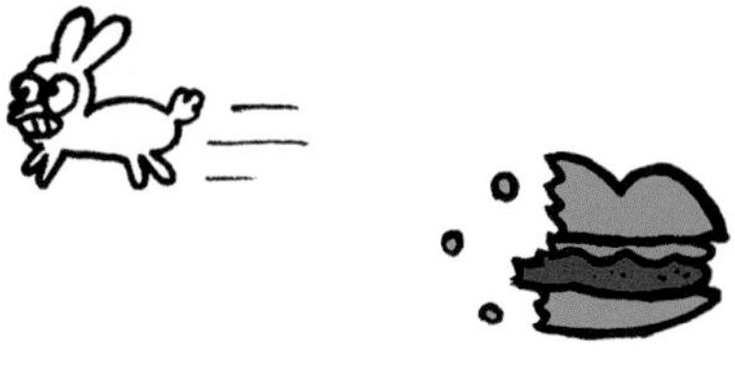

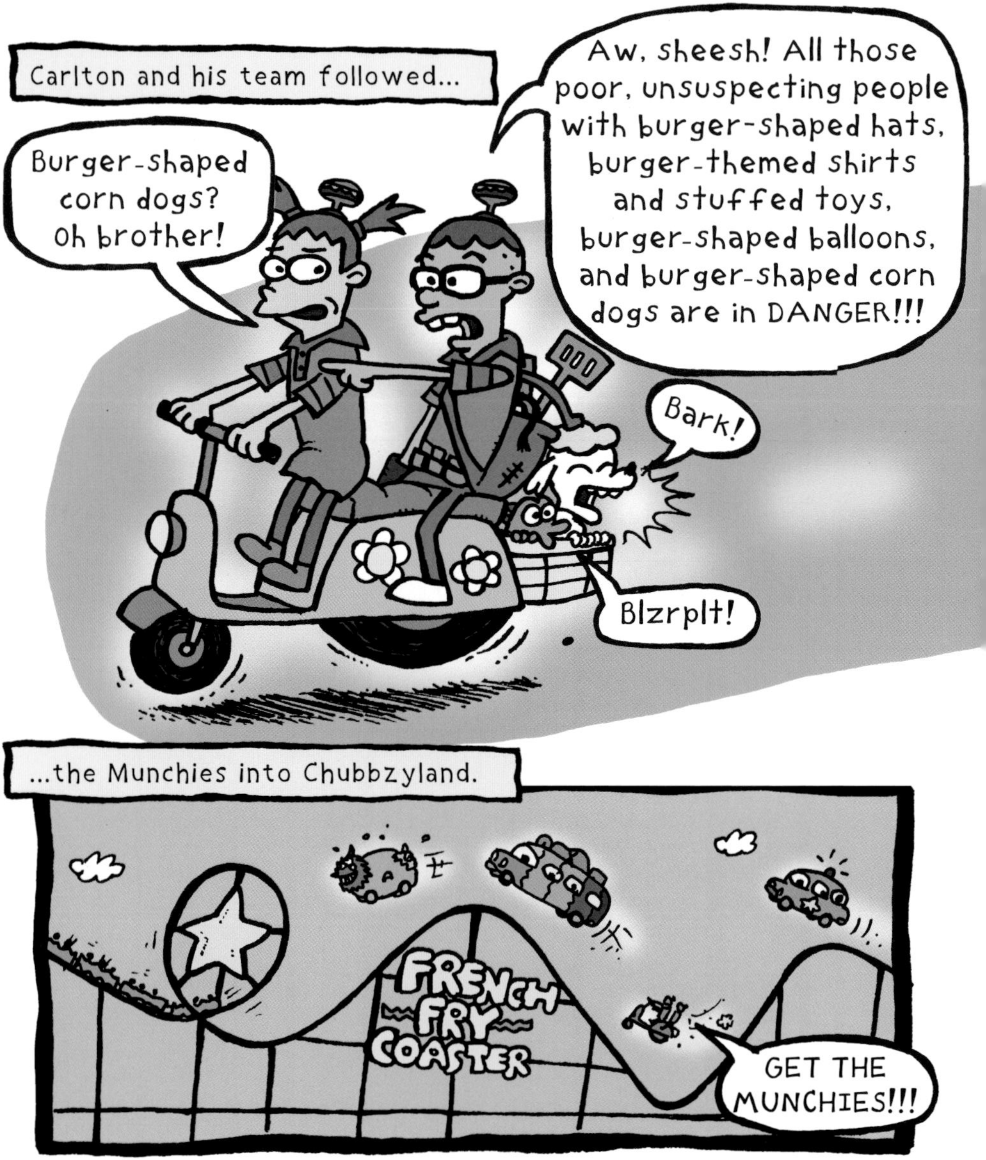
Carlton and his team followed...
Burger-shaped corn dogs? Oh brother!
Aw, sheesh! All those poor, unsuspecting people with burger-shaped hats, burger-themed shirts and stuffed toys, burger-shaped balloons, and burger-shaped corn dogs are in DANGER!!!
Bark!
Blzrplt!
...the Munchies into Chubbzyland.
FRENCH FRY COASTER
GET THE MUNCHIES!!!

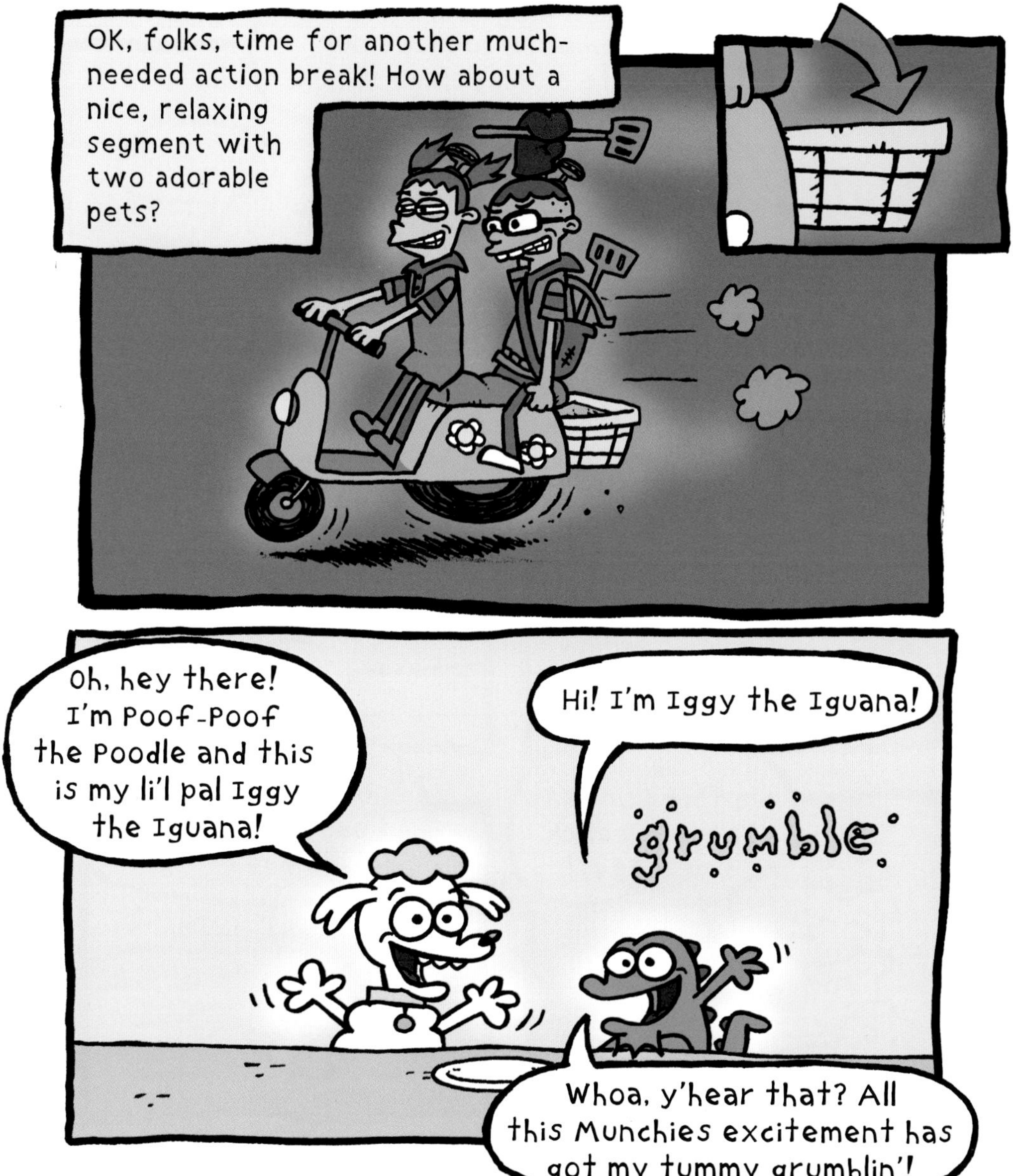
OK, folks, time for another much-needed action break! How about a nice, relaxing segment with two adorable pets?
Oh, hey there! I'm Poof-Poof the Poodle and this is my li'l pal Iggy the Iguana!
Hi! I'm Iggy the Iguana!
grumble
Whoa, y'hear that? All this Munchies excitement has got my tummy grumblin'!

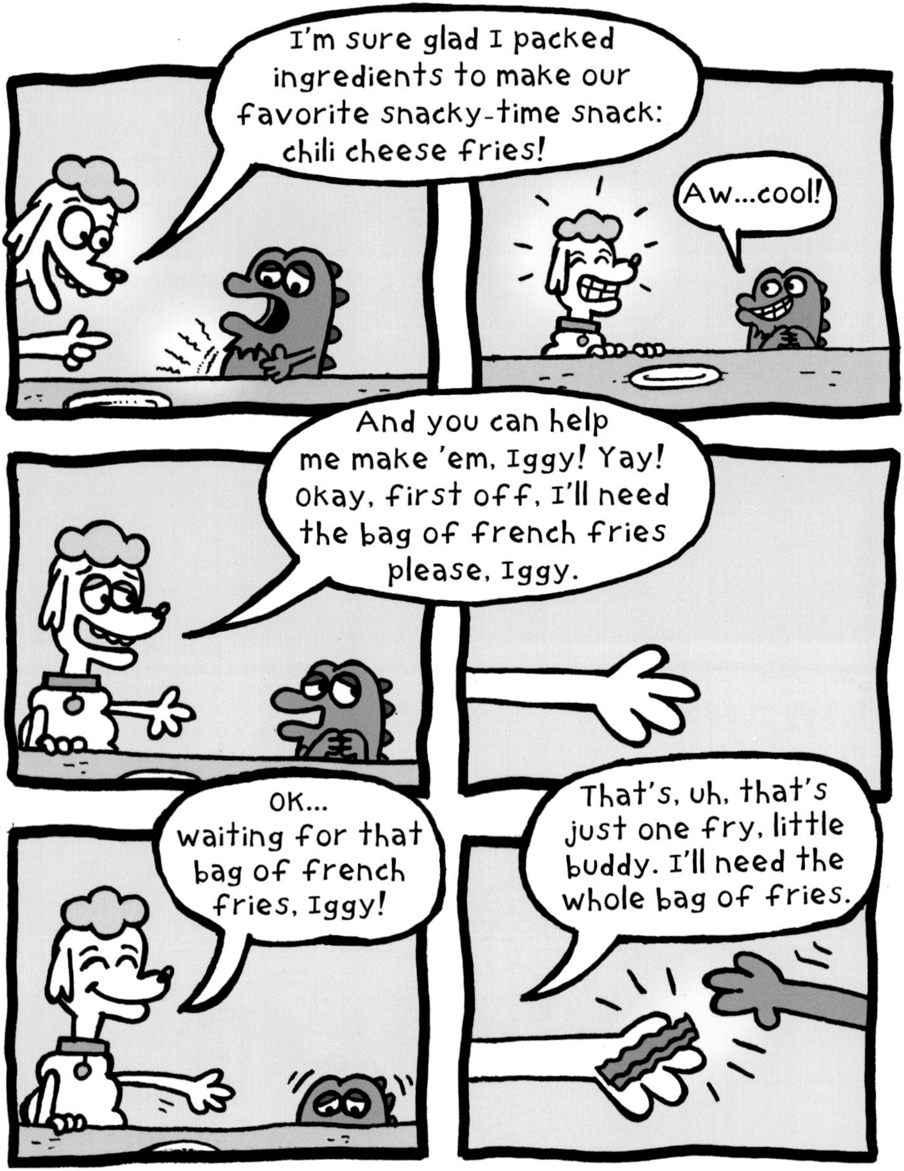
I'm sure glad I packed ingredients to make our favorite snacky-time snack: chili cheese fries!
Aw...cool!
And you can help me make 'em, Iggy! Yay! Okay, first off, I'll need the bag of french fries please, Iggy.
OK... waiting for that bag of french fries, Iggy!
That's, uh, that's just one fry, little buddy. I'll need the whole bag of fries.

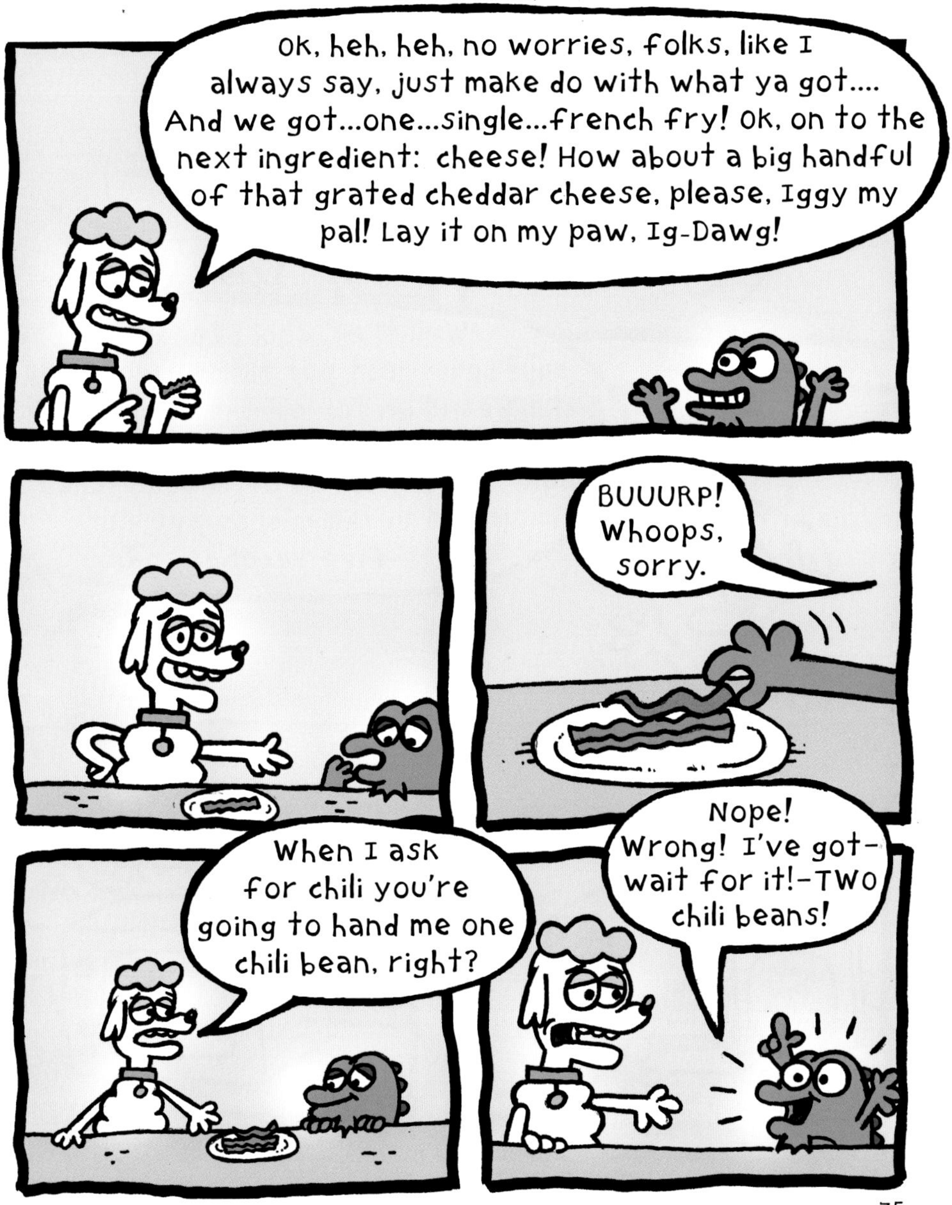

Ok, heh, heh, no worries, folks, like I always say, just make do with what ya got.... And we got...one...single...french fry! Ok, on to the next ingredient: cheese! How about a big handful of that grated cheddar cheese, please, Iggy my pal! Lay it on my paw, Ig-Dawg!
BUUURP! Whoops, sorry.
When I ask for chili you're going to hand me one chili bean, right?
Nope! Wrong! I've got–wait for it!–TWO chili beans!

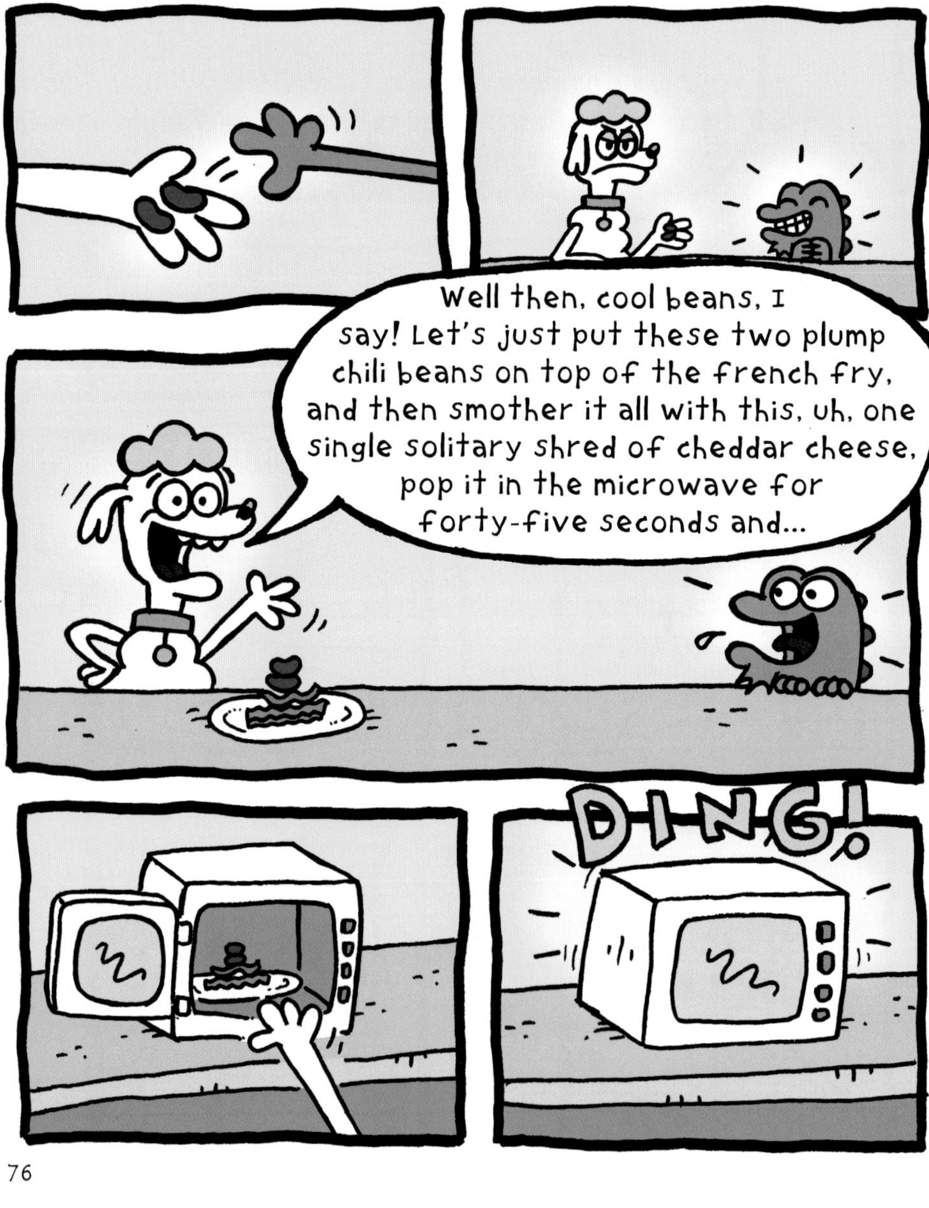
Well then, cool beans, I say! Let's just put these two plump chili beans on top of the french fry, and then smother it all with this, uh, one single solitary shred of cheddar cheese, pop it in the microwave for forty-five seconds and...
DING!

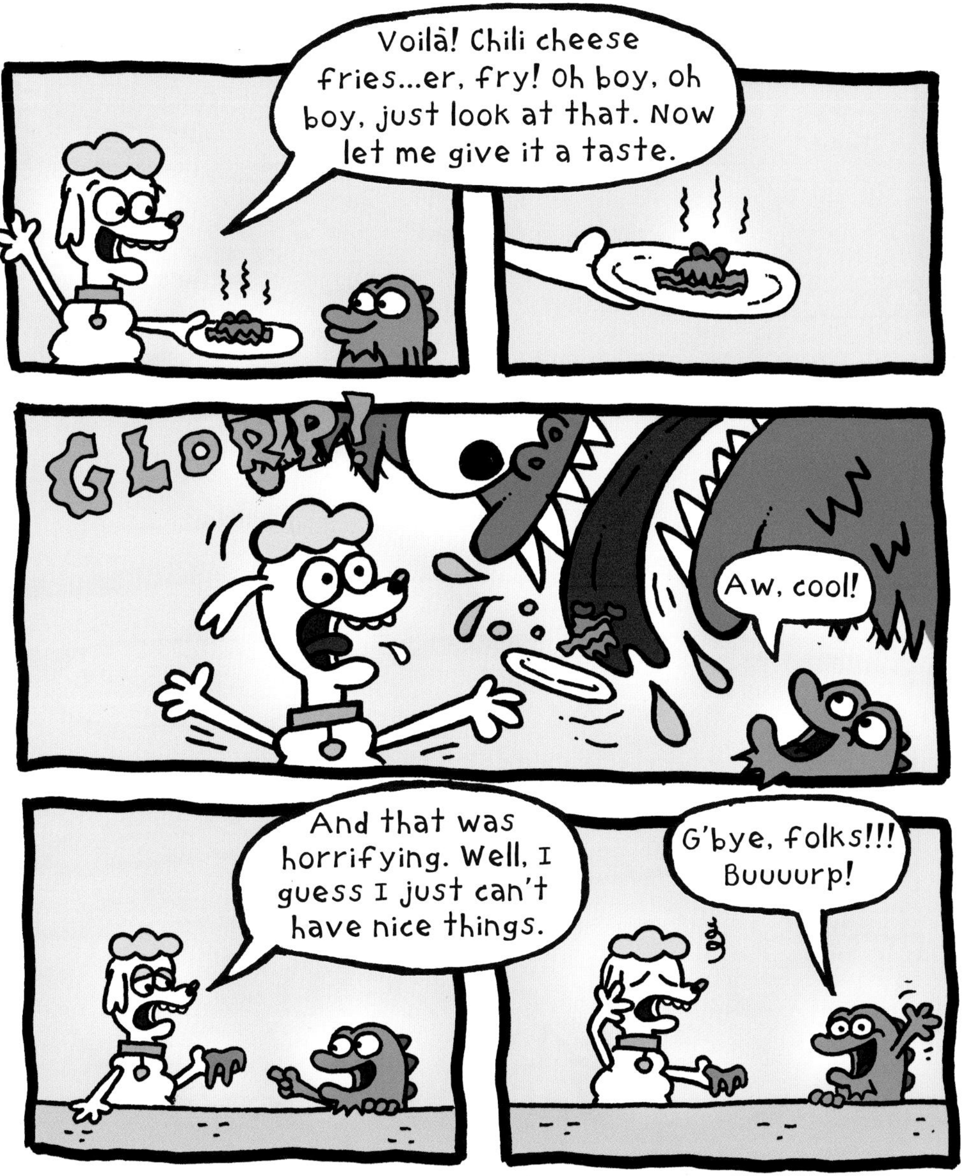
Voilà! Chili cheese fries...er, fry! Oh boy, oh boy, just look at that. Now let me give it a taste.
GLORP!
Aw, cool!
And that was horrifying. Well, I guess I just can't have nice things.
G'bye, folks!!! Buuuurp!

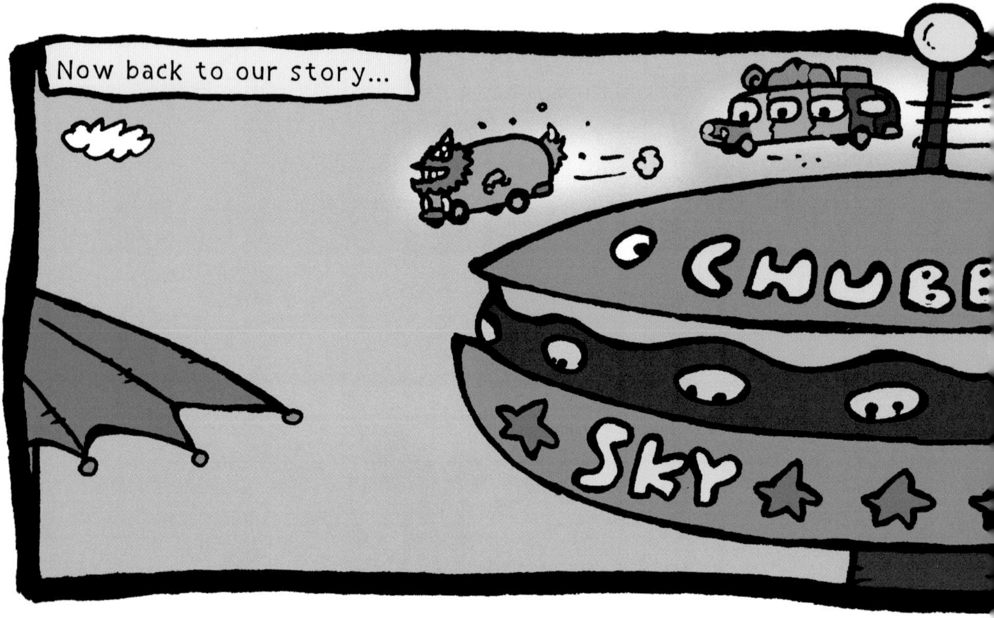
Now back to our story...
CHUBB
SKY

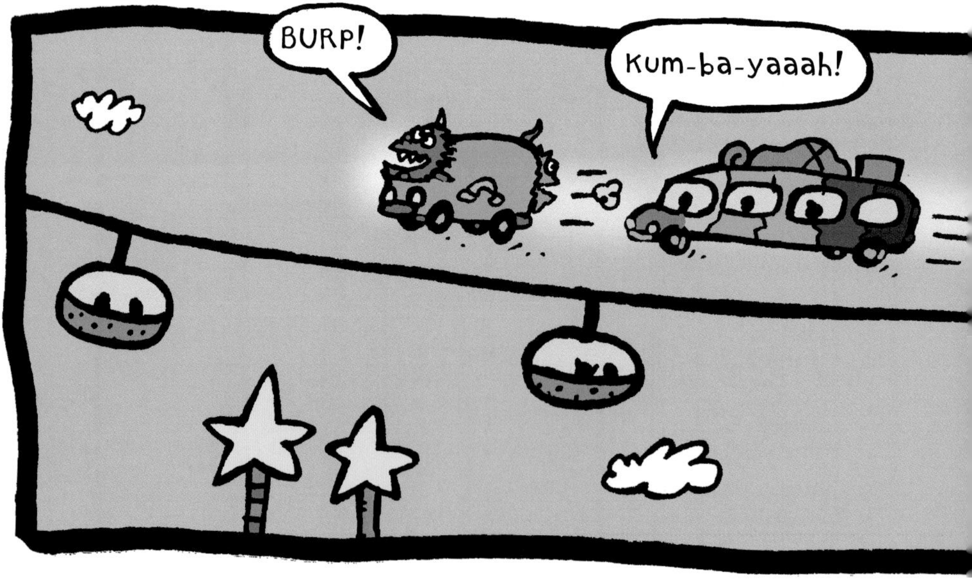
BURP!
Kum-ba-yaaah!

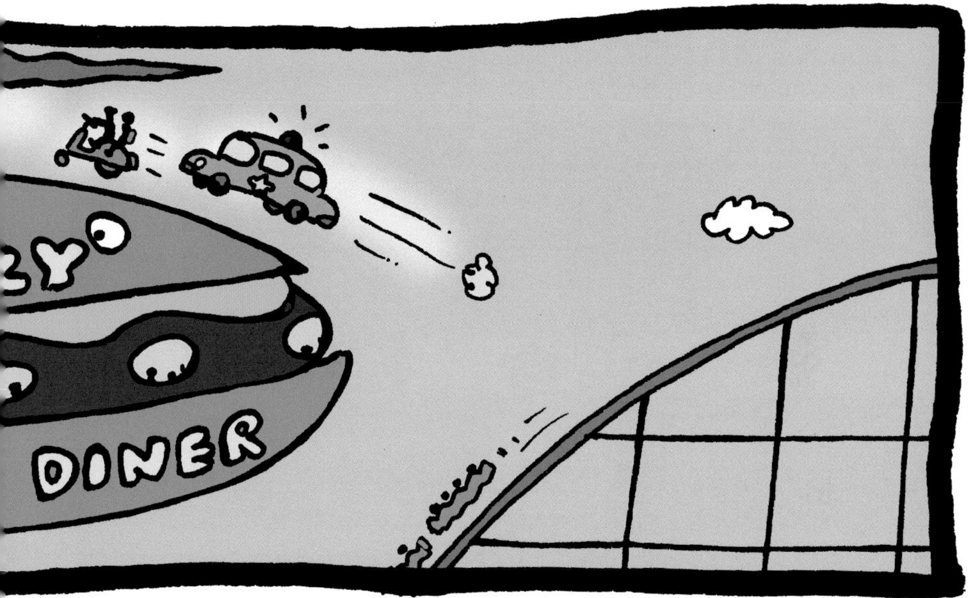
DINER

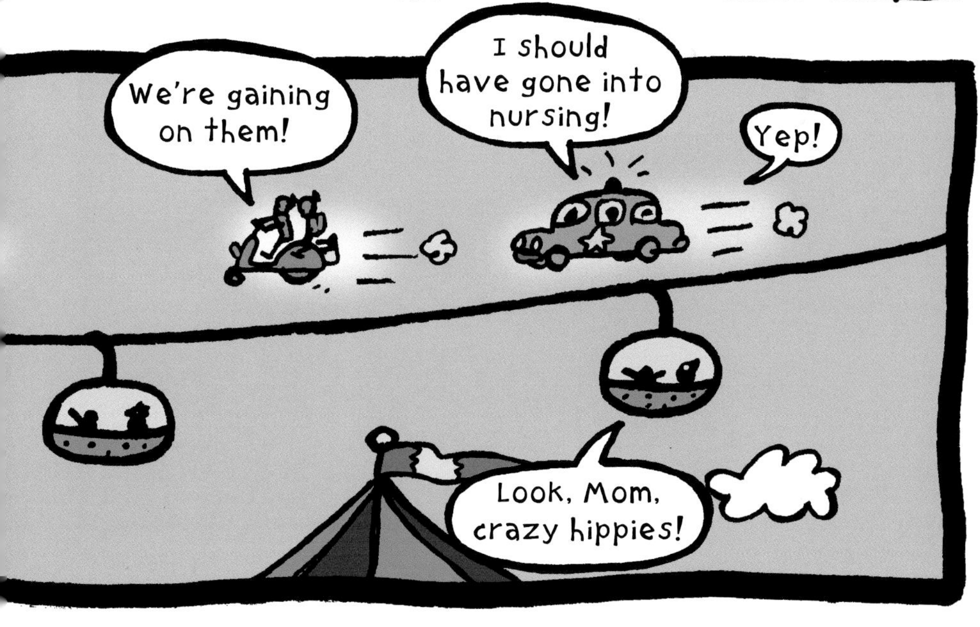
We're gaining on them!
I should have gone into nursing!
Yep!
Look, Mom, crazy hippies!

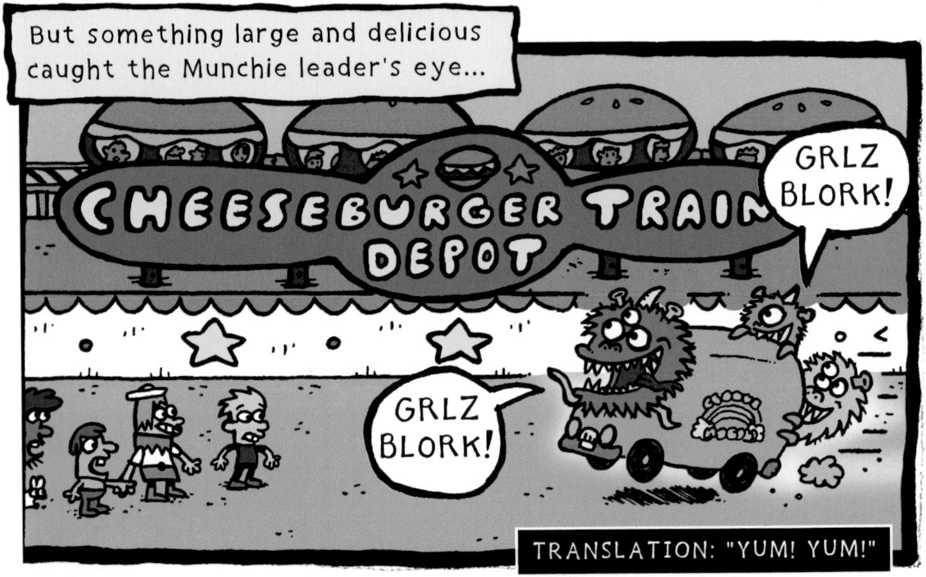
But something large and delicious caught the Munchie leader's eye...
CHEESEBURGER TRAIN DEPOT
GRLZ BLORK!
GRLZ BLORK!
TRANSLATION: "YUM! YUM!"

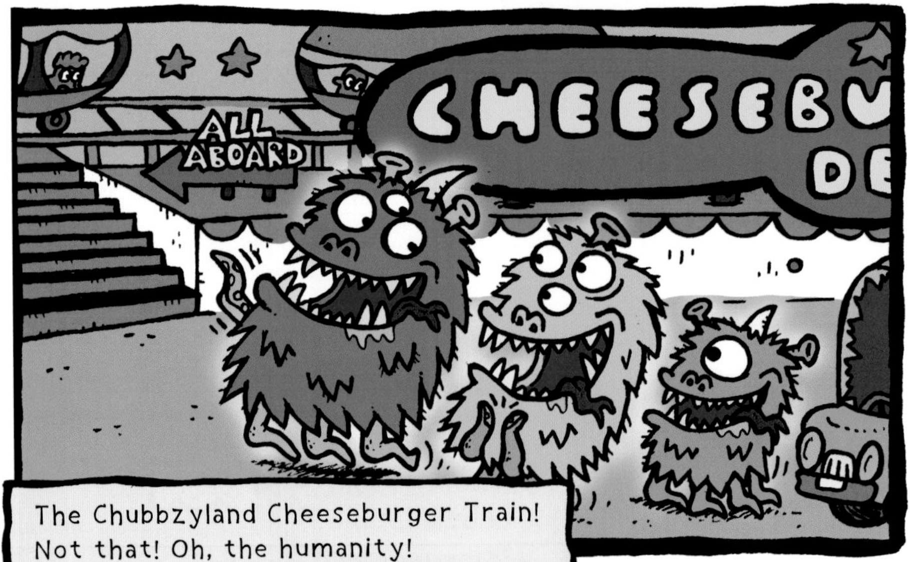
ALL ABOARD
CHEESEBU
DE
The Chubbzyland Cheeseburger Train! Not that! Oh, the humanity!

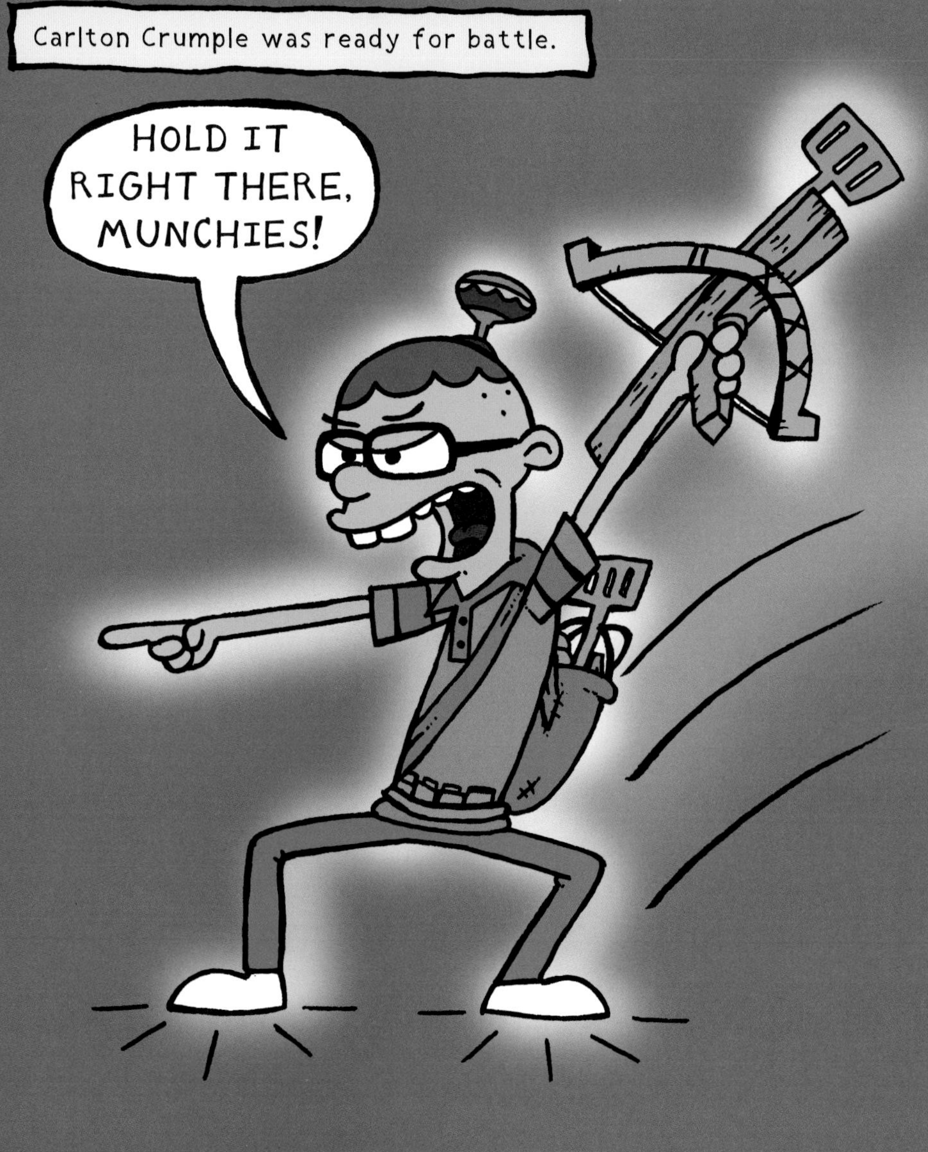
Carlton Crumple was ready for battle.
HOLD IT RIGHT THERE, MUNCHIES!

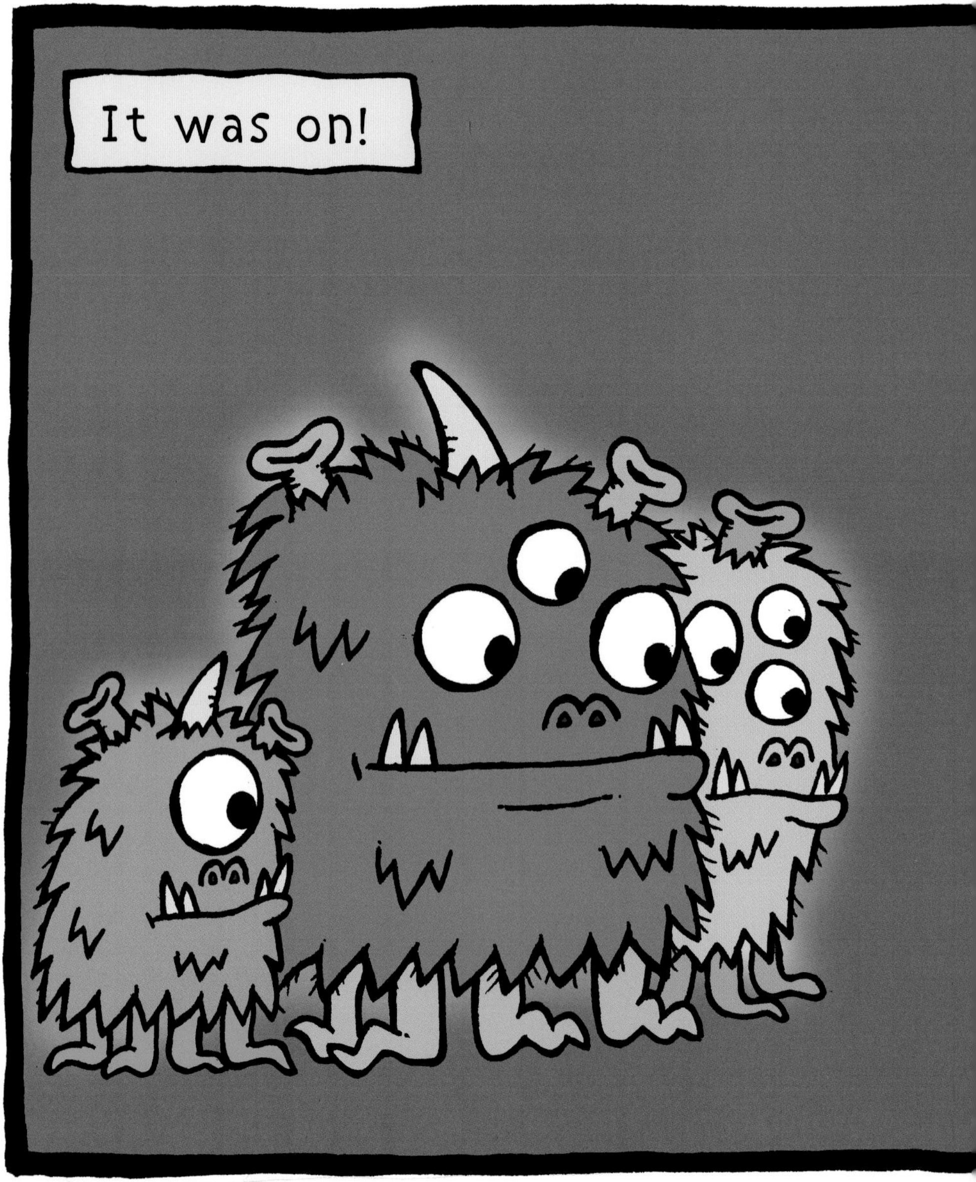
It was on!

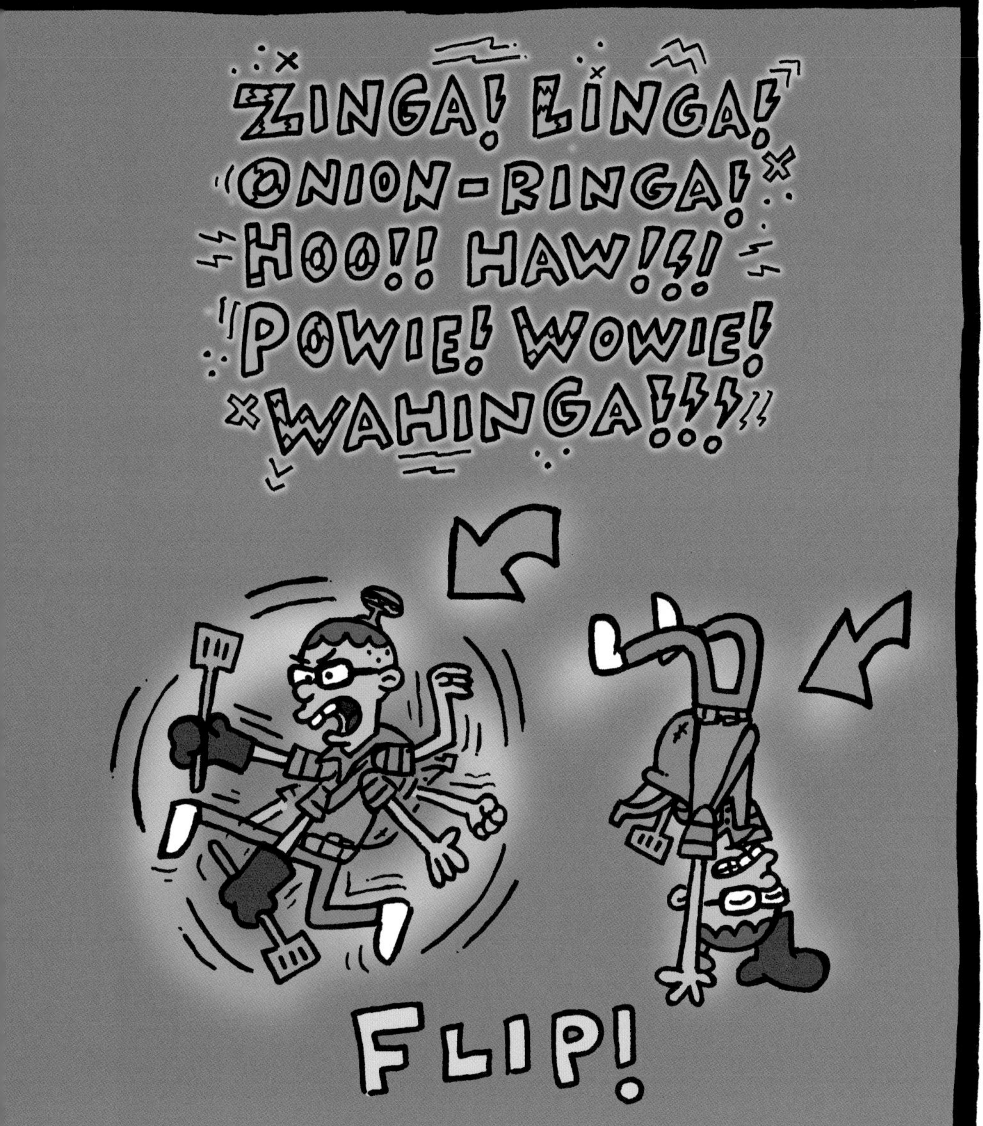

ZINGA! LINGA!
ONION-RINGA!
HOO!! HAW!!!
POWIE! WOWIE!
WAHINGA!!!
FLIP!

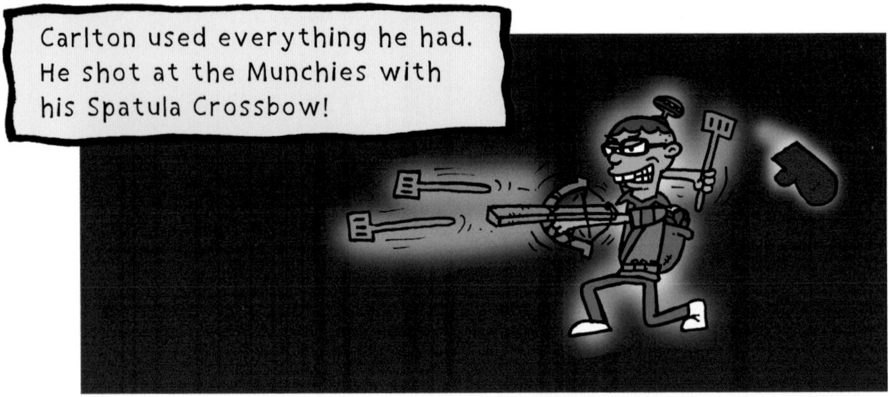
Carlton used everything he had. He shot at the Munchies with his Spatula Crossbow!

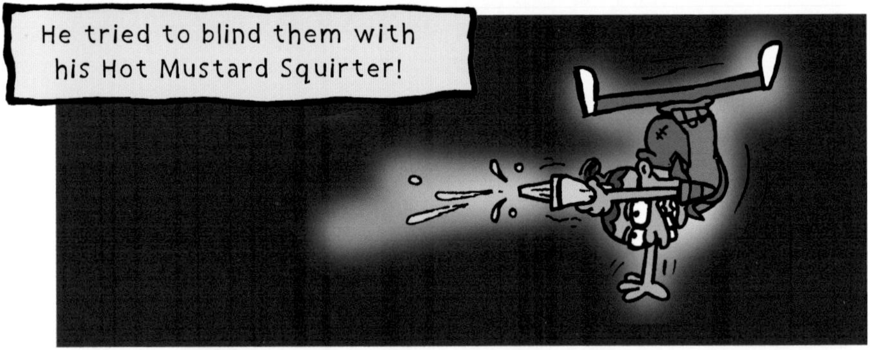
He tried to blind them with his Hot Mustard Squirter!

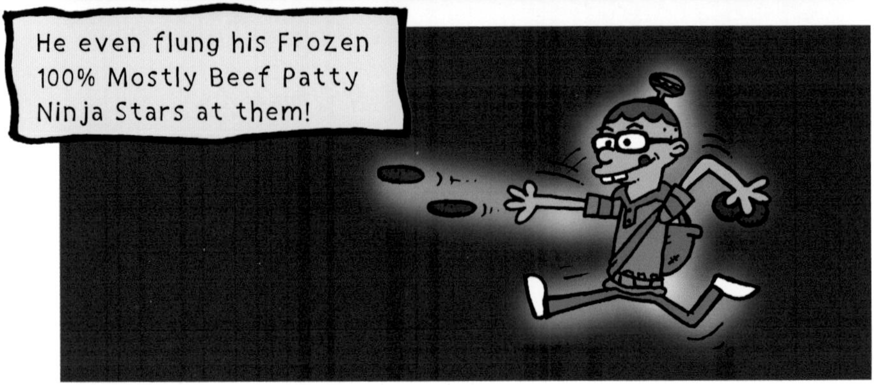
He even flung his Frozen 100% Mostly Beef Patty Ninja Stars at them!

But it was no use. The Munchies just stood there as Carlton's stealth ammo bounced off them. Then they proceeded toward the delicious Cheeseburger Train to chow down!

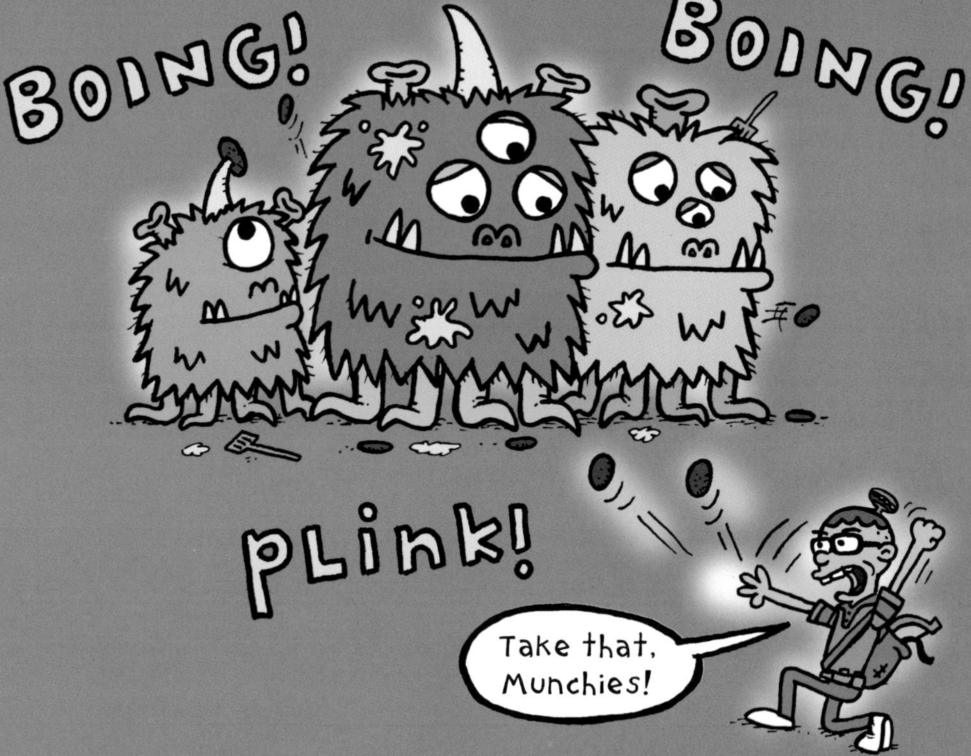
BOING!
BOING!
PLINK!
Take that, Munchies!

CHAPTER 9

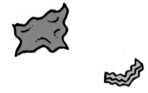

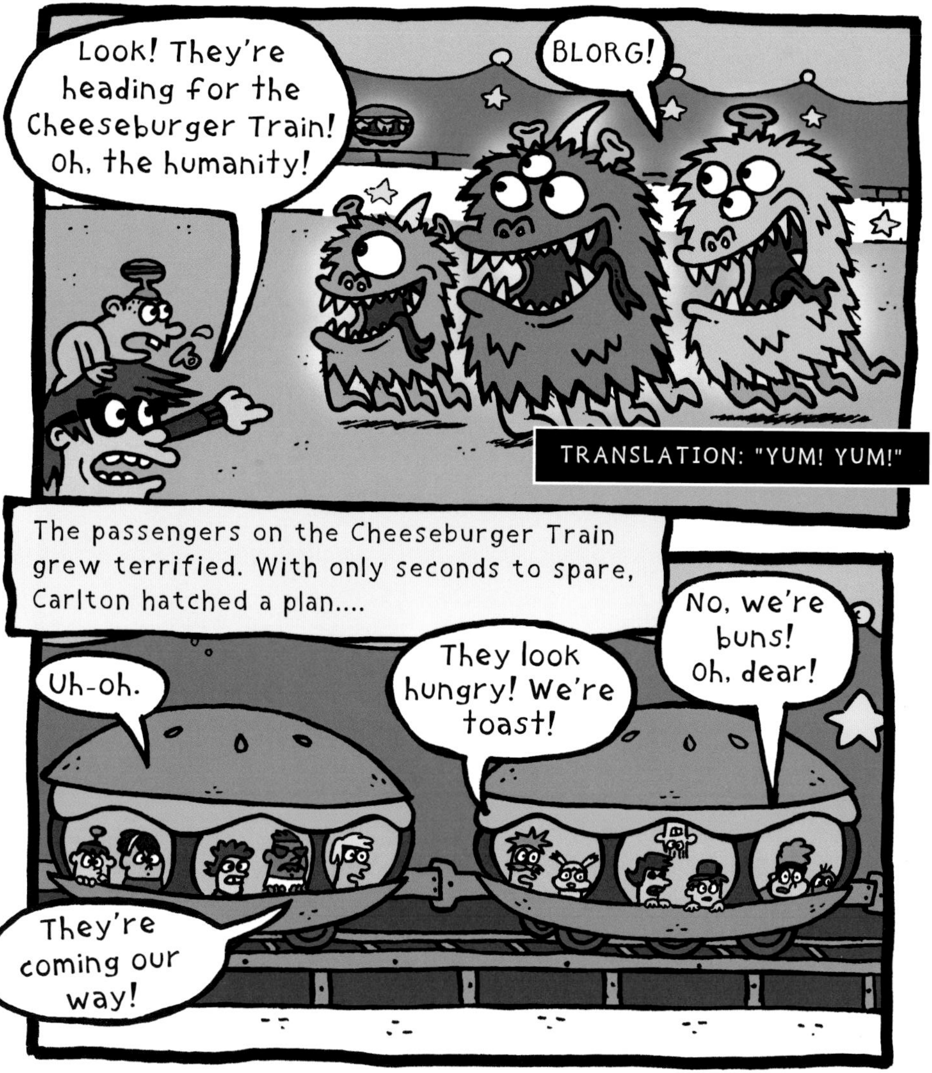
Look! They're heading for the Cheeseburger Train! Oh, the humanity!
BLORG!
TRANSLATION: "YUM! YUM!"
The passengers on the Cheeseburger Train grew terrified. With only seconds to spare, Carlton hatched a plan....
Uh-oh.
They look hungry! We're toast!
No, we're buns! Oh, dear!
They're coming our way!

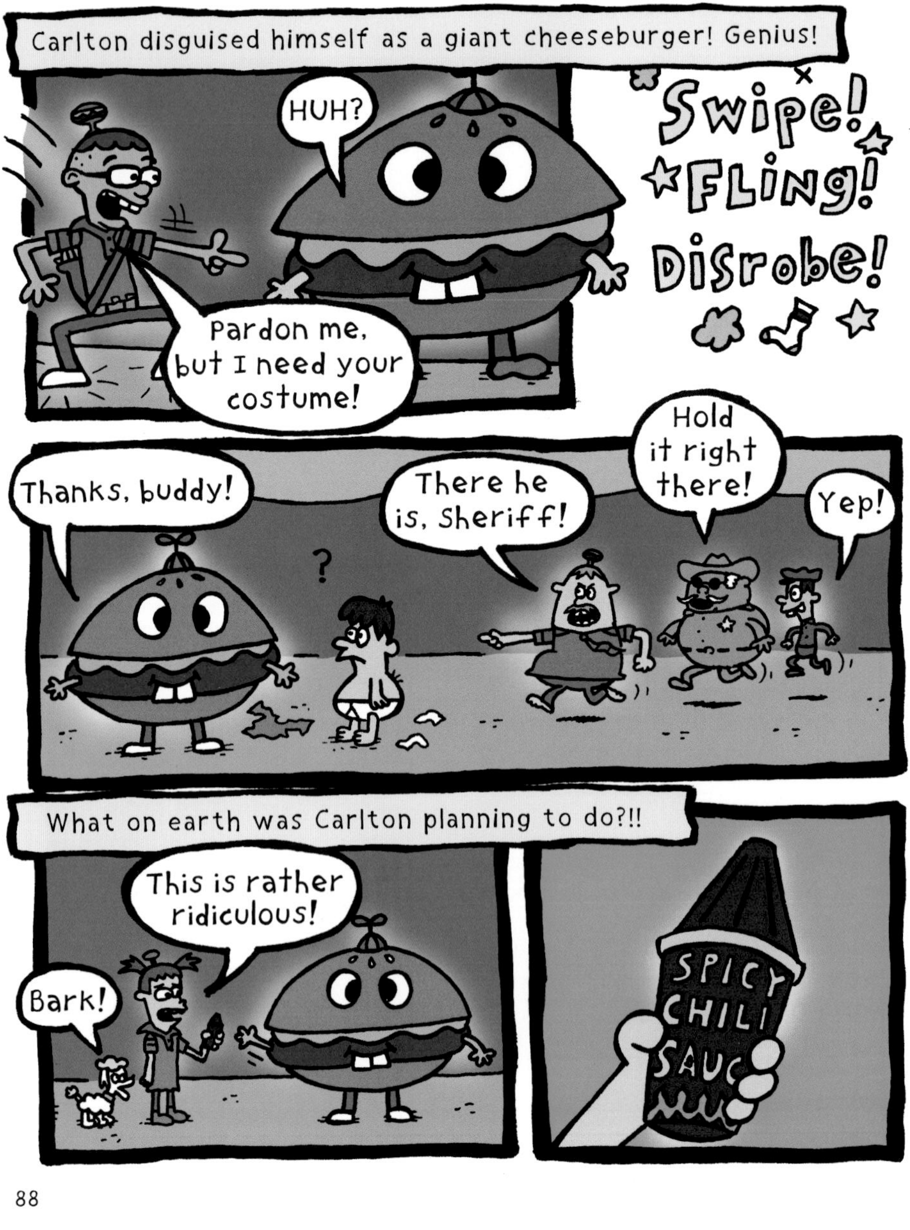

Carlton disguised himself as a giant cheeseburger! Genius!
HUH?
Pardon me, but I need your costume!
Swipe! Fling! Disrobe!
Thanks, buddy!
?
There he is, Sheriff!
Hold it right there!
Yep!
What on earth was Carlton planning to do?!!
Bark!
This is rather ridiculous!
SPICY CHILI SAUC

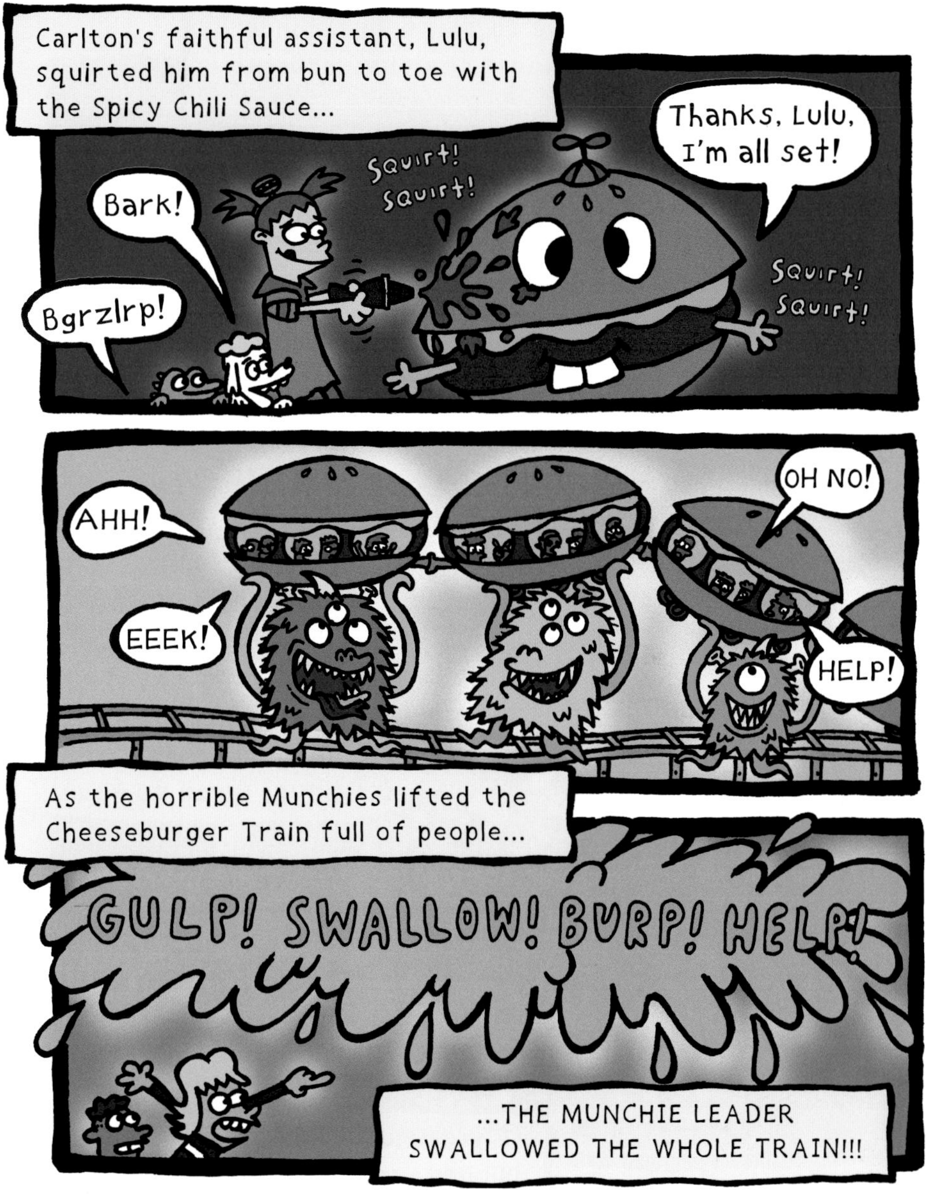
Carlton's faithful assistant, Lulu, squirted him from bun to toe with the Spicy Chili Sauce...
Bark!
Bgrzlrp!
Squirt! Squirt!
Thanks, Lulu, I'm all set!
Squirt! Squirt!
AHH!
EEEK!
OH NO!
HELP!
As the horrible Munchies lifted the Cheeseburger Train full of people...
GULP! SWALLOW! BURP! HELP!
...THE MUNCHIE LEADER SWALLOWED THE WHOLE TRAIN!!!

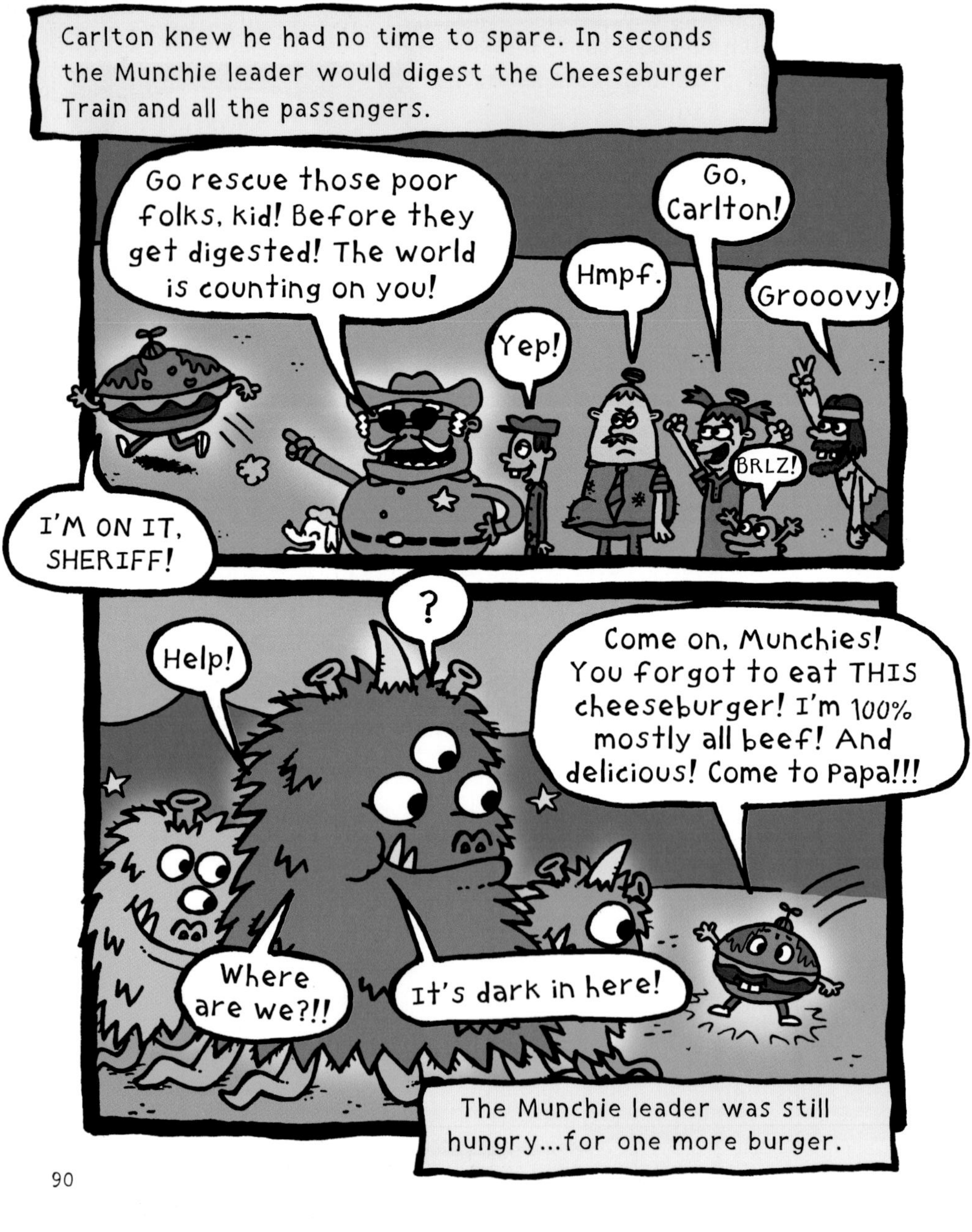
Carlton knew he had no time to spare. In seconds the Munchie leader would digest the Cheeseburger Train and all the passengers.
Go rescue those poor folks, kid! Before they get digested! The world is counting on you!
Yep!
Hmpf.
Go, Carlton!
Grooovy!
BRLZ!
I'M ON IT, SHERIFF!
Help!
?
Come on, Munchies! You forgot to eat THIS cheeseburger! I'm 100% mostly all beef! And delicious! Come to Papa!!!
Where are we?!!
It's dark in here!
The Munchie leader was still hungry...for one more burger.

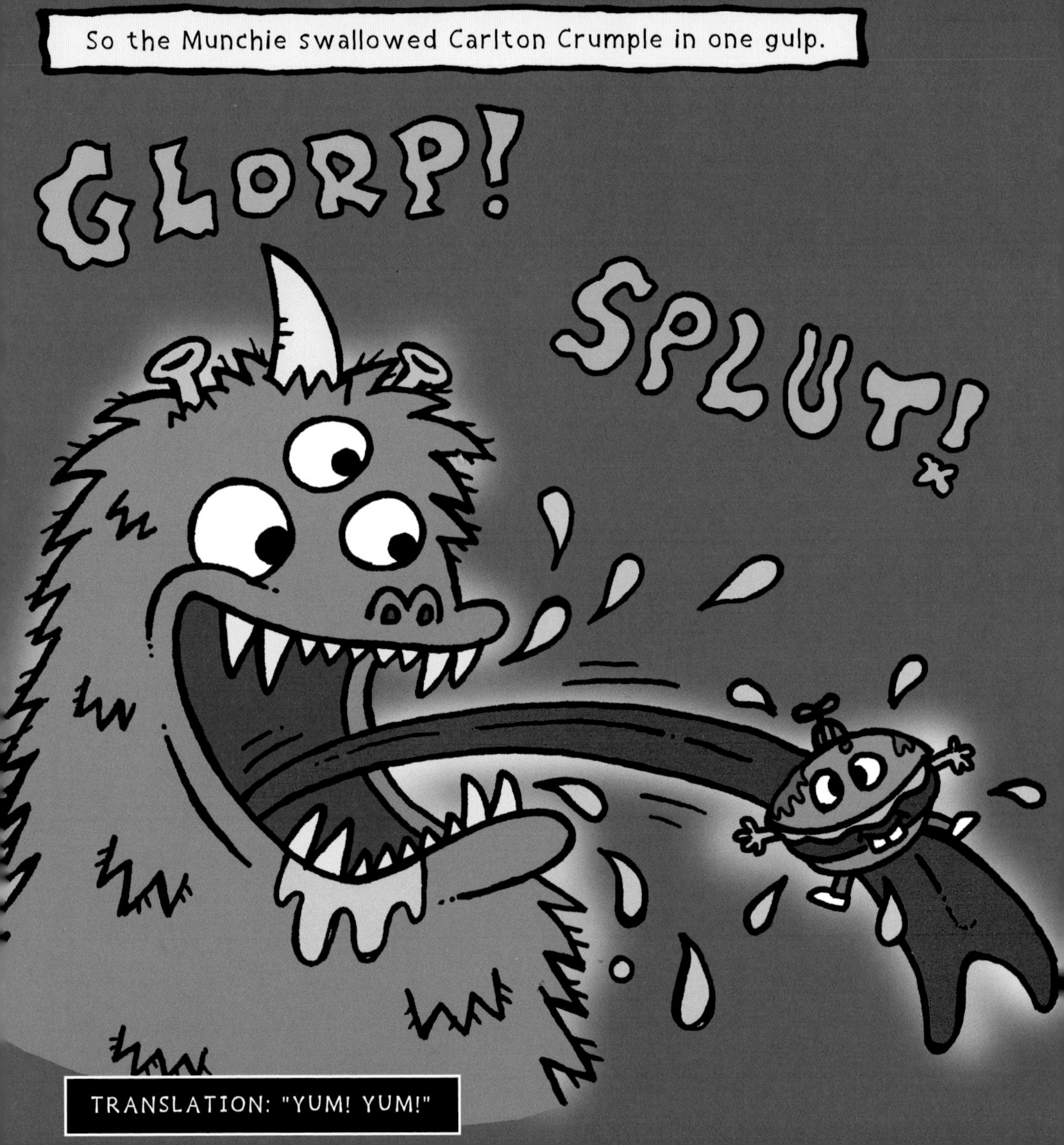
So the Munchie swallowed Carlton Crumple in one gulp.
GLORP!
SPLUT!
TRANSLATION: "YUM! YUM!"

CHAPTER 10

CHUBBZY SAUCE

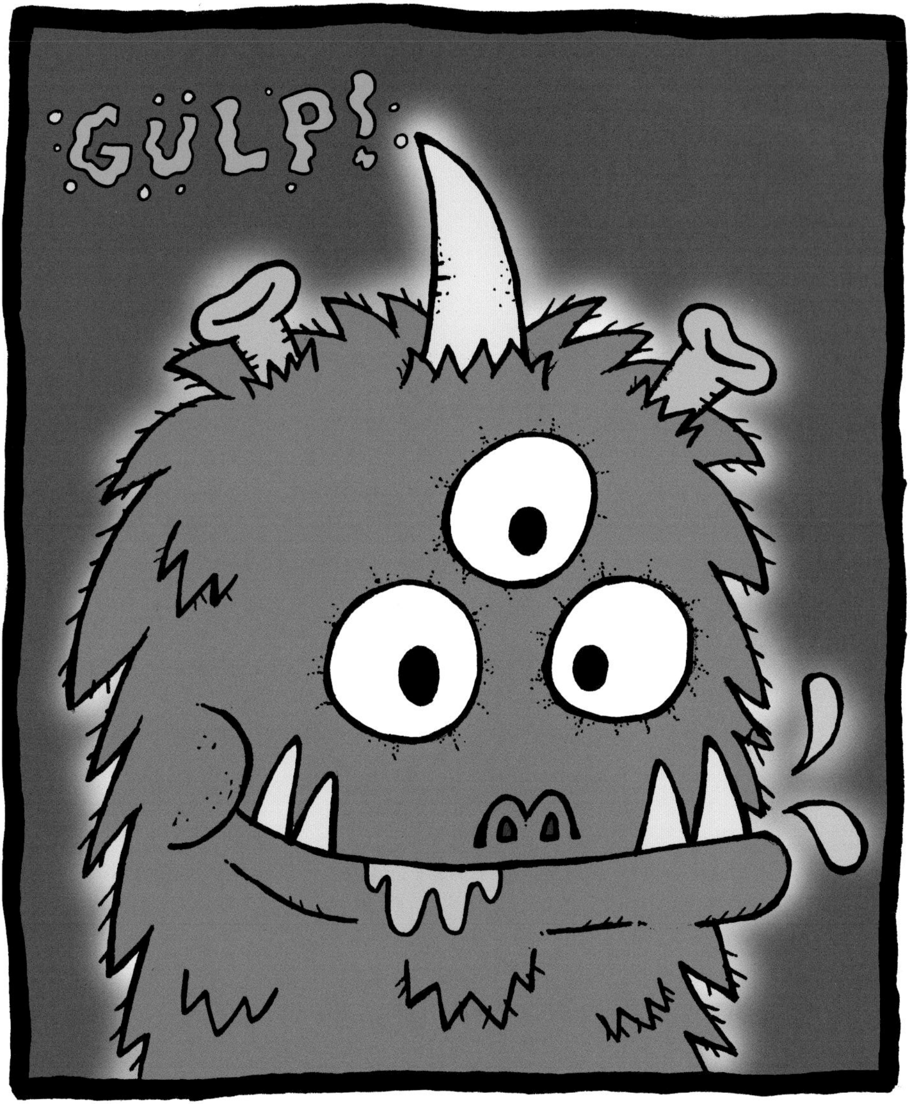
GULP!

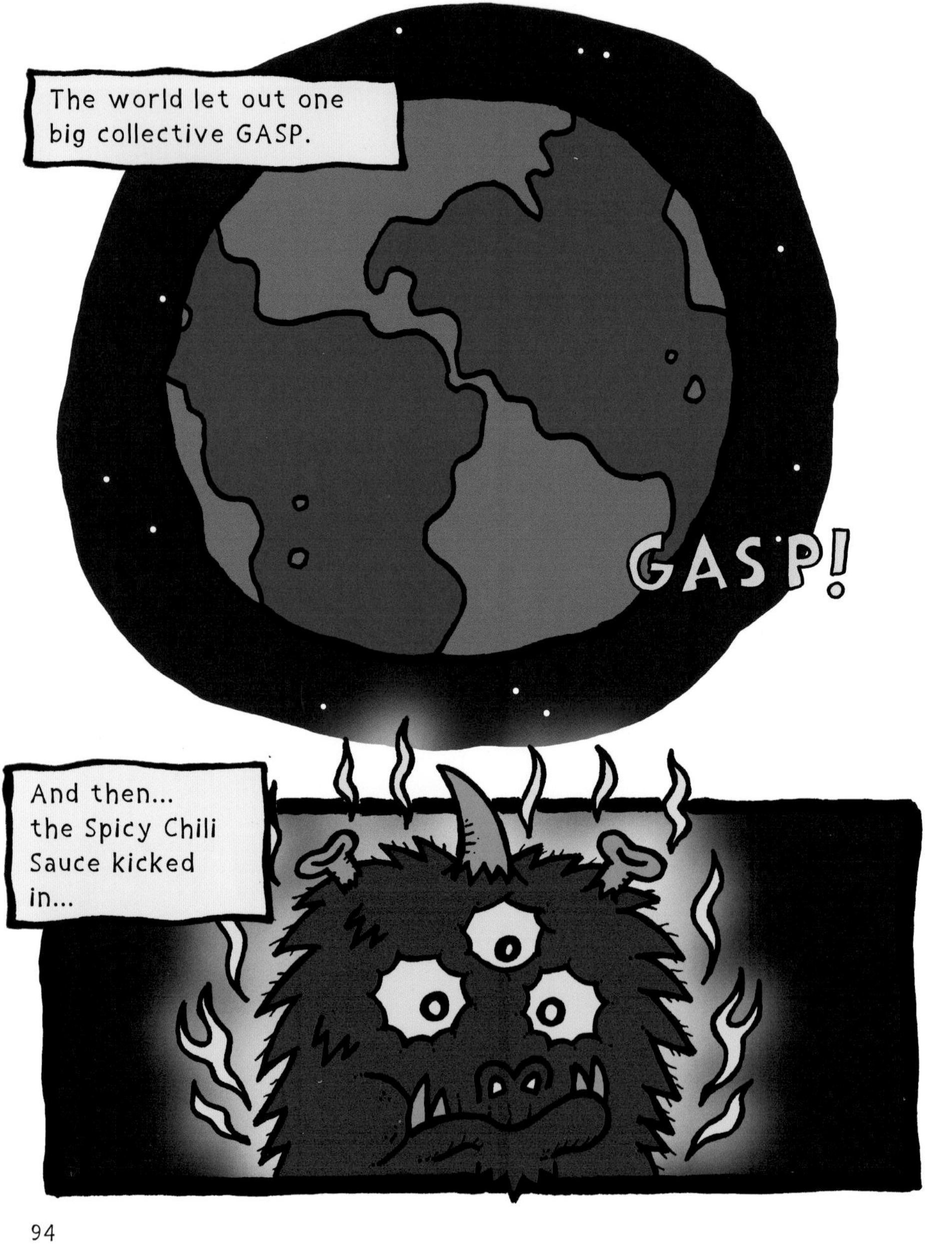
The world let out one big collective GASP.
GASP!
And then... the Spicy Chili Sauce kicked in...

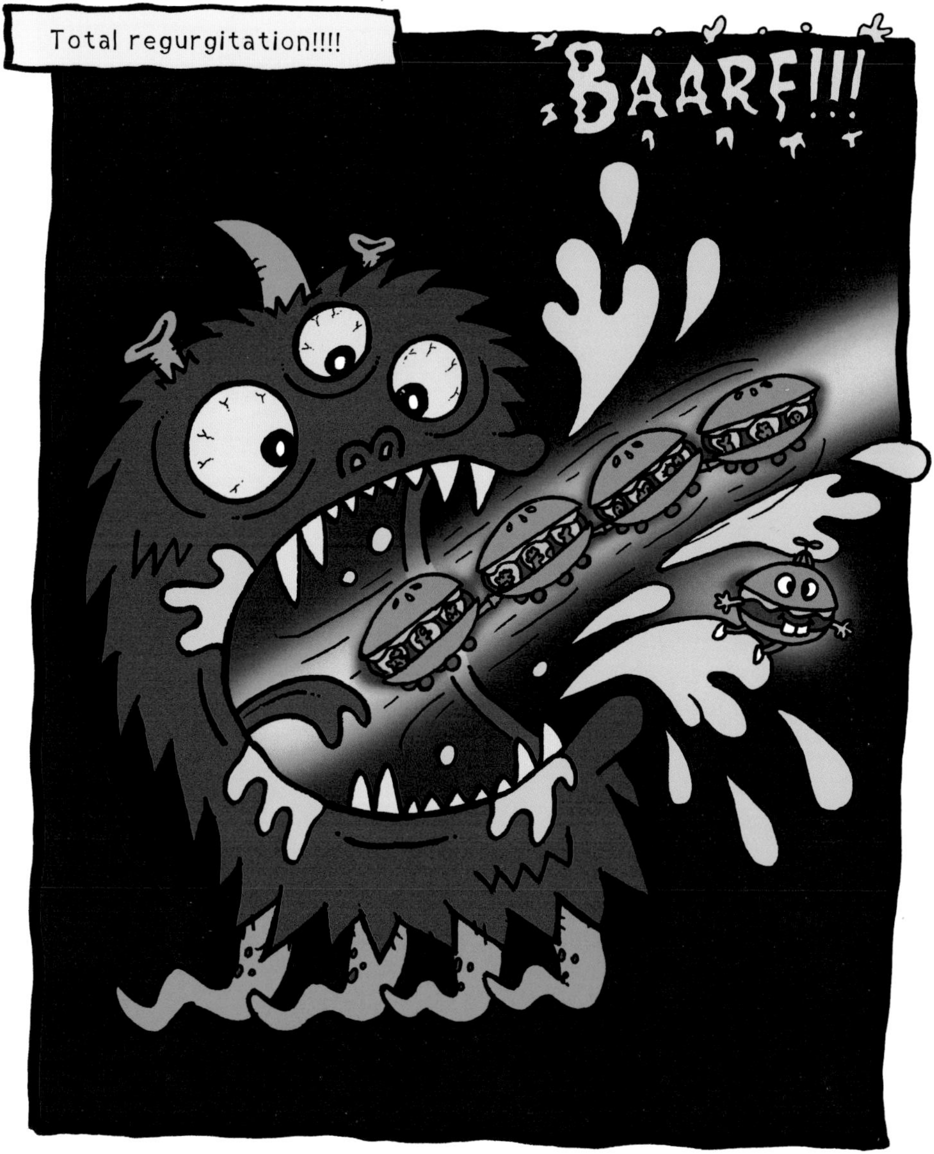
Total regurgitation!!!!
BAARF!!!

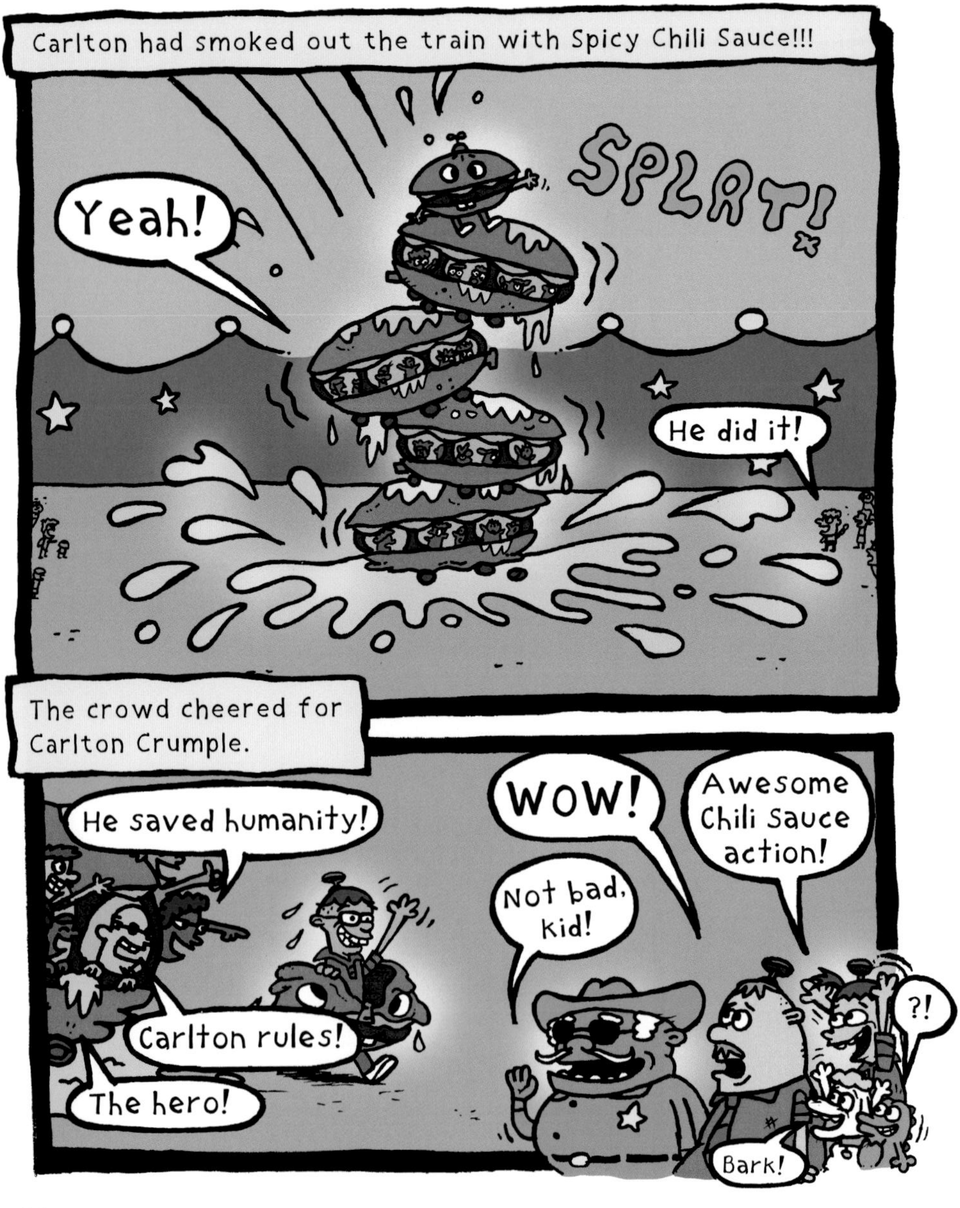

Carlton had smoked out the train with Spicy Chili Sauce!!!
SPLAT!
Yeah!
He did it!
The crowd cheered for Carlton Crumple.
He saved humanity!
Carlton rules!
The hero!
WOW!
Awesome Chili Sauce action!
Not bad, kid!
?!
Bark!

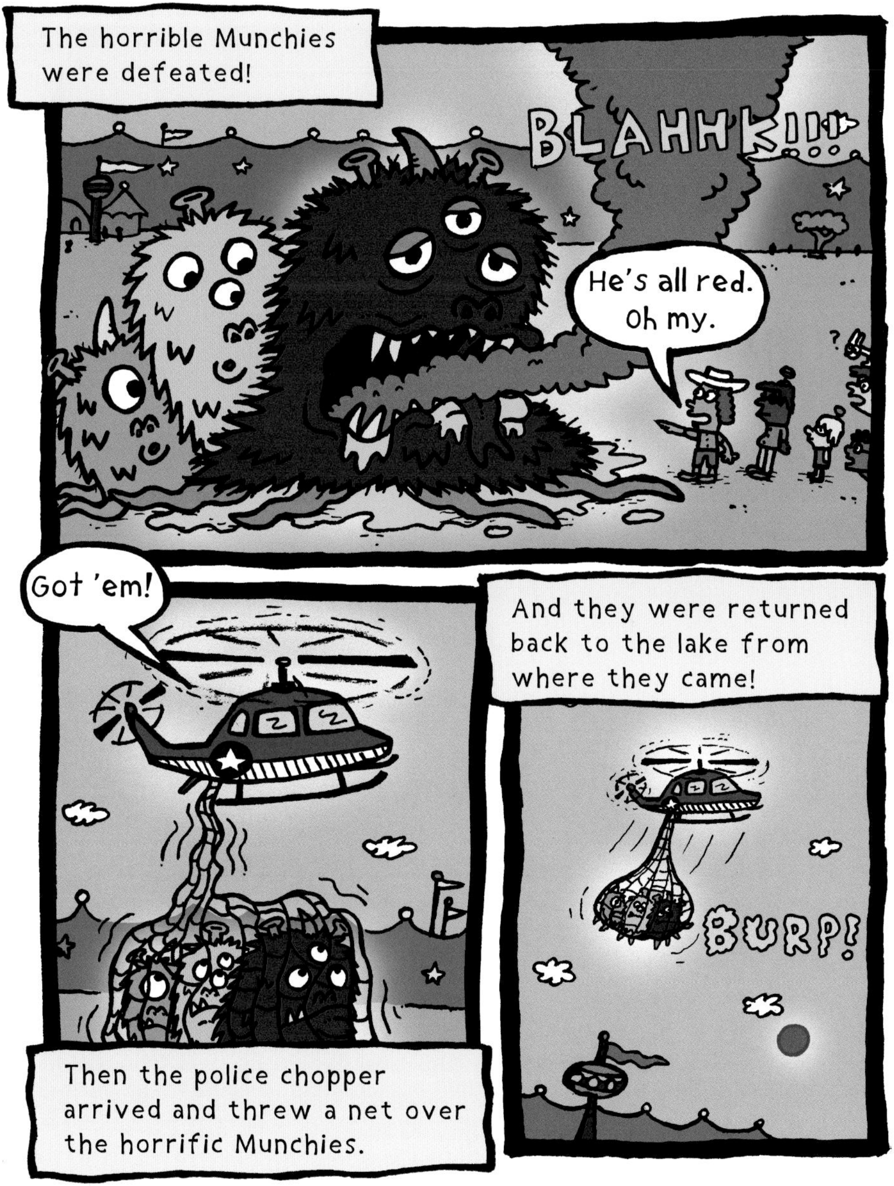

The horrible Munchies were defeated!
BLAHHK!!!
He's all red. Oh my.
Got 'em!
Then the police chopper arrived and threw a net over the horrific Munchies.
And they were returned back to the lake from where they came!
BURP!

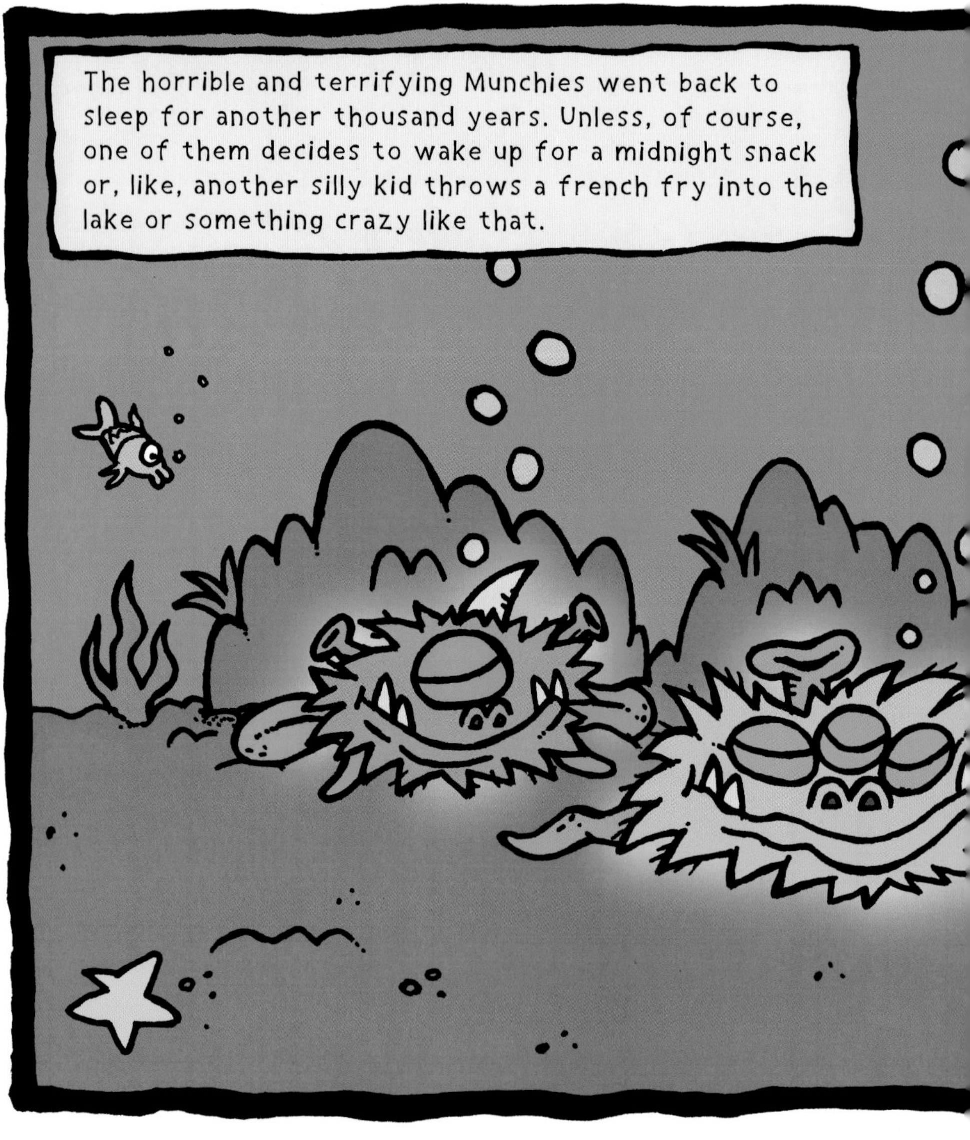
The horrible and terrifying Munchies went back to sleep for another thousand years. Unless, of course, one of them decides to wake up for a midnight snack or, like, another silly kid throws a french fry into the lake or something crazy like that.

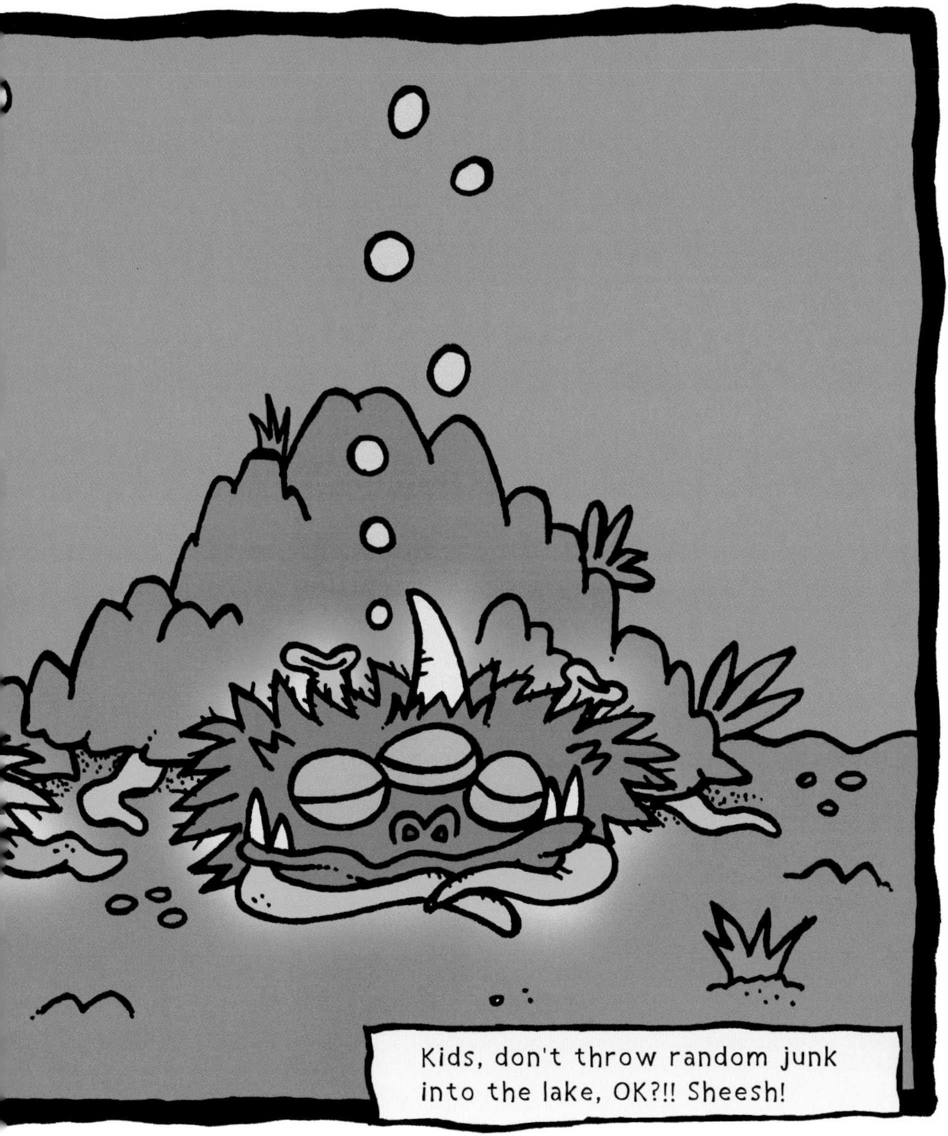
Kids, don't throw random junk into the lake, OK?!! Sheesh!

CHAPTER 11

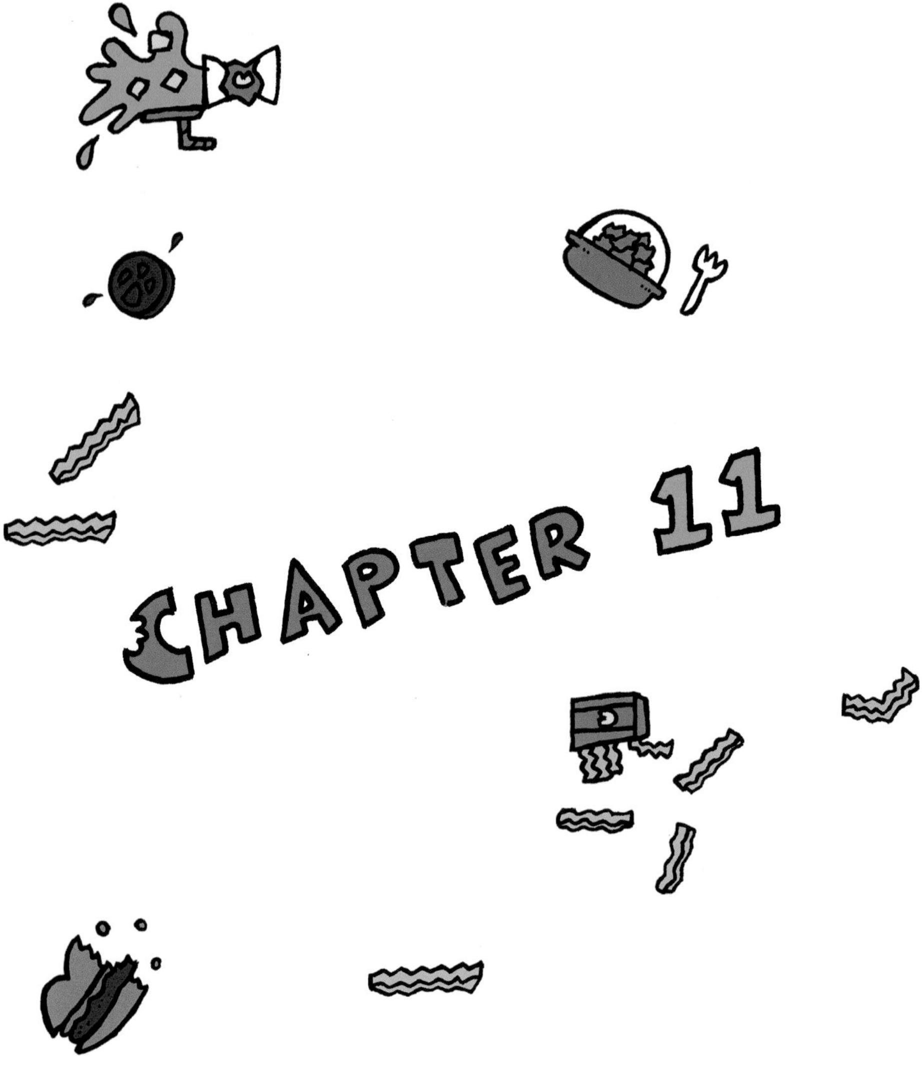

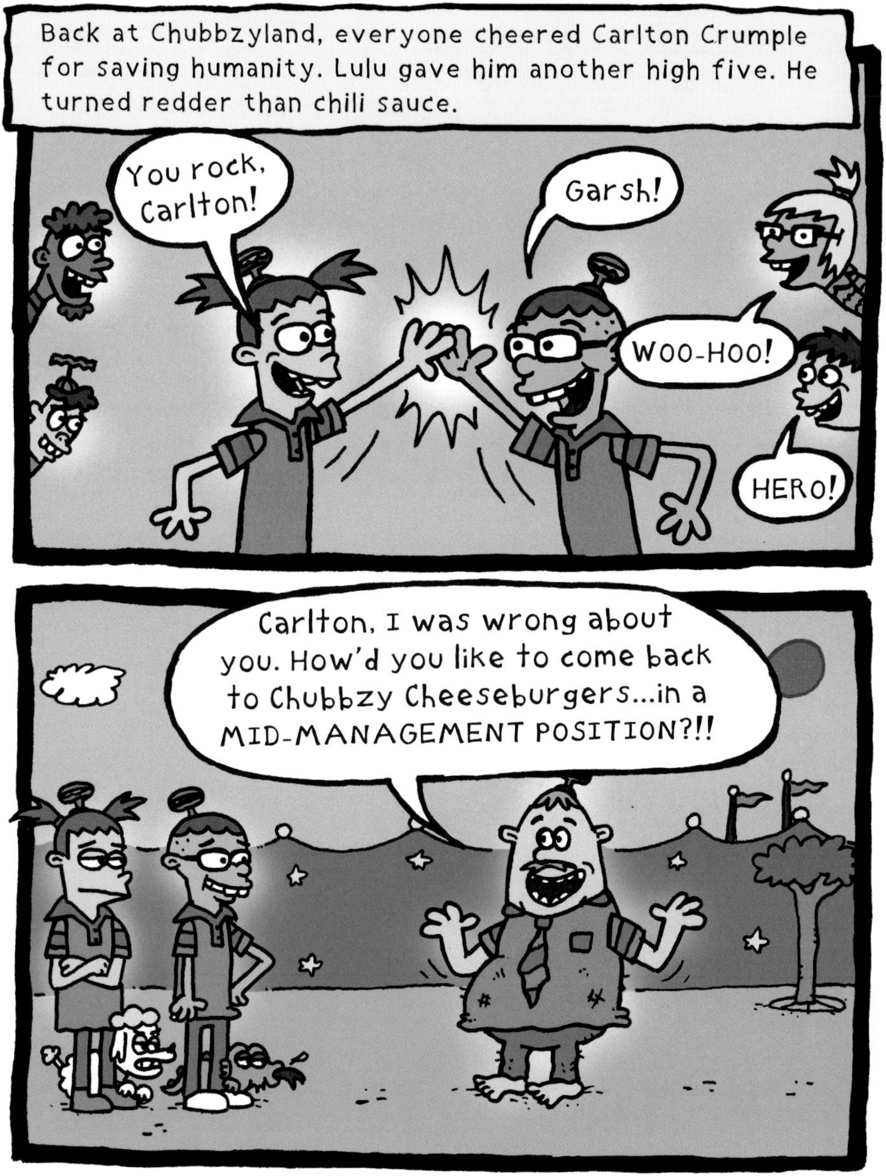
Back at Chubbzyland, everyone cheered Carlton Crumple for saving humanity. Lulu gave him another high five. He turned redder than chili sauce.
You rock, Carlton!
Garsh!
WOO-HOO!
HERO!
Carlton, I was wrong about you. How'd you like to come back to Chubbzy Cheeseburgers...in a MID-MANAGEMENT POSITION?!!

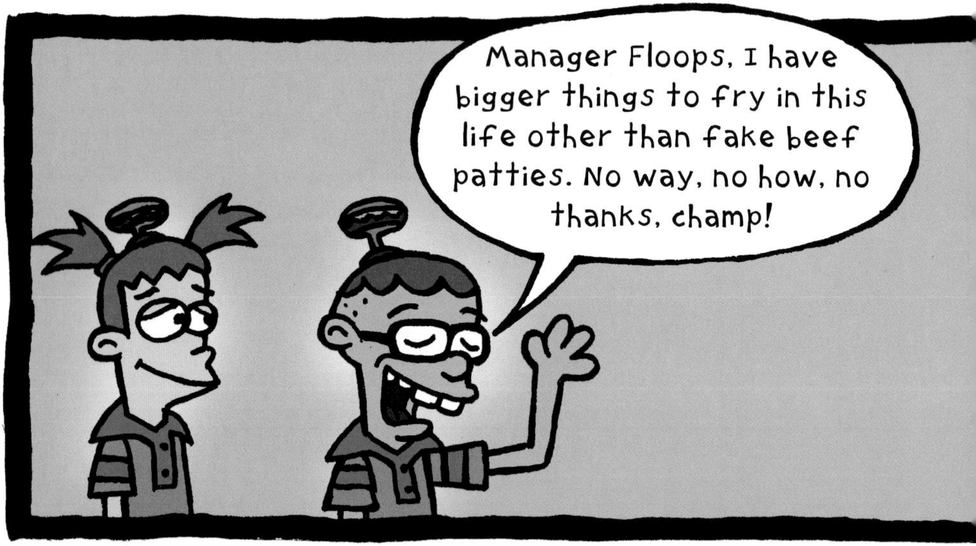
Manager Floops, I have bigger things to fry in this life other than fake beef patties. No way, no how, no thanks, champ!

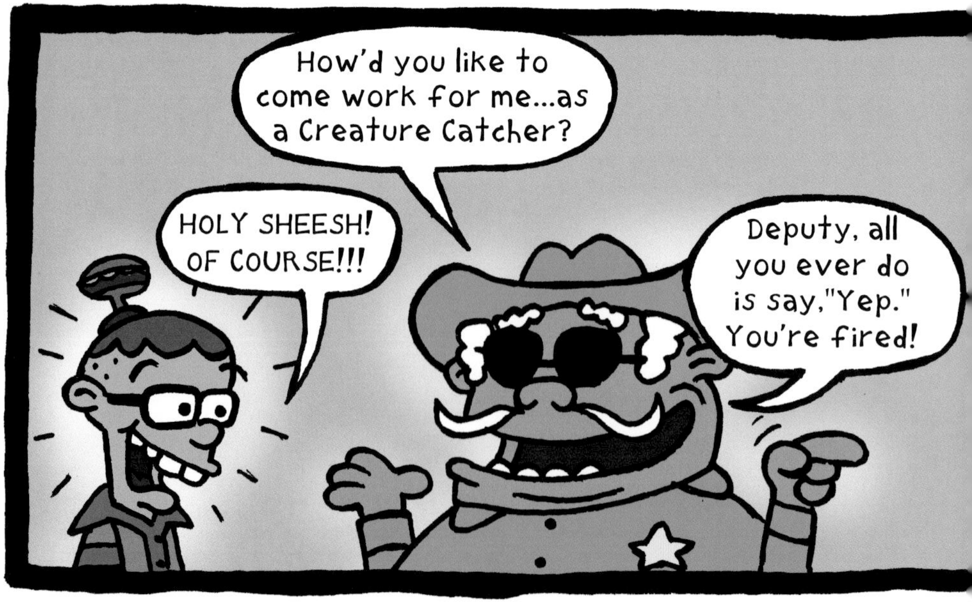
How'd you like to come work for me...as a Creature Catcher?
HOLY SHEESH! OF COURSE!!!
Deputy, all you ever do is say,"Yep." You're fired!

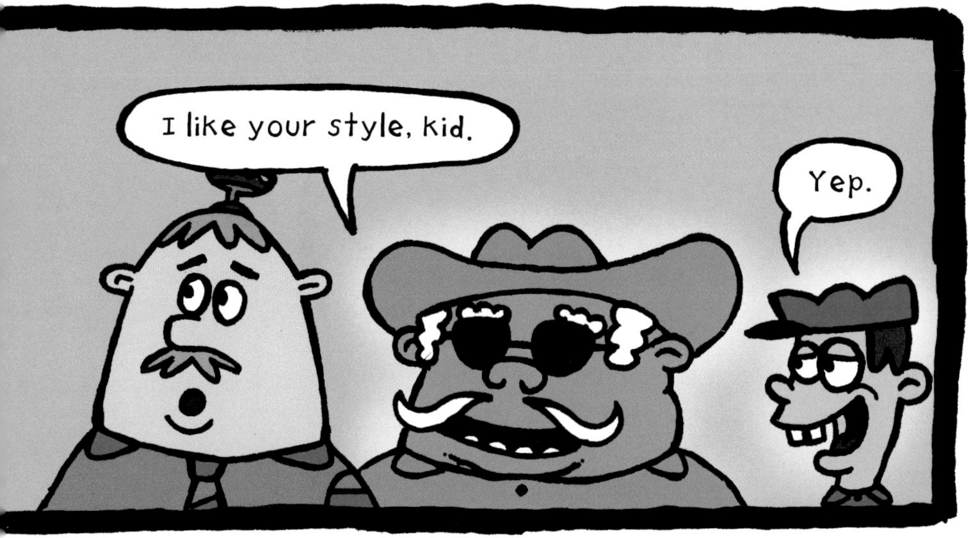
I like your style, kid.
Yep.

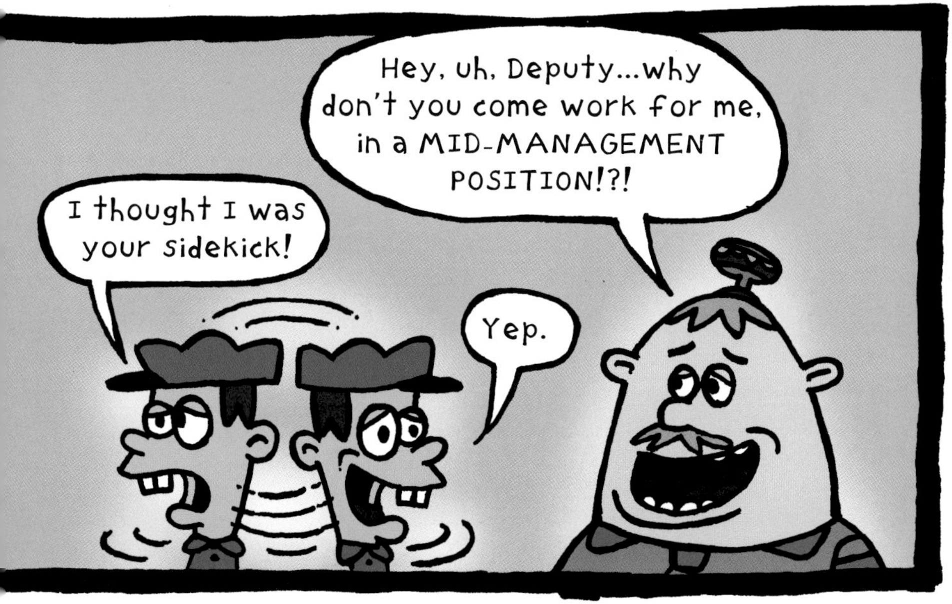
Hey, uh, Deputy...why don't you come work for me, in a MID-MANAGEMENT POSITION!?!
I thought I was your sidekick!
Yep.

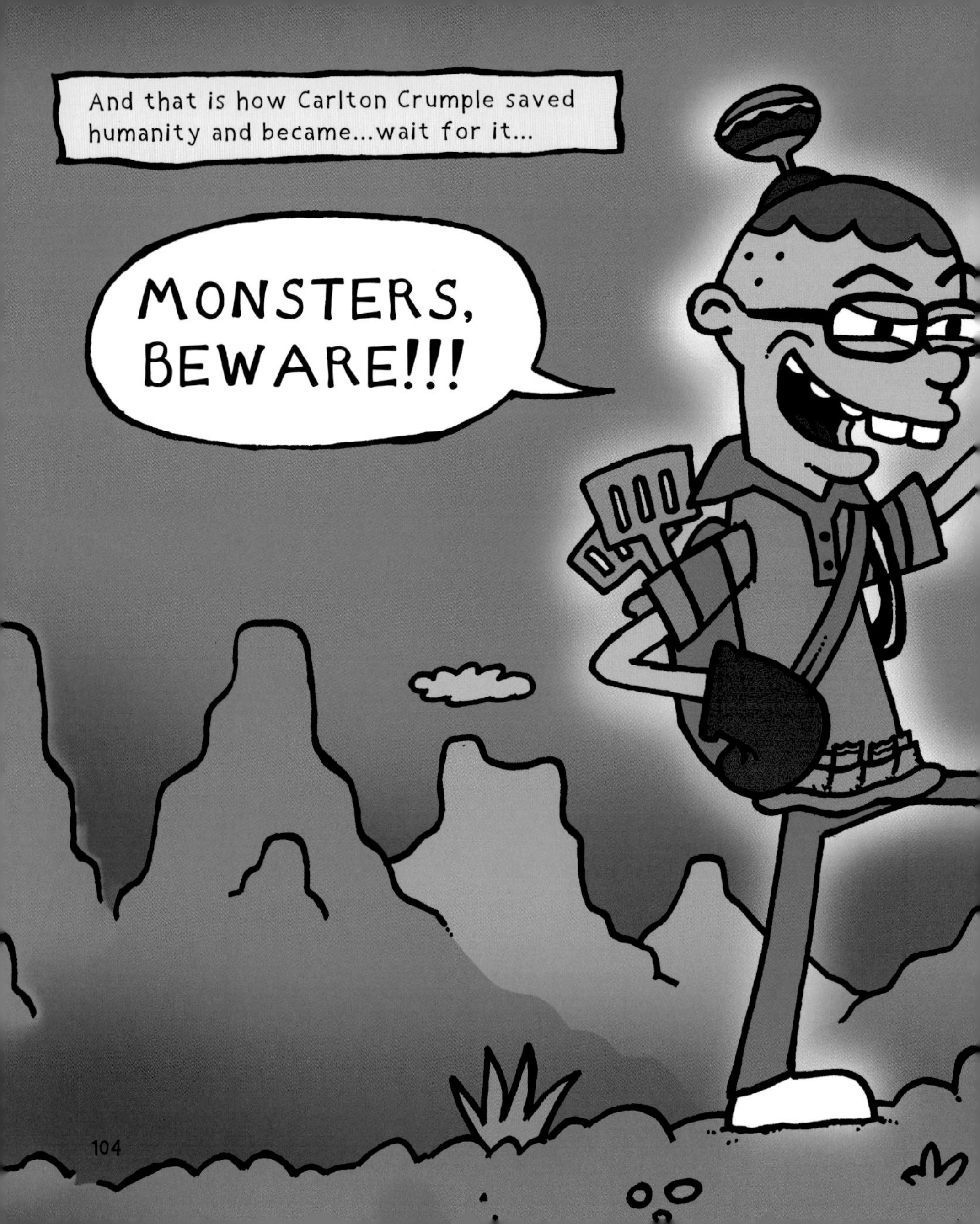
And that is how Carlton Crumple saved humanity and became...wait for it...
MONSTERS, BEWARE!!!

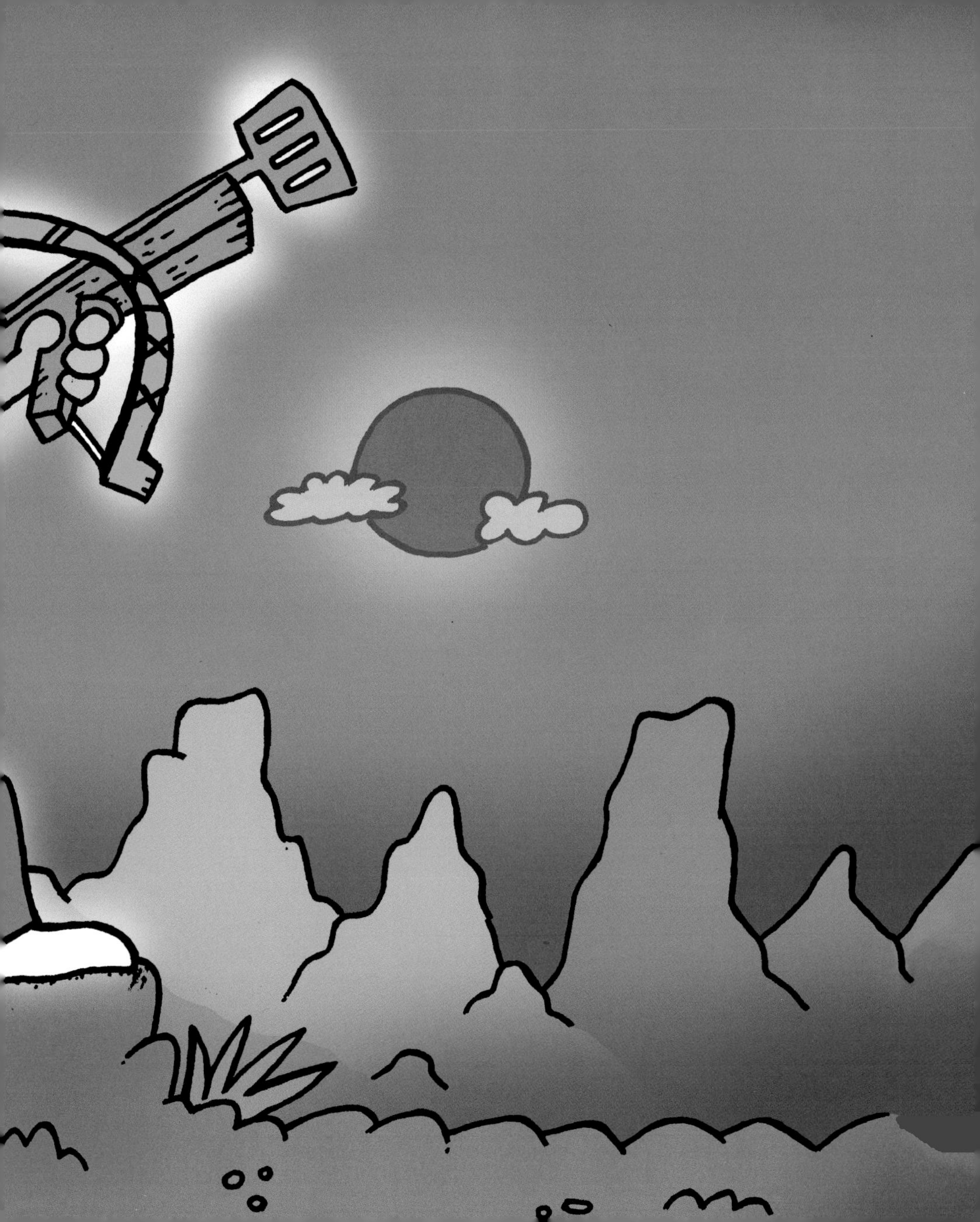

CARLTON CRUMPLE
CREATURE CATCHER!!!

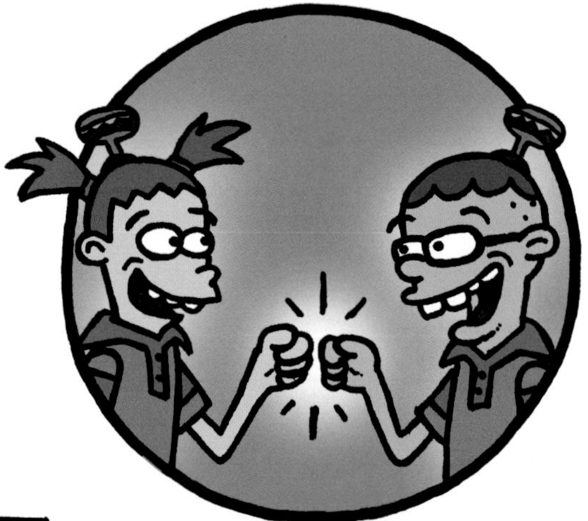

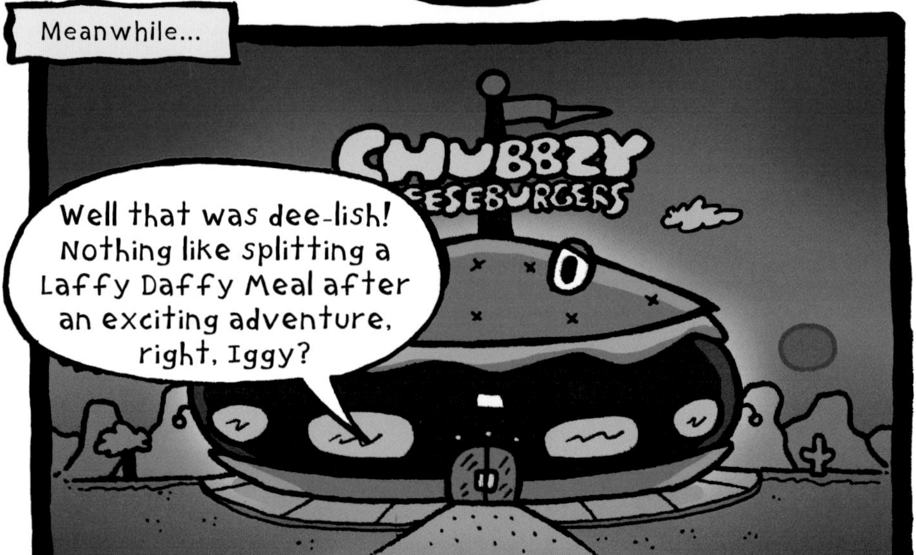
Meanwhile...
CHUBBZY
Well that was dee-lish! Nothing like splitting a Laffy Daffy Meal after an exciting adventure, right, Iggy?

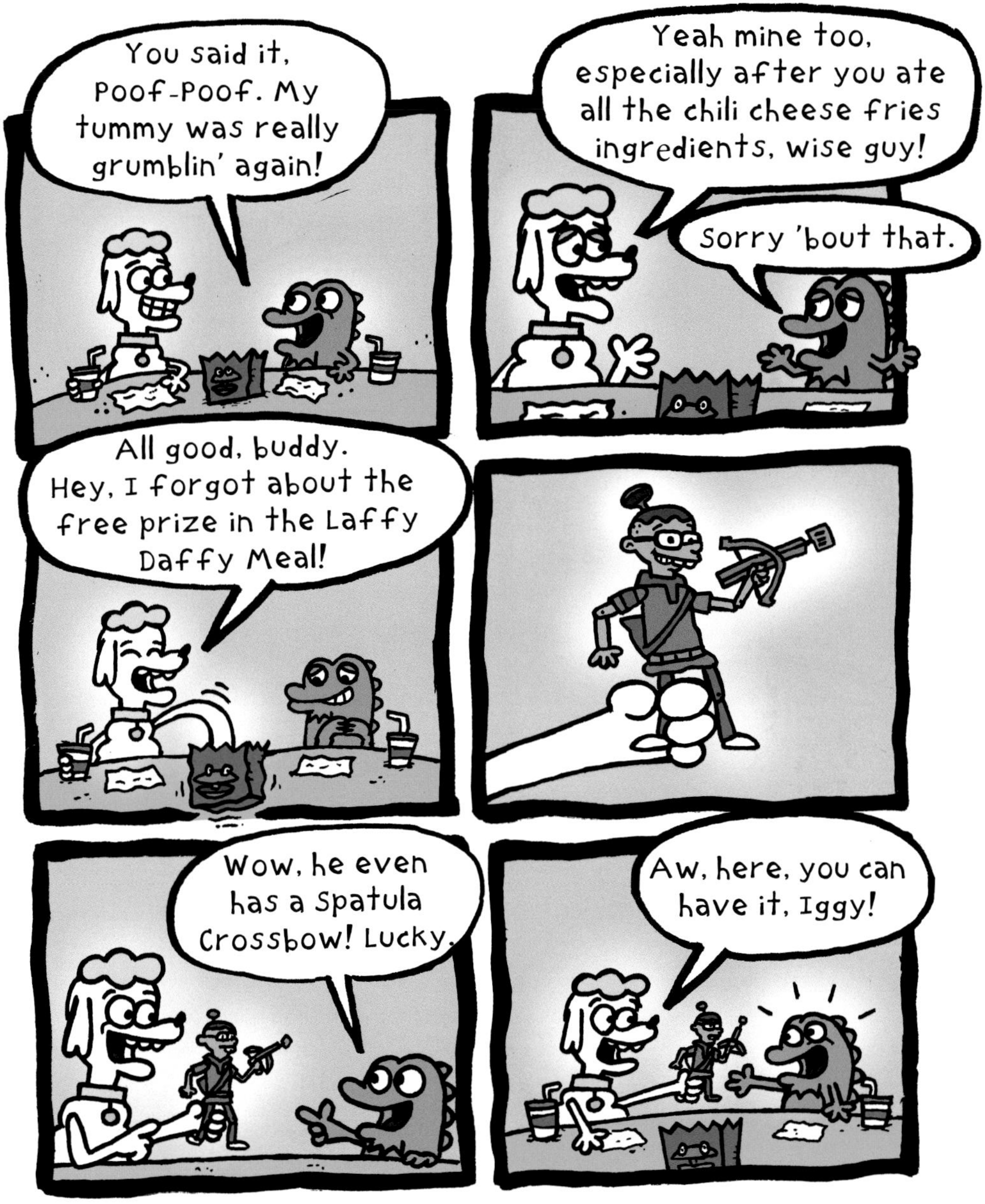
You said it, Poof-Poof. My tummy was really grumblin' again!
Yeah mine too, especially after you ate all the chili cheese fries ingredients, wise guy!
Sorry 'bout that.
All good, buddy. Hey, I forgot about the free prize in the Laffy Daffy Meal!
Wow, he even has a Spatula Crossbow! Lucky.
Aw, here, you can have it, Iggy!

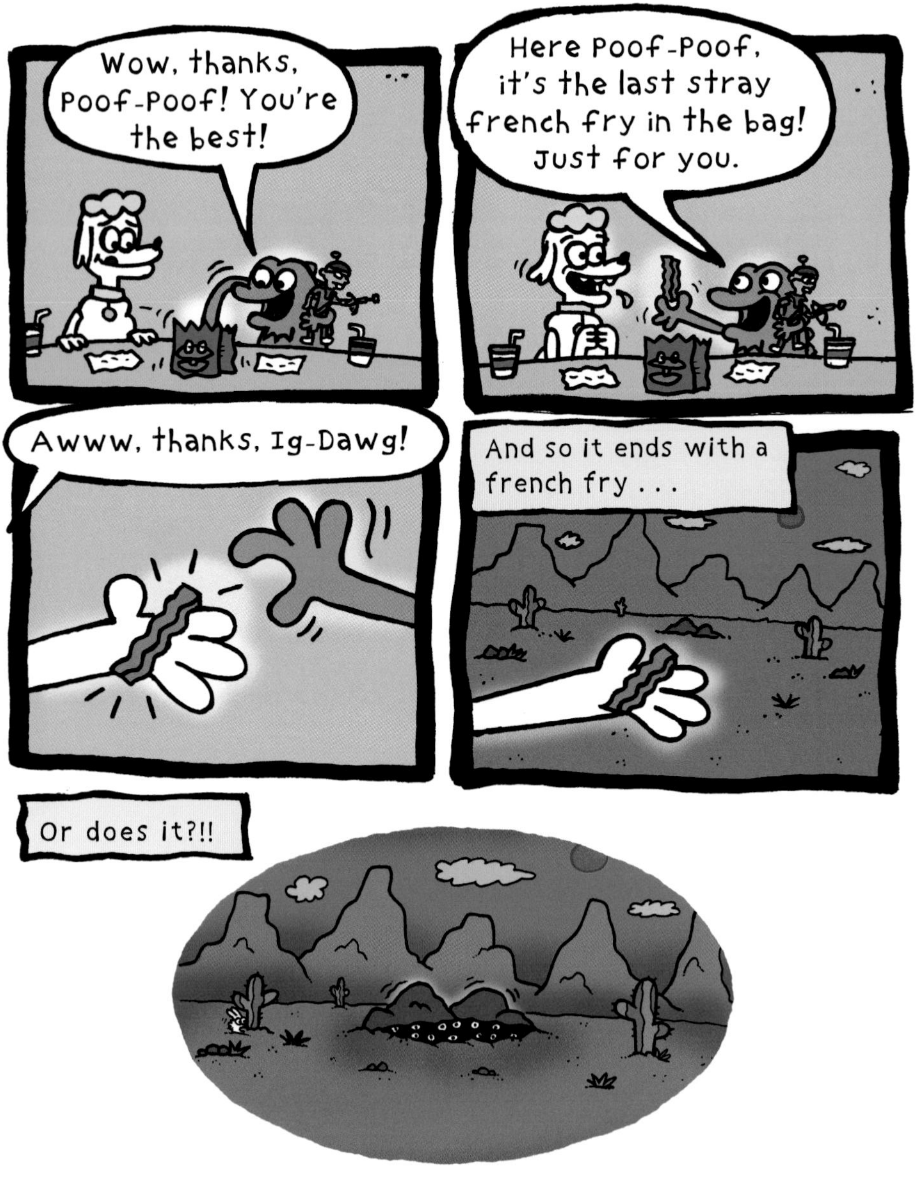
Wow, thanks, Poof-Poof! You're the best!
Here Poof-Poof, it's the last stray french fry in the bag! Just for you.
Awww, thanks, Ig-Dawg!
And so it ends with a french fry . . .
Or does it?!!

Carlton Crumple
Creature Catcher Book 2:
Tater Invaders

Carlton Crumple will do battle with
horrifying underground potato creatures!
Oh my garsh, grab the ketchup!

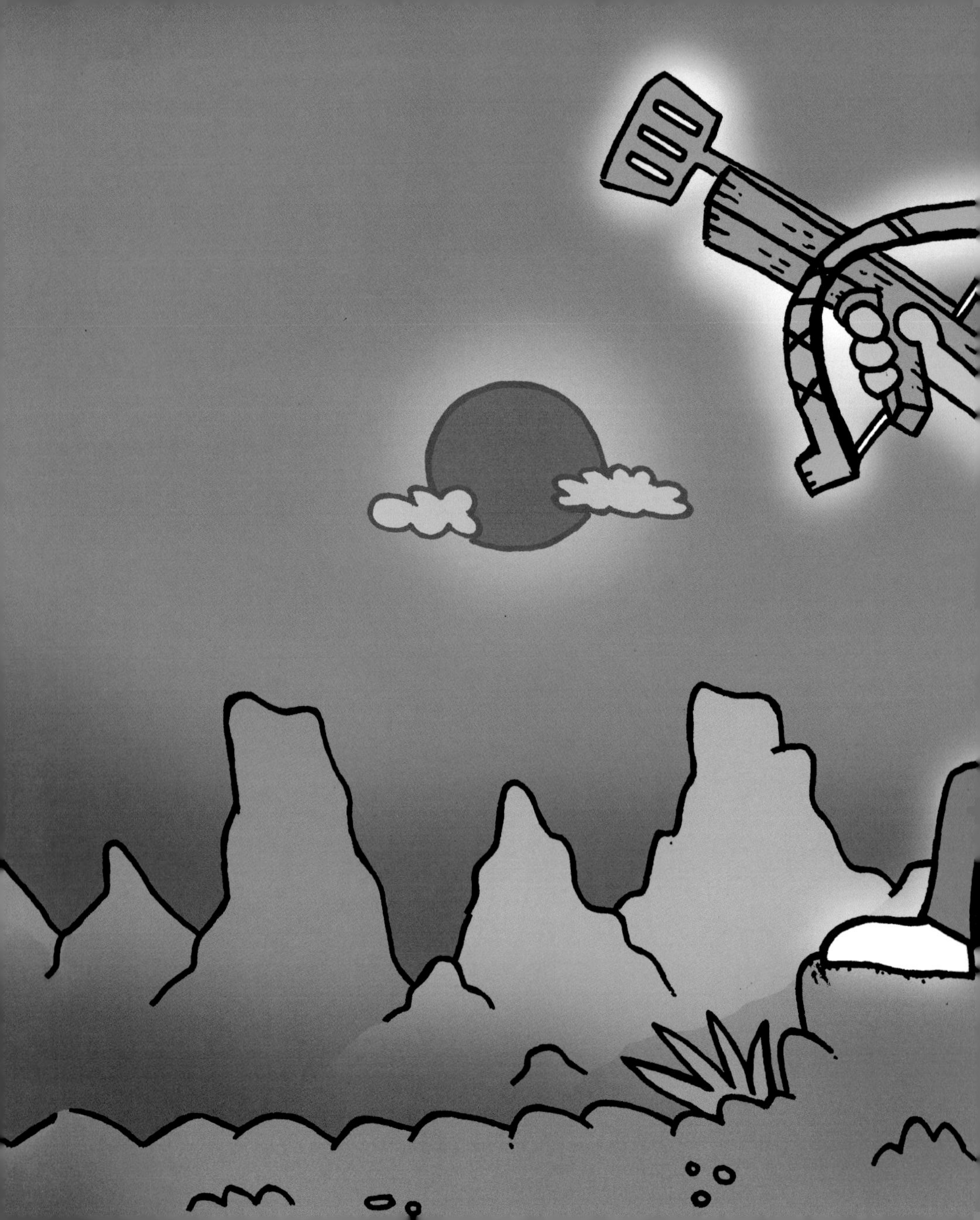

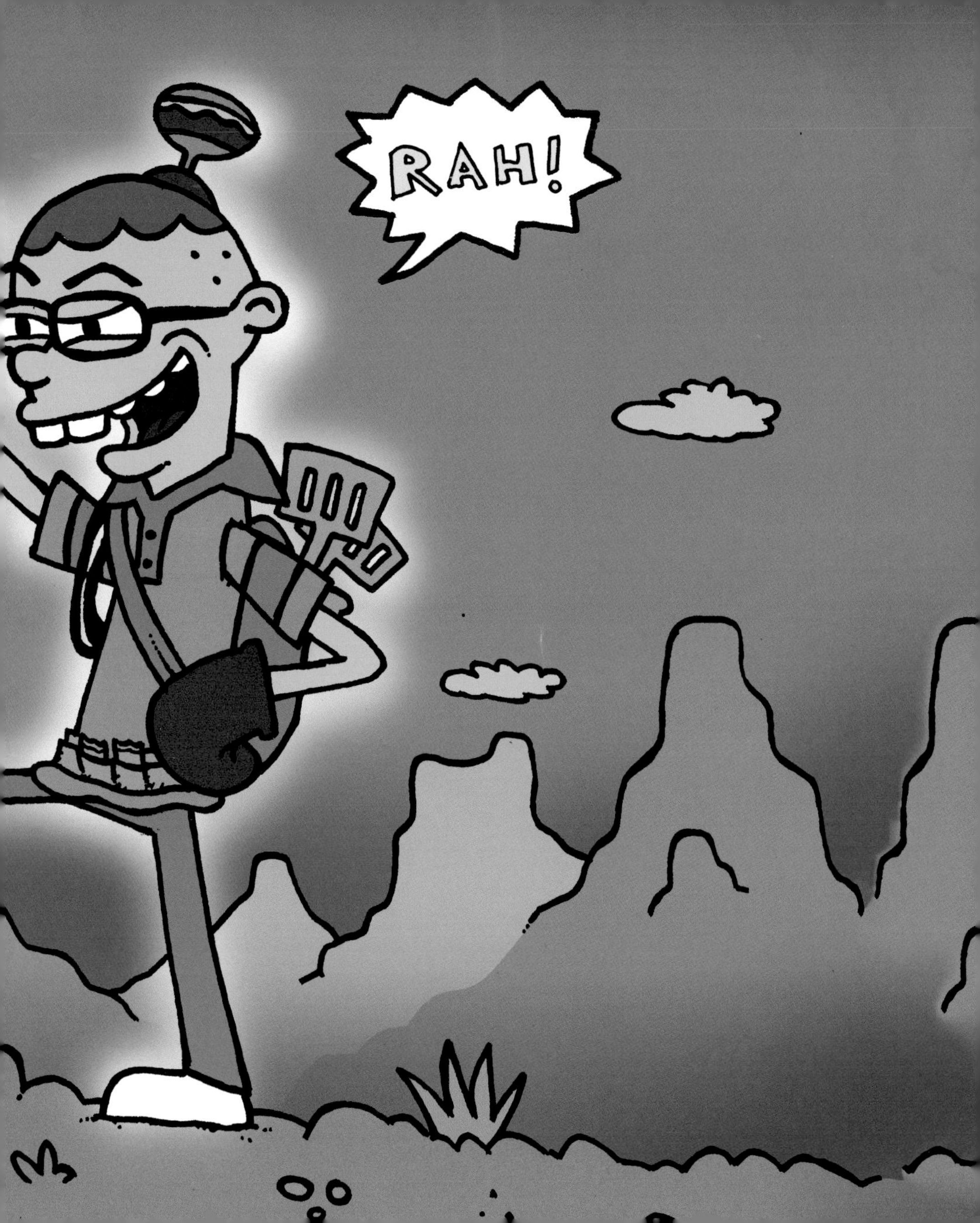
RAH!

ABOUT THE AUTHOR

DAVID FREMONT grew up in Fremont, California—yep, a Fremont from Fremont! He loved watching *Underdog* cartoons, reading comics, and drawing with his brother. When David was eleven, his cousin Steve showed him a super-cool shark comic that he had drawn, inspiring David to start drawing his own comics. When David grew up, he moved across the bay to San Francisco, where he got a job painting cartoons at an animation studio. While at Colossal Pictures, he created projects for Cartoon Network and Disney. More recently, after moving to Los Angeles, he created a pilot for Nickelodeon and an online kids series for DreamWorksTV, called *Public Pool*. He currently lives in Woodland Hills, with his family (and many furry pet creatures!), where he teaches cartooning classes to kids. This is his first book for children.

ACKNOWLEDGMENTS

Double cheeseburgers to all who helped get the Munchies out into the world and make my comic book dreams a reality: Editor-in-chief Bethany Buck for being a believer in Carlton Crumple; Kyra Reppen and all the kind folks at Pixel+Ink, Trustbridge Global Media, and Holiday House; cartoon champion Mary Harrington at Nickelodeon; color rock-star rescuer pal Jimbo Matison; design wizard Sammy Yuen; and legal hero LeighAnna MacFadden. Chili sauce to my author/illustrator friend James Proimos for encouraging me to write and illustrate a book. Super-size fries to my i3 artist friends Eric White and Brad Mossman for lifelong friendship and inspiration. A side of hash browns to Jan Johns for her creature-voiced pep talks. Quesadillas to my siblings Nancy, Lisa, Diane, and Mark for all the homemade munchies, late-night Creature Features, and family road trips that fueled this book. An ice cream sundae with whipped cream on top to my sweet Mom for enrolling me in summertime cartooning classes, and a big baked potato with Salad Supreme to my Dad for telling me to never give up and to "get it done!" Finally, Laffy Daffy meal prizes to my wife, Carol, and children, Milo and Greta, for all their support, love, and laughter.

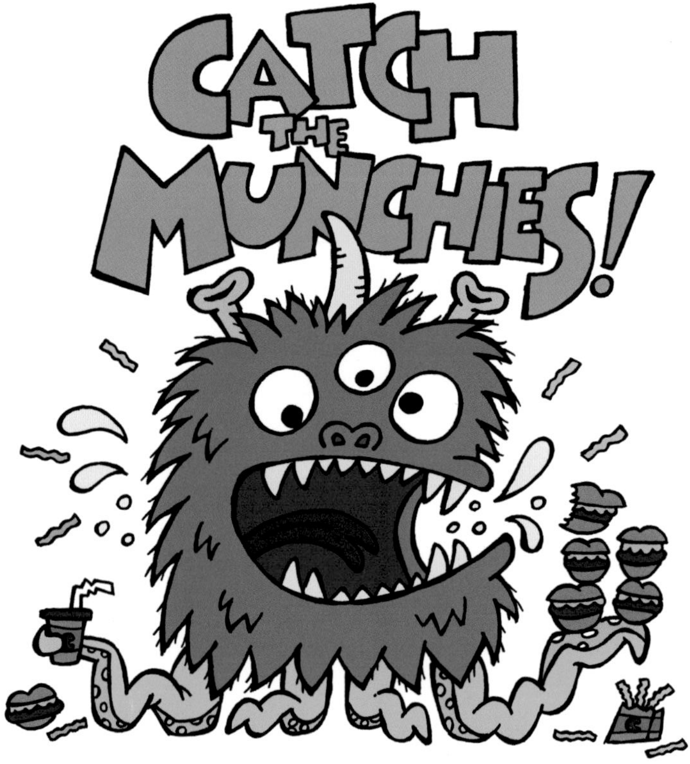
CATCH THE MUNCHIES!